"Steve Neil Johnson returns in top form...the series promises to provide both extremely good reads and a better understanding of gay American life during a very crucial period." --Lambda Literary Review

"Terrific...Steve Neil Johnson writes like a *You Are There* newscaster —breathless, on-the-spot reporting—and paints word images like a Weegee crime photo. His is the voice of a generation of gays who had only just begun, haltingly and courageously, to speak for themselves. Come for the page-turning storytelling, stay for the engrossing journey to a historical era that lies at the roots of modern day liberation. It's a great book." --Eric A. Gordon, author of *Mark the Music: The Life and Work of Marc Blitzstein*

"This is a real treat—believable characters who illuminate the dark just before the dawn of gay liberation. A bonus is the richly detailed backdrop of Los Angeles in 1956, including political corruption, real estate scams, Hollywood scandals and organized crime. I'm looking forward to the sequels." --Peter Cashorali, author of *Gay Fairy and Folk Tales*

## *Final Atonement:*

### Lambda Literary Award Finalist

"Johnson has crafted a literate murder mystery that expands the genre to include deft commentary on the changing face of urban centers."
--Publishers Weekly

"One of the most exciting new detectives in years." --John Preston

## *False Confessions:*

"Steve Neil Johnson may very well turn out to be our queer Raymond Chandler... the plot twists are clean and clever... strikingly original... the best casual reading I've come across yet. Orlando is a great detective... (builds to) a heart pounding climax."
--San Francisco Bay Times

Also by Steve Neil Johnson

The Yellow Canary
*Book 1: The L.A. After Midnight Quartet*

Final Atonement
*A Doug Orlando Mystery*

False Confessions
*A Doug Orlando Mystery*

This Endless Night

*For Young Adults:*
Raising Kane

*For Children:*
Everybody Hates Edgar Allan Poe!

Clutching Hand Books edition, April 2014

BOOK 2

The L.A. AFTER MIDNIGHT Quartet

# THE BLACK CAT

STEVE NEIL JOHNSON

CLUTCHING HAND BOOKS

# December, 1966

## Chapter 1

His eyes stung as he climbed out of the squad car into the airless night. Jim Blake blinked, glancing up through the pale yellow haze that hung low over the city and into the swallowing darkness beyond.

The smog alert had been in effect three days running, but he knew the air quality wasn't the only thing that had left his eyes itchy and bloodshot. As images of the empty house flickered through his mind, Blake could almost hear the solitary click of his heels on the hardwood floor, the echo across the living room, and that haunting loneliness came back. Tommy was gone. She had finally done it. She had left and taken his son.

He shook his personal troubles out of his head and reminded himself he had to work quickly. He'd arrived first at the scene, but other patrol cars were bound to come any moment—and in no time his former partner in Homicide—and then he would be shut out. He had to get what he wanted and get out fast.

Broadway was busy that Saturday evening, the traffic snarled, the unseasonably warm air thick with exhaust fumes and the smell of fried chicken from the stand on the corner. Hustlers huddled in a doorway eyeing him balefully. He felt sticky in his wool uniform, and sweat dampened his armpits. He had forgotten what it was like to dress in blue.

Leaning into the open front passenger window of the cruiser idling at the curb, Blake observed his new partner. Mendolson, not yet thirty, had a baby face, wiry dark short hair and a playful sense of humor Blake admittedly probably once had himself but now found annoying. "Sure you don't mind?" he asked for the second time.

Behind the wheel, Mendolson tossed up his hands and slouched back in the seat. "Be my guest. It's New Year's Eve, our shift is over, I've got a blonde *shiksa* with *Playboy* curves that my mother doesn't approve of for good reason waiting for me in her pool with champagne glasses in hand... but go ahead, take your time."

Blake grimaced amiably at the sarcasm and rapped on the roof with his knuckles in response, then turned toward the theater. Flashing bulbs pursued each other around the perimeter of the marquee. Red plastic letters proclaimed:

Open All Night
ANDY WARHOL'S CHELSEA GIRLS
Smoking in the Balcony

He remembered theaters had offered round the clock entertainment during the war to accommodate those working evening shifts in factories—and soldiers like him coming off ships in San Pedro—but that was more than twenty years ago. He'd been on the force long enough to know the likely reason for all-night entertainment, especially in this area of downtown L.A. with its bars, growing steadily more seedy, strewn along Fifth. The fact it had a balcony was a dead giveaway.

Mendolson stuck his head out the window and tapped his watch. "Did I mention she looks like Brigitte Bardot?"

Blake didn't look back as he proceeded across the sidewalk, took a drag on his cigarette, and bitterly reminded himself he didn't have anyone to go home to. Let

Mendolson's girl wait. He figured his partner owed it to him. A refugee from the 77<sup>th</sup> Street Division, Mendolson had spent every shift since they'd become partners last week endlessly reminiscing about his days in South Central, including the Watts Riots just over a year ago and the smaller insurrection that left two dead last spring. Blake didn't know how much more of it he could take.

"If you just saw how those people live," he'd droned on. "I went there with the best of intentions, you know, liberal Jewish boy from the Westside believing in the Great Society, but when you see what these people do to one another, it changes you." He'd gone into an elaborate description of his intervention in a domestic dispute that went savage when the wife suddenly whipped out a butcher knife and jumped on her husband's back. Mendolson had shaken his head wearily. "If you just saw how they live."

Passing a newsstand plastered with garish glossies of nudes—some male, some female—in provocative poses, Blake's eyes zeroed in on the *Los Angeles Times* headline confirming that the county assessor's death the previous week had been ruled a suicide. That made him stop, and he took a moment to consider what it meant.

So the coroner had stepped in line.

Like everybody else, he thought. He took one last pull on his cigarette and pitched the butt in the gutter. It looked like he was going to be dressed in blue for a long time.

He stepped inside the theater into faded 1920s grandeur. Under an immense chandelier a wide red-carpeted staircase in the center of the lobby stretched up to the balcony. A bank of ornately carved double doors on each side opened into the orchestra section, an art deco concession stand to the right, smelling of stale popcorn and rancid butter, stairs down to the restrooms on the left.

He was vaguely aware these magnificent old palaces along Broadway had started out as vaudeville showplaces in the teens and twenties, converted to movie houses during the Depression and finally, with the nosedive in the population downtown in the last few years, struggled as second run venues with stained carpets and torn seats.

The portly little manager in a mortician's suit was nervously waiting for him at the foot of the staircase. He looked Blake up and down in undisguised appreciation, taking in his height of six feet two and the broad shoulders filling out his uniform. Something happened in his face, something Blake had seen so many times before: his features seemed to brighten, and he had that aching, hopeful sheen in his eyes, as if, for just a moment, he was young again.

"Upstairs," the old man managed breathlessly, swooping forward and planting a hand on Blake's sleeve, letting it linger there, his free hand flying like a pigeon toward the staircase and fluttering in the air. "Upstairs, in the back balcony."

He must have been nearly seventy, and his little mustache and thinning hair were too impossibly dark— black as shoe polish—to be from anything but a bottle. There was a little bit of vaudeville in his flamboyant gestures, and Blake wondered if he'd been on the circuit in his youth, perhaps even headlining in this very theater or other grand relics along Broadway.

Blake glanced at the manicured fingers resting on his sleeve beside his wrist watch and considered how he was going to handle this. Any moment other patrol cars would arrive, and then it would be too late. He gave the old man an ingratiating smile and watched him melt like ice cream on a summer day.

"If you could show me. Can I help you with the stairs?" He offered his arm and the manager's eyes turned impish as he wrapped both his hands snugly around Blake's

4

formidable biceps. He could almost hear the old man purr as they started up the stairs.

"Yes, young man, thank you, you are most kind. My knees are shot from a lifetime on the boards. I'm afraid my dancing days are over. I—"

"You reported a Negro running out of here."

Thick pitch-black eyebrows rose indignantly. "Like a bat out of hell, he came down these stairs." A hand fluttered birdlike again, then landed in a caressing grip on Blake's arm. "Dashed right past me, almost knocked me down."

"You said he had a scar."

The manager cocked his head quizzically and his eyes narrowed, as if the detail wasn't important. "Well, yes, on his cheek, roundish."

"Like a horseshoe, the ends pointing down."

"Yes, that's it."

Blake felt heat course through his veins. It had to be the same one, had to be. Two murders, the same suspect spotted running away. Maybe he wouldn't be in blue that long after all.

They reached the landing, and the old man nodded to the left. Blake pushed through a velvet curtain and into the vast dimness beyond, hesitating a moment while his eyes adjusted. Reluctantly, the manager released his arm with a wistful little sigh.

A large screen flickered gray light in the distance. It was split in two black-and-white images: on the right a chubby woman on the phone, on the left two men in bed, one in a robe, the other in briefs only.

Blake glanced down into the orchestra section; few of the seats were taken. The balcony was where the theater made its money. Young couples with nowhere else to go made out in the worn and broken seats, hardly coming up for air. Nobody seemed to be watching the movie. Blake glanced back at the screen. Two beautiful women with long hair entered and tied up the man in briefs with a belt. As one woman rolled him to the side, the camera zoomed in on his crotch. The sound was so tinny Blake couldn't understand a word being said.

Now that he could see better, Blake gazed up to the aisle separating the upper and lower sections of the balcony. Above the area dominated by squirming young couples, another world loomed in the smoky haze. A handful of dark figures dotted an expanse of empty seats. It was very still up there, and most of those who sat there, sat alone.

A place for men, Blake thought.

As soon as several of the solitary figures in the upper balcony spotted his uniform, they stiffened with panic then darted for a distant exit. No matter. The suspect was long gone and the man Blake was interested in wasn't going anywhere.

Blake started up the stairs; the old man followed, taking the opportunity to cling to his arm again. The smell was worse up here, the fog of tobacco smoke mingling with a whiff of forbidden sweetness, the stale odors of popcorn and butter joining the aroma of something darker, musky and male. In his years in Homicide he had learned the technique of breathing but not breathing in.

When they were halfway up the back balcony, a hand squeezed Blake's forearm.

"Down this row," the manager whispered.

Gazing through the blanket of dimness, cut by a smoky silver wedge of light from the projector's booth, Blake focused on a figure sitting alone in the middle of the row, his head hanging forward as if he had fallen asleep, his chin on his chest. When the screen momentarily lit up, his balding crown shone silver.

"Are you sure he's dead?"

"Oh, my, yes, I'm afraid he's very dead," the manager replied, wringing his hands. "People fall asleep in here all the time. We're open twenty-four hours a day. But when the colored fellow ran out of here, I became suspicious. And when I went to investigate... it was the, uh, rope that brought him to my attention."

Motioning for the manager to remain where he was, Blake started along the row of empty seats toward the dead man. The soles of his shoes stuck to the floor, and Blake figured grimly it wasn't just from spilled Coca-Cola.

As he approached, he noted the ligature around the man's neck. He quickly sized up the victim: short, hardly taller than a child, middle-aged, in a conservative suit. That his head had dropped forward didn't entirely account for his hunched posture and Blake concluded he had suffered from a disease of the spine.

Blake was about to feel for the victim's pulse when something lying in the shadows under the next seat caught his eye. He reached down and picked it up. A hardcover book. Blake looked at it curiously, but it was too dark to read the title, and he slipped it under his arm to examine later.

Returning his attention to the dead man, Blake leaned over him and put a finger gently on his neck, attempting to find the carotid artery. A mixture of disgust and pity overcame him. Who had he been, this pathetic little man, to end up dead in a place like this? In his bleakest moments, after he'd come home to the empty house, lying sleepless on a blanket on the floor, Blake had feared that in the end this would be his fate, to die alone and in the dark.

Just then he was startled by the sound of a horrid intake of breath and the skin beneath his finger flinched away from his touch. Blake stumbled back in surprise as the head of the man suddenly bobbed up and let out a strangled cough, his eyes opening wide.

"Help me," the man wheezed.

◇◇◇

Paul Winters gazed out the back seat window of the limo and hoped the interminable ride wasn't going to wrinkle his tuxedo. Leaning forward, he tapped on the glass divider. "What's the holdup?"

"It's L.A.," the driver explained in monotone patience. "And it's New Year's Eve."

Throwing up his hands in exasperation, Paul turned to Jeannie in the seat beside him. "We could walk at this rate."

"Not in these shoes, sweetie." She tilted her head and looked him over critically. Her pert little nose was already shiny from the sticky night air, but her eyes still twinkled with excitement over his invitation to accompany him that evening. "Your bowtie is crooked."

"That's David's revenge. He tied it for me."

"Aha. Here, let me fix it."

His lover David Rosen was fuming that he hadn't been invited to what the gossip columns were calling the social event of the season, a fundraiser at the recently opened Music Center in downtown. Jeannie had always been his beard for office parties, but tonight's festivities were of a higher profile, promising Hollywood luminaries, from Kirk Douglas to Doris Day, as well as city and state politicians. Even the new governor had promised to attend. "Surely," David had insisted, "straight arrow deputy district attorneys occasionally bring a male friend along to a party." Then he'd sniffed, "New Year's Eve, and we don't even get to spend it together." He had sulked until his friend Billy asked him to check out a new bar in Silver Lake that evening. To placate David, Paul had invited the whole gang to his house in Brentwood for a late-night bash after midnight. He would make it up to David then, he thought, though he wondered why, after ten years together, they had never entirely come to terms with how unalike they were. If anything, when their relationship should have been coasting into middle-aged boredom and grudging acceptance of each other's foibles, tensions seemed to rise out of nowhere lately, especially since David had started hanging out with that scruffy radical crowd that met at the Hub and were hell-bent on changing the world.

"There," Jeannie said, nodding at her handiwork. "Perfect."

"Is Pat running with the bulls tonight?"

Jeannie's girlfriend of fifteen years was a landscaper and gardener by day who had taken up amateur Roller Derby by night. The team's latest tournament had even been broadcast on local TV.

"There's a beer bust at the Daily Double in Pasadena tonight. The whole team will be there. But she'll meet us at your place later."

"Good. Your hair looks nice."

"It's a wig, silly. Did you think I grew this overnight?" Jeannie's Twiggy cut, short as a boy's, had been supplanted by a towering auburn coif encircled by stiff curls and the scent of Aqua Net. She was a make-up artist who freelanced at several movie studios and regularly sneaked out flashy dresses for nights on the town. "Do you recognize the dress? I borrowed it from the costume department. I wanted the little black number Audrey Hepburn wore in *Breakfast at Tiffany's* but I couldn't get my hands on it. Stella Stevens wore this in *The Silencers*, you know, the Dean Martin movie?"

"I must have missed it."

The last time David had dragged him to the movies, they saw something mod and British about a photographer who thought he witnessed a murder, a two hour movie in which

9

absolutely nothing happened. Next time, Paul had told David firmly, we go to a Bond film.

After glancing impatiently at his watch, Paul leaned forward again and suggested to the driver, "How about if we go down Sixth then take a left on Broadway?"

"Relax, will you?" Jeannie scolded gently. "We get there when we get there. Why are you so uptight?"

He was getting a little annoyed at how often his friends had been asking him that question lately. Sometimes he felt like they had all gone off on an extended holiday and he was stuck tending to the problems of the world. But she was right, he *was* tense, and it wasn't just because of his little tiff with David.

Perhaps it was that cryptic conversation yesterday with his boss, District Attorney Anthony Bulgetti, that had left him on pins and needles. The D.A. had taken him aside and said he wanted to speak to him at the fundraiser tonight. Paul didn't doubt for a moment it was about something important. Surely it wasn't to tell him the D.A. was finally leaving his position, and to offer his support to Paul in his own campaign for the office. After his disastrous run for governor last spring, where Bulgetti had placed third in the Democratic primary, he wasn't going anywhere fast. In fact, the biggest obstacle to Paul's lifelong goal of becoming District Attorney seemed to be the possibility that the current D.A. would never leave office, and Paul, his heir apparent, would molder away like a prince forever in line for the throne.

Or, he wondered, could his malaise just be the inevitable descending pall of middle-aged blues? He had to admit a deep vein of dissatisfaction cut its way through most aspects of his life, leaving him restless and anxious. Where was the fire—the passionate sense of following a calling— that had driven his early career? When had everything become so maddeningly routine? Maybe he just had to accept that his best days were over. He was forty, after all, not a kid anymore, and you couldn't be the rising star forever.

As the car turned onto Broadway, flashing lights up the block drew Paul's attention and he rolled down the window and stuck his head out to get a better look.

Three police cars and an ambulance, its lights flashing, were parked haphazardly in front of a theater, blocking a lane and causing northbound traffic to snake at an agonizingly slow pace around them, with each passing car pausing to get a voyeuristic peek. Paul observed several uniformed policemen surrounding a stretcher being rushed by attendants out of the theater entrance toward the waiting ambulance. Something about one of the officers caught his eye, and Paul leaned his head farther out the window.

"Pull to the side," Paul said to the driver. He turned to Jeannie. "I'll just be a minute."

He was out of the car and striding down the sidewalk before he realized why the officer seemed so familiar. He felt the pluck of a taut string in his chest, and for the briefest moment considered turning on his heel and slipping unseen back into the limousine. Then Jim Blake's eyes fell upon him from the knot of officers around the stretcher and he knew it was too late. Their eyes met, and Paul could see recognition, then pain, in Blake's eyes before he lowered them and continued with the bustling entourage into the street. By the time Paul reached the theater the attendants were about to hoist the stretcher into the back of the ambulance.

Paul hung back, watching as Blake raised his hand, requesting a moment, and leaned over the victim, trying to get a last word out of him before he was whisked away to the hospital. Over the swish of traffic, Paul could barely hear Blake's soft-spoken but resonant voice speaking in the victim's ear.

"The man who did this to you, the Negro, the one with the scar on his face, do you know who he was?"

The balding man on the stretcher, covered by a sheet tucked at his chin, stared blankly at him. He opened his mouth to speak, seemed to think better of it, then closed his eyes to shut Blake out. Two of the attendants shrugged at Blake and slid the stretcher into the ambulance. As they jumped in after, Blake stepped back, crossing his arms and shaking his head in frustration. A third attendant slammed the double doors then rounded the vehicle and climbed in the driver's seat.

Before the ambulance could take off, a black sedan pulled up and stopped in the middle of the street, halting southbound traffic. A chorus of horns blared angrily behind it. A tall, reedy man in a gray suit and hat, with a long, roughly assembled face got out, the lights of the ambulance flashing on his pale skin.

Paul knew Sergeant Pete "Mitch" Mitchell, LAPD Homicide, from a few murder cases they had worked on together over the years. He was a good cop, a meticulous witness, with a serious demeanor leavened only occasionally by biting humor and a raucous laugh that seemed to erupt out of nowhere. Paul had never heard any rumors about him as he did with so many other officers, hints of payoffs, planting evidence, and brutality. Even so, their relationship had never been more than professionally cordial. Paul had burned far too many bridges and prosecuted far too many bad cops to ever be trusted—even by the honest ones.

When the sergeant's eyes came to rest on Blake, they registered weariness, and perhaps anger.

"You shouldn't be here, Jim."

Blake broke away from the cluster of uniforms and approached him tentatively, his voice tense, excited. "Mitch, I'm here for the same reason you are. It can't be a

12

coincidence. Colored guy with a scar like a horseshoe on his cheek running away from the scene. We need to interview this man to see what he knows. If I can just have a minute—"

The sergeant's face hardened and he shook his head. He took Blake aside, voice low, his hand on his shoulder. "For God's sakes, leave it alone," he hissed. His face leaned closer to Blake's and softened. "Just shut up and do your time and you'll be back in Homicide before you know it. Let it go."

Then Sergeant Mitchell reached over and slapped his hand against the side of the ambulance, signaling for it to leave. The driver waved from the window, the siren wailed, and the vehicle took off up the street.

"Mitch—" Blake began to protest.

"Go home, Jim. You're done for the night." He looked up and addressed the rest of the officers who were watching silently in the street. "We're finished here," he announced.

While the other uniforms proceeded to their cruisers, Blake remained, working his jaw muscles, then headed Sergeant Mitchell off as he turned toward his car. "Mitch, let me go with you to the hospital."

"I'll handle it," Mitchell said stiffly. His eyes were warning. Blake must have taken the admonition seriously, because he stepped back, unblocking the sergeant's path.

As Mitchell pulled open his door, he recognized Paul watching from the sidewalk. He angled his head, a puzzled but friendly smile creeping across his lips. "Deputy D.A. Winters, what brings you out tonight?" His eyes rose to the theater marquee. "Enjoy the movie? I didn't know that sort of thing was black tie."

Paul was standing below the marquee and couldn't see the film's title. He glanced over at a poster near the entrance—a drawing of a naked woman with windows strategically placed around her breasts and an open doorway between her spread legs. He felt his cheeks flush, but before he could answer, Sergeant Mitchell threw his head back and laughed, then slipped into his car.

Blake stood in the street watching the sergeant's sedan drive away, his face tight, then hesitated a moment before sauntering with that confident gait of his over to Paul on the sidewalk. As he approached, Paul took in how he had changed since the last time he'd seen him. He was still an impressive, powerfully built man, especially dressed in blue, and Paul found his breath catching in his throat. That wasn't new. That hadn't changed. He saw the years showed in little ways, in the streaks of gray at the temples of his once unruly black hair, now buzzed to a crew cut, and in the eyes Paul could never forget: deep blue flecked with coal black, but more turbulent now, creased with dark circles.

Paul didn't know what else to say, so he said, "Are you okay?" For the first time he noticed a book with a dark blue cover snugly tucked under his arm.

"I've been better. Looks like you're going to a party."

"Oh, the Music Center. It's a fundraiser."

Blake had a hard time looking at him, his eyes shifting everywhere except to Paul's face. It had been like that the last time they had spoken. Ten years ago. Paul had forgiven him for everything that had happened back then, but that hadn't been enough. Sometimes, he came to realize, the hardest person to forgive is yourself. In the intervening years it had been easier to avoid one another, averting their eyes on the rare occasions their paths crossed at City Hall. The last time he'd seen him, a few years back, Paul had been with David and several friends at the Brown Derby when Blake had walked in. He had stopped in the doorway, spotted Paul and quickly slipped back out the door. Every time Paul ran into him he felt a tug deep inside and a sense of loss he couldn't explain.

14

Blake dug a flip-top box out of his pocket and offered him a Chesterfield.

"No," Paul said. "I quit." He smiled wanly. "You know, the Surgeon General's warning." The bombshell report three years before conclusively linking smoking to cancer—and David's gentle-at-first, then more insistent, nagging—had convinced him to give it up. He missed it, though, especially at times like this, when he didn't know what to do with his hands.

Paul watched Blake strike a match and light up. He had forgotten how big Blake's hands were, and the black hairs thick on his wrists. His fingernails had been bitten to the quick, and Paul wondered if that was a new habit, or if it had been so long that he simply no longer remembered. "I thought you were in Homicide. What are you doing in uniform?"

Blake chuckled sourly and exhaled a stream of smoke out of his nostrils. "That's a long story."

An awkward silence fell between them, Blake studying the sidewalk, Paul gazing beyond his shoulder at smog halos around streetlights and neon signs up the block.

"Where are you living now?" Paul asked finally to break the silence.

Paul had heard he'd gotten married, had a kid.

"I'm over in Hollywood, on Sierra Lane, off Canyon Drive, the very last house on a little dead-end street that shoots up into the hills. Tiny, but it has quite a view. You?"

"Brentwood still. But I bought a place a few years back, just up the block from where I used to be." He realized then that Blake had never been to his old apartment, that their most intimate moment had occurred in the back seat of a Hudson Hornet on a night-shrouded cliff overlooking the lights of the city.

15

The horn of the only squad car still parked in front of the theater honked and a handsome young cop stuck his head out the driver's window. "Does my girl have to ring in the new year alone? Or is somebody going to get his fat ass back in the seat?"

"Well," Blake said, shrugging, "I'd better be going."

"See you, Jim." Paul felt a pang inside and wanted to tell him it didn't have to be like this between them, but he couldn't get the words out. Instead, he nodded and walked away.

When he reached the limo, Paul looked back to catch a last glimpse of Blake, but he had already ducked into the patrol car. Paul hesitated a moment as an inexplicable wave of sadness washed over him. What was it about that guy that always got to him, that lingered uneasily in the back of his mind and wouldn't let go? He bit his lip as he watched the black-and-white merge with traffic and disappear up the street. As Paul slid into the back seat, he felt a spear of regret that he had decided to stop in the first place.

# Chapter 2

The party was in full swing when Paul and Jeannie arrived at the Music Center. The tuxedo and evening gown crowd spilled out from the lobby of the new Dorothy Chandler Pavilion—five stories of sparkling glass and tapered columns showcasing monumental chandeliers inside—into the plaza and around the fountain, which spurted graceful arcs of spotlighted water. The theater had been named after the woman who had led the campaign to build a permanent home for music and the dramatic arts in the city in the belief that without it Los Angeles, long derided as a cultural wasteland, would never become the great metropolis it was destined to be. When complete, the complex would house three theaters for the performing arts and rival those of any municipality in the world.

In what was undoubtedly the largest urban renewal project the city had ever seen, the entire Bunker Hill neighborhood was being transformed into a vast business and cultural center. Gone were the mad, rambling Victorians, like sweet elderly dowagers of another era covered in delicate lace. Once the homes of wealthy citizens, they had fallen into disrepair over the decades and had been divided into rooming houses for the working poor. Among the rubble of the bulldozed mansions, chrome and glass high-rises were reaching up gaunt against the sky, beneficiaries of the city's recent repeal of height-limit laws. Little was said of the nearly ten thousand who had been forced from their homes, or the groceries and shops and movie theaters that catered to them, now closing from a lack of customers. Even the large department stores were suffering, and with the advent of malls sprouting up all over the city, their days were numbered. Haunted by cars and parking lots and skyscrapers, this part of downtown Los Angeles was rapidly becoming a shining ghost town by nightfall, a soulless place to escape from at the end of the business day, but not a neighborhood.

"Paul!" District Attorney Bulgetti called to them, waving his hand. He was a big man with a big personality and a big waist to go with it. The taut fabric of his tux jacket strained against his stomach, the button ready to pop. He excused himself from a group of men who looked none too pleased to be straightjacketed in formal wear, bounded over with energy belying his age of sixty-three, and kissed Jeannie on the cheek with obvious pleasure.

"So good to see you, Jeannie." He shook Paul's hand vigorously then stood back and nodded with approval. "I have to say, you two kids make such an attractive couple."

Paul and Jeannie had their act down to a T from years of experience. A more affectionate and doting couple you would never meet. He had been bringing Jeannie to Christmas parties at the D.A.'s office for over a decade now, and they always got a good laugh out of how everybody fawned over them and chirped what an adorable pair they made.

A waiter glided by with wine and hors d'oeuvres on a tray and Bulgetti handed them both long-stemmed glasses. "Now, Jeannie, is it all right if I borrow your fella for a few minutes?"

"Of course," Jeannie said. "I have to go powder my nose anyway."

"What she really wants," Paul grinned at her, placing his hand on the small of her back in a casual but carefully calculated proprietary gesture, "is to meet the new governor." While he played along with their easy rapport, his apprehension continued to grow over what his boss wanted to discuss with him. He took a quick sip of the wine hoping it would settle his nerves. His awkward encounter with Jim Blake tarried in the back of his mind; the unfinished business between them was the last thing he wanted to think about now.

Bulgetti smiled indulgently. "Ah, giving comfort to the enemy. I do believe he is over by the fountain with Nancy. I'm sure he'd love to meet you." Bulgetti continued to smile benignly as he watched her go, then all pretense of affability quickly faded and his face fell, accentuating his sagging jowls. "That damned Republican bastard. Not even sworn into office and already he has his eyes on the Presidency in sixty-eight. Can you believe it?" Bulgetti was equally embittered toward his Democratic rivals after his miserable showing in the primary election, but both he and Paul agreed the new governor was a disaster for the state.

Paul shrugged. "A lot can happen in two years." Reagan had sailed into the governor's mansion on the winds of white resentment against rioting Negroes, government welfare handouts, and conservative backlash over growing campus unrest at UC Berkeley. As a candidate Reagan had referred to the student protestors as "beatniks, radicals and filthy speech advocates" and accused them of turning student dances into sex orgies. It had been that kind of campaign. He'd won by a landslide.

"Come," Bulgetti said, putting his arm around Paul's shoulder. "We need to talk."

They strolled past the fountain, where Jeannie had joined an animated group surrounding the Reagans, and crossed the plaza to where another theater was still under construction.

"Jeannie's such a sweet girl," Bulgetti mused fondly, apparently forgetting politics for the moment. "How long have you been going out now?"

"Oh, quite a while."

"You don't find them like that every day. You really should marry her."

"Yes, Jeannie is wonderful," Paul said with a breezy noncommittal air he had mastered over the years.

Bulgetti stopped short and his arm dropped from Paul's shoulder. "I'm serious," he said, his eyes meeting Paul's and holding, his tone suddenly blunt. "You should marry her."

Crimson heat seared his face and Paul looked away at the view unfolding from the plaza down the hill to where the night-lit City Hall towered above the rest of downtown. Was this what his boss had wanted to talk to him about? He felt a sinking deflation in his chest and a sudden fear that Bulgetti and the rest of his colleagues at the District Attorney's Office had known his number all along. Who was he kidding? He was middle-aged. Despite his continuing charade escorting Jeannie to office parties surely there was already talk behind his back. Nobody dated for ten years. How much longer could he expect to play the role of carefree single man about town? Sometimes his ambition felt like a noose tightening around his neck.

He scrambled for a response, but Bulgetti changed gears before Paul could say a word. "I mentioned there was something I wanted to talk to you about. I've been offered a post in Washington, D.C. in the Department of Justice. After careful thought, I've decided to take it."

Suddenly Paul understood and swallowed hard. "I don't know what to say." Several thoughts battled for his attention at once, from hopeful to euphoric. Bulgetti's mention of marriage was probably not a warning, just solid advice. A married man running for office always appeared more stable to voters, he reasoned, than a single one. Crowding that realization out, and the relief that came with it, was the understanding that after all the years of waiting to run for office, his moment had finally arrived. This was it. He felt so light his feet hardly touched the ground. A rush of pride flooded through him and all he wanted to do was call David and tell him.

"You don't have to say anything. I'll be officially announcing my resignation in the next few weeks. There will be a special election in the spring. You've been my right hand all these years and the public knows it. A good part of the success of our office has been because of you." Bulgetti appraised him and nodded knowingly. "It seems like yesterday that I was in the same position you are in. Don't tell me you haven't dreamed that one day this moment would come. It's your turn to run for District Attorney, Paul. This is your time. You earned it. Just keep your nose clean, and it will be smooth sailing."

Paul shook his head in disbelief and laughed. "I can't believe it. Tony, really, yours will be big shoes to fill."

"Aw," Bulgetti said, patting him on the back, "stop buttering up the old man. Say, I want you to meet some people, some very important people." He winked. "Be on your best behavior."

He ushered Paul through the crowd until they came upon a gathering of three men and a woman sipping their wine and chatting quietly with the air of casual exclusivity possessed only by the very rich. While they stood among so many others, somehow they were a world unto themselves. How did everyone else instinctively know, Paul marveled, that they were not to be approached without a proper introduction? Paul found himself shaking the hand of a balding man with red hair and translucent skin scattered with middle-aged freckles.

"Charlie Barnes is the president of the California Real Estate Association." Bulgetti grinned. "A hell of a lot of the skyscrapers sprouting up like mushrooms all over downtown are his fault."

"Now, now," Charlie laughed, "once we're done Los Angeles is going to have a modern downtown that will attract business from all over the world. And our beautiful Music Center is a part of that."

"And this," Bulgetti said of a tall jowly man in his sixties with a thick head of silver hair and eyebrows white as snowdrifts, "is Buck Chandler."

He squeezed Paul's hand in a powerful grasp that could only be interpreted as a play for dominance at the very first moments of acquaintanceship. But his horsey smile was friendly, his voice folksy and deep. Only his narrowed eyes, pale blue and assessing, kept Paul on guard. He struck Paul as the kind of man who was always calm, even when he was crushing you under his heel. "Good to meet you, Paul. I've read quite a bit about you in the papers…" and here his smile turned into an ironic grin, "can't quite recall which one."

A polite chuckle rippled through the group. Despite all the attention and praise bestowed on Dorothy Chandler for spearheading the drive to erect the Music Center, she was hardly the only one in the family to make a mark on Los Angeles. Paul knew the extended Chandler family was one of the richest and most powerful in the city, and if any one family could take credit or blame for how L.A. had developed over its first century, it was the Chandlers. They owned a diverse real estate and business empire, with the *Los Angeles Times* its crown jewel.

Paul felt utterly obsequious grinning back and saying, "The *Times* is on my doorstep every morning," even though it was true. Better get used to it, he thought, this is what campaigning is all about. To his surprise, bitter lines formed at the edges of Buck Chandler's wide mouth and Paul knew he'd said the wrong thing.

"Too bad it isn't the paper it once was."

There was an awkward silence, then an alarmingly slender woman standing next to Chandler dove in. "But at least we were able to get an endorsement for Ronnie this fall. But even that was a struggle, wasn't it, dear?" She patted Chandler affectionately on the sleeve.

"This is my wife," Buck Chandler said, "Agnes."

She offered Paul a bird-boned hand and a tight but amiable smile. "Agnes Wingate Chandler." She had a tight face, too, shrewd eyes, narrow lips glossed with pink lipstick, and blonde hair stiffly piled high. She looked twenty years younger than her husband, which would put her somewhere in her well-preserved forties. She spoke with the clipped enunciation of a private east coast women's college grad, but incongruously had the raspy voice of a woman whose best friends are whiskey and cigarettes.

"Delighted to meet you, Mrs. Chandler."

Paul turned to the last person in the gathering, a man in his late thirties with a bristly flat-top crew cut whose hard, compact body and military bearing couldn't be hidden under a tux, but before Paul could extend his hand, the man stepped back as if he was not part of the group. Paul had been a prosecutor long enough to recognize a cop, even in a stylish tuxedo; perhaps he was moonlighting as a bodyguard for the Chandlers and was expected not to socialize with the leisure class.

"Thanks in large part to Paul's prosecutions," Bulgetti began, as if dictating an election flyer, "the organized crime problem that plagued this city in the fifties is largely a thing of the past."

Buck waved his wine glass. "You've driven the gang-sters off Sunset Boulevard, now if you could just do the same with these damned long-hairs. Ever drive down there on a Saturday night? Can you believe the way these kids dress? The boys look like girls, and the girls look like boys."

They all chuckled dutifully, and while a couple came up and drew the others' attention, Agnes leaned toward Paul and laid her hand, light as a feather, on his arm. "You know, I'd like to put together a little informal party for you, so you can get to know some of our friends. People who would like to get to know you."

"That would be great, Mrs. Chandler." He could feel Bulgetti beaming at him as if he'd just won the lottery. He had the feeling he wasn't the first to hear that the District Attorney would be leaving office soon.

"After all," she said, giving him a knowing smile, "spring isn't that far off." She paused thoughtfully and pursed her lips. "I suppose we'll be electing a new assessor at the same time. You heard the news, that his death was ruled a suicide."

"Wesley Durkin? Yes, I read about it in the paper." Paul recalled a mild little man with a slight build who was prone to wearing cardigan sweaters and reminded him of the children's television host Mister Rogers both in appearance and temperament.

"I never met him personally, but my husband supported his campaign when he ran for office. It's a sad thing, you know, from what I understand he was still a fairly young man."

"Yes, it was quite a shock for the city, Mrs. Chandler."

"Please, call me Agnes," she said, her voice a throaty purr. "Oh, about my little get-together. How about next week, say, Tuesday at eight at Chasen's?"

"I'll look forward to it."

She leaned in closer to his ear. "We've been watching you," she confided, "and we like what we see."

◇◇◇

After Paul had excused himself and broken away from the Chandlers, he'd wandered through the crowd, enjoying mingling with movie stars and the political elite. The fact that David wasn't there to share it with him was the only thing marring the heady feeling he was experiencing.

"It looks like somebody has come up in the world. I didn't know you hobnobbed with the Chandlers."

Paul turned to find Marvin Botwinick teetering beside him, a smoldering pipe he never left home without in one hand and an empty wine glass in the other. Stout with a stubby beard streaked with gray, he looked miserable in a tuxedo.

"And it looks like *you've* had a few."

"I've only just begun." He grinned crookedly. "Easy for you, Paul. You look like Double-O-Seven in a tux, you handsome bastard. I'm an ugly, short little man who is uncomfortable socially at parties, especially wearing a monkey suit, which makes me sweaty in all my unpleasant crevices, surrounded by California Club types who wouldn't let a commie Jew radical like me on the premises of their golf course even if I was dressed as a plumber and came in the back door. Show me some compassion."

Botwinick was a reporter Paul worked with occasionally who had become a casual friend. Ten years before Paul had given him the story on corruption in city government that had made his career. After that, every paper in the country had wanted him, but Marvin had chosen to stay with the small liberal paper that had broken the story. When his paper crashed and burned in the early sixties along with several other L.A. dailies—victims of increased production costs and competition from television news— Botwinick had been plucked from the unemployment line along with the cream of other dying papers by the brash new publisher of the *L.A. Times*, Otis Chandler.

Paul waved over a passing waiter. "Another drink for the gentleman." He handed a fresh drink to Botwinick, who smiled at him gratefully from behind his thick beard.

"Ah, you're a good man. But do you know what makes it all worthwhile?"

"Tell me, before I have to call you a cab and send you home to your long-suffering wife."

"*That.*" He pointed with the hand holding his wine glass, barely spilling a drop, at the theater under construction at the other end of the plaza, which would be dedicated to experimental drama. "The Mark Taper Forum. Named after a big Westside Jew who donated a million bucks, and there's nothing the bluebloods at the country club can do about it. They'll be gritting their capped teeth every time they see a play."

While she hadn't exactly brought the WASP establishment and the Westside Jewish elite together in raising funds for the center, Dorothy Chandler had gladly taken from both, and in refusing to have any planning sessions at venues like the California Club that excluded Jews, she had struck a blow against well-entrenched discrimination in the city. There were some who would never forgive her.

"Hmmm, now look at that." Marvin tilted his head. "Where are the photographers when we need them?"

Across the way Paul recognized Dorothy Chandler, with curls of gray hair, a white dress with a bow and white gloves, exchanging pleasantries with Agnes Wingate Chandler.

"What's so special about that? What are they, sisters-in-law, right?"

"There's bad blood between Dorothy and most of her in-laws going way back to when she married into the family in the twenties. The entire Chandler family treated Dorothy like dirt because she came from a department store family—successful, but not in the Chandler's league, not by a long shot. They drove her to a nervous breakdown, but later Dorothy showed them all, first by campaigning to save the Hollywood Bowl in the fifties, and now this. But Agnes hates her most of all because Dorothy pressured her own husband to bypass Buck as the next publisher of the *Times*. Instead Dorothy insisted the job go to her own blond goldenboy son, Otis. Buck was supposed to be next in line for the job, so the rest of the family was livid."

Otis, the young scion of the Chandler clan was boldly refashioning the family paper from a right-wing rag— notorious for anti-union rants and dedicated to promoting the Republican Party and unbridled business growth—into a reputable and fair journal. He believed that without a great newspaper, Los Angeles would never become a great city. Under his tutelage the *Los Angeles Times* had gone from being considered the third worst paper in the country to one of the top ten, with a Pulitzer in its pocket, all within a few years. Paul now understood his *faux pas* in mentioning the *Times* to Buck Chandler. Undoubtedly the liberal direction his nephew Otis had taken the paper in wasn't the only sore spot.

"Considering how much they hate each other," Marvin went on, raising his eyebrows conspiratorially and sipping his drink, "the big mystery is why Agnes suddenly got her husband to donate loads of money at the last minute to the Music Center."

Before Paul could follow up with another question, Jeannie came over to them, eyes wide and gushed, "He's like a sitcom dad on TV, but with very greasy hair. He said it was okay to call him Ronnie. He says 'golly' a lot. And when he smiles and his eyes get all crinkly and moist, it's hard not to like him."

"Better not let David hear you say that," Paul warned. Reagan had vowed to veto any attempt by the legislature to repeal California's lifetime prison sentence for homosexual sodomy, and David had campaigned furiously against him. Paul glanced at his watch. "Look, it's almost midnight, and I need to make a call." He excused himself while Botwinick took the opportunity to snatch two drinks from a passing tray for himself and Jeannie.

"Cheers!" Marvin called after him.

Paul felt buoyed by the news he had to tell David, and wondered if he should wait until the party at home tonight to announce it to everyone. No, he wanted to tell David before anyone else. He knew how proud he'd be.

He found a booth on the sidewalk on Hope Street on the northwest side of the plaza, but it was already occupied. Because the man in the booth had his back to Paul, it took him a moment to recognize the guy with the military demeanor who had been with the Chandlers. Even though Paul stood back at a polite distance, and the door to the booth was closed, the man glanced back sharply, as if to ensure he couldn't be overheard. When their eyes met Paul felt a little jolt. The man had still snake eyes in a battered boxer's face. After spitting a few more words into the phone, he hung up angrily, then strode so closely past Paul their shoulders brushed. It was such an unprovoked act of aggression in such an unlikely venue, that Paul turned with a puzzled expression on his face to watch the man thread his way back through the crowd. The heavy scent of the man's cologne, a cheap variety advertised on television, lingered after he was gone.

Paul stepped up to the pay phone, dropped a dime, and dialed the number of the bar. He let the phone ring and ring, but nobody answered. He supposed the bartenders might be busy serving drinks, but surely someone would pick up eventually. But no one did. He held the phone away from his ear, looking at it doubtfully, a line of concern etching his brow, and slowly replaced it in its cradle.

Now that's strange, he thought.

# Chapter 3

It was two minutes to midnight at the Black Cat.

David leaned against a wall in the back corner of the bar beside the juke box with a bottle of Coors in his hand and tried not to feel hurt and depressed. It always seemed worse when everyone was having a good time except him. He took a swig of beer and looked moodily about the packed room. The costume contest at the bar down the street had ended earlier and an influx of festive drag queens jostled their way through the crowd, holding court, flirting for drinks, and demanding to be admired, while a trio of Negro girls called the Rhythm Queens sang jazz-rock at a microphone. Beyond shiny party hats perched jauntily on patrons' heads, three decorated trees left over from Christmas glittered and colored balloons covered the ceiling.

Taking another sip from the bottle, David wondered gloomily what Paul was doing now. Probably joking around with movie stars—it was reported that Cary Grant and David Niven were going to be there—while waiters in black tie and tails clamored to refill his champagne glass. Paul had looked so striking that evening in his tuxedo with his dark brown hair, cut with razor precision, aquiline nose and powerful jaw, the strong lines of his face softened only by his sympathetic brown eyes. It had dawned on David while he'd helped Paul with his cuff links that in all the years of their relationship they'd never once gone to a function in formal dress together. And here he was, once again, celebrating the New Year without him.

He glanced over at Billy, who was standing next to him swaying to the music in his tight blue jeans, a polo sweater and sneakers. David had taken him under his wing years ago when Billy was still a lonely teen who had begun hanging around the office of *ONE Magazine*, where David had volunteered his artistic skills in the layout of the periodical.

Billy jabbed an elbow in David's side, nodding his head, his long blond bangs cascading across his forehead. "That guy is checking you out."

David scanned the crowd and spotted a man next to the pool table in a checkered shirt and leather vest with shaggy hair and a droopy little mustache grinning at him from across the room.

"I'm already taken."

"Uh-huh, and where, exactly, is that boyfriend of yours? Since Mr. Right has abandoned you for the night, how about Mr. Right Now?" Billy's baby-blue eyes peered through his bangs. "You know, that guy's actually kind of cute. He's better than that crabby old fuddy-duddy you're married to." Billy had had it in for Paul for years, since he was a teenager sneaking into bars with a fake I.D. and cruising parks in his Capri pants and shirt tails knotted at the abdomen like a calypso dancer. All he'd ever gotten from Paul were stern paternal warnings about the dangers of getting picked up by older men and the threat of arrest by vice cops. And, of course, condemnation for the flamboyant way he'd dressed in public. If Paul had simply told him it was easier to get laid wearing masculine apparel, he would have done it long before. He'd found that out after seeing *Rebel Without a Cause* and on a lark mimicking James Dean's outfit. Suddenly he turned heads everywhere he went. In the end, he realized, it was *all* drag. Now that he was twenty-six, he grudgingly acknowledged Paul had only been trying to protect him, but he still got a kick out of giving it back every chance he got.

"You're a troublemaker," David observed. "And anyway, Paul is only seven years older than me."

"Yeah," Billy drawled, "like I said, officially ancient. Forty… isn't that the age when your penis falls off?"

A hush of anticipation came over the crowd and then everyone began to shout the countdown chant. *"Ten— nine—eight—"*

"Oh, my God," Billy cried suddenly. "Do you see who that is over there? It's the Man in Black!" Long ago Billy had had a crush on a man his friends had suspected was a male hustler, but he'd disappeared from the scene years ago as mysteriously as he had first appeared. But in all this time Billy had never stopped talking about him. "I'll be right back." He pushed his way through a gaggle of drag queens and vanished into the crowd.

"Thank you for leaving me alone at midnight," David muttered to no one in particular.

*"—three—two—one—Happy New Year!"*

A bartender pulled a string and balloons on the ceiling began to fall and confetti sailed in all directions while noisemakers squawked and men kissed to ring in the New Year.

Just as the colored girls began to sing a rock version of "Auld Lang Syne," the jubilant atmosphere in the bar changed in an instant when a scuffle broke out in the center of the room. The music abruptly stopped and David heard a scream and a shout as a wave of fear and confusion rippled across the bar. A discordant murmur rose and suddenly he felt himself lifted off the ground and slammed against the wall as the crowd pushed and shoved to get away from the melee.

Across the room a casually dressed man who had been playing pool violently grabbed the bartender and hiked him up by his collar and dragged him over the bar. Beer bottles went flying and glass exploded on the floor. As the bartender was hustled out the front door, he shouted, "If you're the police, you have to identify yourself!"

The man hauling him to the door whipped out a gun and shouted back, "This is the only I.D. I need."

When the front door momentarily opened, David glimpsed uniformed cops posted outside, and he knew the place had been infiltrated by plainclothes vice cops and this was a raid.

A man in a red sweater not far from David grabbed a patron and threw him headlong into the juke box with such force the impact rocked the machine away from the wall. As David tried to jump out of harm's way, he lost his footing and fell on all fours to the floor. The last thing he saw before he went down was the front door bursting open and a troop of uniformed cops charging inside swinging their batons to the screams of customers in the bar.

Something struck him hard on the back of the neck and he fell flat, his head swimming, and a cold dark fear gripped him that if he didn't get up fast he would be trampled to death. The soles of someone's shoes stumbled over him, then he felt the sharp jab of a high heel on his thigh. He frantically climbed to his hands and knees and forced his way through a sea of stampeding legs to the wall, where it took every effort to slide up into standing position.

Everywhere he looked now he saw chaos. Cops indiscriminately swung their clubs while customers dodged and ran. A vice cop tore ornaments from a Christmas tree and tossed a nearby chair in the air. A stout queen in a red wig, full-length gown and sequined high heels was on the floor face down straddled by a vice cop who was cuffing him behind the back. Handcuffed drag queens were being prodded by a uniformed policeman out the front door.

David had experienced bar raids before, but they were generally quiet, humiliating affairs, usually leaving little more than anger that burned inside him long after the incident was over. If you put up with being carded and a bit of verbal abuse, and maybe being herded outside, you might be lucky enough not to be one of the handful of guys randomly arrested and shoved into police wagons and whisked to the nearest precinct house for a miserable night in jail until the bail bondsman showed up. But this was different and the pandemonium terrified him. He knew he had to get out quickly before he got crushed by the crowd or beaten by cops. He craned his neck looking for Billy. Had he been arrested already and dragged outside?

He pushed his way to the front of the bar where others were crowding the door to exit. Once outside, he found safety in numbers—the sidewalk was jammed with people trying to escape—and slipped along the art-deco façade of the bar, a painted-over window featuring a grinning black cat, and made his way stealthily down Sunset.

Patrol cars were pulling up in front of the bar and several customers and bar employees were being forced to lie face down on the sidewalk. Among them David spotted two bartenders and a couple of drag queens he had seen earlier in the evening. A boy in taffeta leaned spread eagle against a squad car while a uniform frisked him. But David couldn't see Billy anywhere in the gathering.

He was halfway down the block when he heard a voice call to him from behind.

"You, come back here, honey."

David froze and a hard knot tightened in his stomach. He turned slowly and faced a young, short cop a dozen yards away, a club in his hand and a sizable belly protruding over his belt. Their eyes locked and David involuntarily swallowed, an adrenaline rush coursing through his veins. He pondered his options only a moment, then broke into a sprint down Sunset. He heard an angry shout and then heavy footfalls behind him.

"I'm going to fuck you over good if you don't stop, you little faggot," the cop shouted.

David glanced swiftly over his shoulder but kept running, his heart beating so fast he thought it would burst. Despite the cop's girth, rolling like a wave, his feet pounding the pavement like bricks, David feared he was losing ground. He wasn't convinced he could outrun the cop on Sunset for long, but dreaded venturing onto the dark tree-lined residential streets feeding off the boulevard, where he could be beaten in the shadows. At least the rows of small businesses along Sunset were well-lit and offered the possible protection of witnesses who might cause the cop to show restraint. Then it came to him that there were easily a dozen gay bars along this stretch of the strip in Silver Lake that he could lose himself in. The bar called New Faces was just up ahead on the far corner across Sanborn, and he raced toward it.

"Stop right there!" the cop hollered.

David was nearly across Sanborn when he saw two officers kicking a man in a bartender's apron lying on the sidewalk in front of the bar, and knew the Black Cat wasn't the only establishment under attack that night. In the gutter another man was being stomped by cops flashing batons.

He hesitated only a moment, but it was enough for the cop to catch up and he felt the searing blow of a club on the back of his head. In a surge of fury David spun around and socked the cop in the face. The cop stood there for a moment, stunned, his fleshy mouth hanging open. They stared at each other stupidly, then the cop gulped, his Adam's apple jumping, and reached for the gun in his holster.

David bolted forward, pushing through the bar's door, then stopped short the moment he was inside. He recognized the owner, Mrs. Leroy, sitting sprawled on the floor, a stunned expression on her middle-aged face, her hair disheveled, her dress bloody, as a young man stooped to help her up. Her hand clutched her cheek as if she had received a blow.

"Hide me!"

The young man pointed to a dark curtained doorway beyond the bar and David scurried past the few other patrons still in the place and dove through it.

He found himself in a dim back room crowded with beer and wine crates. His heart pounded and his breath rasped heavily in his ears. He could see a door with a window in it at the far end. He made his way quickly over to it, wrestled with the lock, and slipped back outside, closing the door behind him. He stood for a moment on a rickety wooden porch at the back of the building, his mind racing, and tried to catch his breath. He felt a strange exhilaration at the memory of punching the cop, and a triumphant little smile wavered briefly on his lips.

David slowly descended the porch stairs and peered around the corner. His breathing had slowed but his chest still burned. He watched four cops hoist the handcuffed bartender, who appeared bloody and unconscious, into the back seat of a waiting patrol car on the corner. The man lying in the gutter, left alone for the moment, moaned and rocked back and forth. David couldn't see the officer who had pursued him, but figured he was in the bar searching for him.

Silently David moved from the shadows onto the sidewalk then strode rapidly away from the bar up the residential street of lazy bungalows and into the night.

◇◇◇

The limo turned on Tweed Lane, a cul-de-sac just north of San Vicente Boulevard in Brentwood, and dropped Paul and Jeannie in front of his house, a forties ranch-style with a garage around the back, an orange tree in the front yard, and wisteria vines climbing on the shade porch. The curtains were drawn in the picture window, but he could see the lights were on and music blared from inside. He had his key in the lock when he breathed in a cloying sweetness that didn't come from any of the flowers in his yard.

"Goddammit," he said under his breath.

Parker Huston was lying on the living room floor by the couch smoking a joint with a mashed bag of Fritos resting on his chubby torso. He stared fixedly at a color bar test pattern that shone brightly on Paul's new television as the Beach Boys harmonized good vibrations from the console's high fidelity stereo. All the networks had gone to color prime time programming that season and Paul and David got a kick out of having friends over to watch shows in living color.

"You missed Guy Lombardo's countdown," Parker announced, blinking and taking a final hit on a slobbery twisted doobie before crushing it in an ashtray on the carpet.

Paul waved his hand irritably to cut the smoke curling in the air. "Do you really have to smoke dope in my house? You can smell it all the way down the block. What happens if my neighbors call the police?"

"And hello and Happy New Year to you, too, Paul." Parker observed him through heavily lidded eyes. His cheeks were red from too much booze. "You are so square. First, your neighbors are smoking it too, in their pools with their neighbors' wives. And that's before the orgies start."

"And could you please turn that thing down?"

A Neil Diamond song came on the stereo and Parker shuffled over to the console, singing along, "Cherry, Cherry, Cherry, baby." He turned down the volume. "I tell you, the man is a poet."

Jeannie went over and kissed Pat, who sat slumped in a recliner, her straw hair lank as ever, wearing jeans and a red and white Roller Derby jersey with the number 17 embroidered on it. She offered a smoldering joint to Jeannie.

"You're as bad as he is," Paul scolded, but with considerably less bite.

Pat pulled Jeannie down into her lap and patted her bee hive wig curiously. "You made my girlfriend into a Barbie Doll," she said, shooting a stream of smoke toward the ceiling, "and you begrudge me getting high?"

Paul nodded at Jeff Dupuis, who lounged on the couch with a glass of whiskey resting on his knee. He had grown his hair out in a Natural, which made his head look a little like a liquid shoe polish dispenser with a round sponge top, and a sparse mustache and whiskers sprouted on his lip and chin. Lately, it seemed he did all his shopping at Army-Navy Surplus stores, down to his snug-fitting bell-bottomed button-flied dungarees.

"Jeff's been brooding all night," Parker blathered, "because you didn't invite enough cute white boys to the party."

"I'm doing fine, Parker," Jeff countered with a drunken grin. "You've kept me busy. I enjoy observing the decadent white man in his native environment, you blue-eyed devil."

"Oh, I almost forgot. Pat, I have something for you." Parker fumbled with his jacket, which hung over a chair. "My latest. *Sorority Sisters' Sins.* Hot off the press. You're gonna love this." He waved a paperback at her. The cover showed a woman in butch apparel leering over a seated pretty girl, while a man gazed at them in the background. Parker was a librarian who worked at the downtown library on Fifth, but for extra bucks at night he churned out pulp novels at an alarming rate with titles like *Truck-Stop Tarts* and *Shame Alley*. Cheap paperbacks with sensational subject matter had proliferated going back to the early fifties, but since a series of Supreme Court rulings striking down many obscenity laws, the potboilers had exploded in popularity—including those with gay themes—though prosecutions for salacious material continued and publishers still found their businesses threatened by mountains of legal fees required to defend their books.

Groaning, Pat fumed, "The only ones that are any good are written by women. The rest are horrible. Why does the lesbian always have to die in the end?"

"Who cares if she dies or not?" Parker asked, a puzzled expression coming to his face. "It's *how* she dies that makes it poignant. In my book a bull seduces a young co-ed, but when the girl spurns her for the campus jock, the dyke splashes acid in her face and runs out into the street where she gets hit by a Mack truck." He looked pensive. "It's really a tender story of unrequited love."

Loosening his bow tie, Paul asked, "Where's David and Billy? Aren't they here yet?" He pulled off his tux jacket and headed down the hall to the bedroom. He hung up the jacket and tie, and was about to change his shirt, when he heard the front door burst open. A trill of excitement ignited in his chest at the thought of telling David about his conversation with D.A. Bulgetti that evening. Everything he had worked for all these years was finally going to pay off. He couldn't hear what David was saying in the living room, but his tone was strident, and with growing concern Paul strode back down the hall.

"They raided the place," David was saying, the front door still wide open. Jeff sat up straight on the couch, and

Jeannie, still in Pat's lap, put her hand over her mouth. David's curly dark hair, long enough to touch his ears, was disheveled and he had a wild look in his brown eyes. "They beat the fucking shit out of everybody and they arrested at least a dozen guys, maybe more. A pig chased me down the street and bashed me on the head."

Paul came over and held him tightly, and David sank into his arms.

"Let me see."

"No, I'm all right."

"Let me see."

David allowed him to examine the back of his neck, and Paul could see a bruise and swelling at his hairline. "Come into the kitchen. I'll get you some ice."

David pulled away from him and there was anger in his voice. "You've got to go down there and get them out."

Paul figured those arrested had been taken to the new Rampart Station on Temple. It had been a while since he'd heard of such aggressive tactics by the LAPD, in fact some believed an unofficial truce existed lately between the department and gay establishments. That hadn't stopped entrapment arrests, of course, but Paul hadn't heard complaints about this level of wholesale brutality in some time. Since it wasn't election season—always a bad time for gay businesses—Paul suspected the new captain of the Rampart Station was trying to make a name for himself, maybe even angling to be noticed when the next police chief was chosen.

"Where's Billy?"

"For all I know he got arrested or he's hurt. I lost track of him before the cops busted in."

Paul led him down the hall to the kitchen and made him sit at the table. He went over to the fridge and opened the door to the freezer. The ice cube trays were empty. Of course, Paul thought. The party had been going on in the

40

living room all night. He found a frozen steak and held it up for David to see.

"I guess this is going to have to do."

"Forget it. I'm okay. Paul, I know you worry about getting involved in stuff like this, but you've got to tell the D.A. what's happening," David said. His voice had taken on that urgency that always made Paul wary. "Tell him what the police department is doing in the bars. Make him drop all the charges. You've got to prosecute those cops for what they did."

For years Paul had quietly given advice to gay men caught in vice stings and lesbians harassed for wearing male apparel. He had likened his involvement to balancing on the edge of a razor. Any whiff of open support toward homosexuals at the District Attorney's Office could only lead to his downfall. He thought about the increased scrutiny he would be under campaigning to become the next District Attorney, and the financial contributors he would have to please.

Paul sank into the chair across from him.

"I can't do that."

David stared at him. "What do you mean?"

Paul reached across the table and took David's hands in his. "I have to be very careful for the next few months. Something happened tonight. Bulgetti told me he's resigning from office. There will be a special election in the spring. David, this is it. This is what we've waited all these years for." He leaned forward and tightened his grip, and his eyes took on light. "Think of the impact I can have. Think of what the authority of my office can bring to really change things for all of us."

David blinked thoughtfully and leaned back in his chair. "How can you possibly change things when you can never speak out for fear someone somewhere will think you're gay?"

"That isn't fair, David."

He saw David's jaw clench and he knew they were going to have a fight.

"You know, I think I'd better go home. I don't think I'm in the mood for a party tonight."

Paul held tight to David's hands. "I don't want you to go. You're in no condition to drive, especially all the way over to Hollywood—" he stopped himself and shut his eyes for a moment in dismay. He realized he had just taken the conversation in a dangerous direction. Like throwing gasoline on a flame. David had been complaining for quite a while about the long trip over to Brentwood and how Paul never stayed at his place and how great it would be if he gave up his apartment and moved in with Paul.

"When are you and I ever going to live together?" David asked quietly. He pulled his hands from Paul's and crossed his arms.

"That has nothing to do with this."

"It's been ten years. Ten years that I've waited for you."

Paul felt his anger rise. It always came down to this. David knew full well that was impossible, that he would never be District Attorney if he shacked up with another man, that it was ridiculous and unfair for David to constantly bring it up as if facing the reality of his work situation was some kind of moral failing.

"You've known from the very beginning that that's not going to happen. You've known that all along."

David's lower lip quivered. Paul might as well have slapped him. It was as if a truth that had always been evident had finally become clear to him. An expression of such crushing humiliation came over David's face that Paul regretted it as soon as the words came out of his mouth.

"I guess that about says it." David threw up his hands and without another word got up and left the room.

Paul sighed and put his face in his hands. He had dreamed for so many years about this moment, and now that it had come, he had made a huge mess of it. He was stung by David's curt dismissal of what was undoubtedly one of the most important events in Paul's career, and that he had belittled the impact Paul could have if he became the next District Attorney. And yet he knew what he had said to David was inexcusable. He got up slowly and splashed water in his face from the sink.

When Paul returned to the living room a minute later, the party was already breaking up. He couldn't help but feel everybody was eyeing him accusingly, or not looking at him at all. As usual all their friends seemed to be on David's side. Jeff was pulling on his pea coat and David was already halfway out the front door.

"Look," Jeff said, "I'm going to mosey down to the Rampart Station and see if those guys have a bail bondsman yet." Jeff had been a cop for several years before graduating from law school. He had a one-man law office in South Central. "Don't worry, David, I can take care of it."

David nodded at Jeff, then without looking back at Paul, disappeared out the door.

Parker stumbled to his feet and went for his jacket. "I was going to crash here tonight but the vibes are definitely a downer. I'm out of here."

"Yeah, it's getting late," Pat said, sighing. She trailed Jeff and Parker out the door. On the walkway, she held up her palms. "Hey, I feel drops. I think a downpour is on the way. Maybe it'll get rid of the smog."

Before following the others, Jeannie hung back for a moment, giving Paul a sad smile. She gently cupped his cheeks in her hands, her eyes etched with concern. "Poor Paul. You worry me." Then she turned and slipped out the door, and he was left standing alone in his living room.

# Chapter 4

He paced back and forth until he couldn't stand it anymore, then Paul went outside and rolled opened the garage door.

Sliding into his year-old Thunderbird, he sank into the red-and-black leather bucket seat. He was tired and angry but he knew he couldn't sleep and all he wanted to do was get out on the road to clear his head.

He headed north to Sunset then east into the city, not knowing, not caring, where he was going. Rain began to spatter against the windshield. Except for the occasional drunk making his way home from a party, the road was deserted at this hour of night, a bright yellow line shining in the beams of his headlights on the curving blacktop. He sped with ruthless intensity, flashing through intersections just before the light turned red, reliving his argument with David and how the evening had careened out of control.

He had always pictured celebrating his candidacy for District Attorney with David and their friends, and here he was alone with everybody apparently annoyed with him. He felt badly about the cold-blooded tone he had taken with David, and yet he knew in his heart everything he had said was true. They could never live together. It was just too dangerous. David had always known what he was getting into by dating him. And suddenly he was furious that David had taken *his* moment of triumph, the one he had waited years for, and turned it into another one of his political crusades, with Paul expected to take all the risks.

Easy for David, he had nothing to lose. Sometimes Paul found it difficult to contain how frustrated and disappointed he was with him. David was thirty-three years old—middle-aged, for God's sakes—and what had he done with his life? In the past ten years he had squandered his considerable artistic talent in advertising working odd jobs in little agencies, when he really should be in New York making a name for himself.

Paul knew David had never gone after his dreams because a New York career meant leaving Paul behind, but the guilt he felt just rankled him further. Even in L.A., David could have done *something* more. Instead of focusing on his career, he had flown around the country participating in protests rarely numbering more than a dozen or so in front of the U.N. and the White House. Paul could still remember the picket signs. *Stop Castro's Persecution of Homosexuals! End the Federal Government's Ban on Homosexual Employees!*

David's most recent obsession was a tiny local newspaper reporting on the latest gay news put out by the radical group he belonged to. It wasn't even a newspaper. It was a newsletter. An ink-smudged mimeographed newsletter at that. Some revolution, Paul thought savagely.

He had driven all the way to Hollywood, the rain now pounding the rooftop, the windshield wipers slurping, before he asked himself where he was going and when he should turn back. In the rear of his mind he told himself if he had planned to go to David's house, he would have turned south nearly a mile back.

His mouth was dry and it was as if someone else was steering the car as he turned up Canyon then found the narrow lane nestled among tall hedges. There were no streetlights on Sierra and all the houses running up the hill were dark. He coasted to a stop at the top of the dead end and cut the headlights.

Paul hesitated a moment, then got out of the car, shut the door, and leaned back against it, gazing up at the last house, perched atop a steep vine-covered incline, connected to the road by a long wooden staircase. The rain pelted down and in no time he was wet, his hair sopped, drops running in rivulets down his cheeks, his tux shirt soaked. What the hell are you doing? he chastised himself, what are you thinking? What if his car engine had woken somebody up, Blake's wife or his kid? He told himself he had to get out of there before anybody, especially Jim Blake, noticed. He couldn't explain even to himself why he was here.

But he didn't move from the spot.

And then, in the black-as-night front picture window, he saw the brief flare of a lighted match and the red glow of a cigarette and realized his presence had been observed all along. He stared but couldn't make out the shape of the person holding the cigarette. He heard a lock mechanism tumble and the door opened into a gaping black hole, inviting him inside.

He was across the street and climbing the stairs before he could think about what he was doing. His heart began to pound harder as he climbed but he knew it wasn't because of the steep incline.

Only as he reached the porch did Blake's tall broad-shouldered figure take form against the darkness, framed by the doorway. He was still in his police uniform, the shirt open and the shirttails out, his chest a mass of black hair. They stared at each other a moment, not saying a word, Paul still standing in the rain, and then Blake swung the door open wider and stepped aside to let him in. Blake didn't ask what he was doing there at that hour of the night, and that told him they understood each other.

"I'm sorry, there's no place for you to sit. My wife left and she took everything. I can offer you something to drink, though. Some whiskey?"

"On ice, if you have it."

Paul could see the living room was a dim expanse of hardwood with no furniture, just a snarl of blankets in the middle of the floor that looked more like a nest than a bed. Blake headed for the kitchen, the heels of his shoes echoing on the hardwood. He flipped a switch and a narrow carpet of light streamed across the floor. Paul could hear the clink of ice in glasses as he stood looking out at the view from the front picture window, a swath of rich darkness sprinkled with the lights of the city. He waited for the beat of his heart to quiet.

He felt Blake's presence beside him but wasn't ready to look him in the face again, and both men stood silently watching the sprawling canvas of night below. A sudden twitch of memory reminded him that the same lights had shone just as brightly ten years ago through the windshield of Blake's Hudson Hornet on a cliff above the city.

"The place isn't much," Blake said finally, "a little cracker box really, and the stairs to the front door are a pain, but we couldn't resist the view."

Blake handed Paul a glass, and they turned and faced each other. Now that they were up close, Paul realized he had forgotten Blake was a good three inches taller than he was and how he had always felt a bit intimidated by his size. In the dimness the years were erased from Blake's face, and it was hard to believe a decade had passed. And it was hard not to stare at the hair curling thick on his chest.

"You didn't tell me what happened to you." Paul cleared his throat and took a drink, the ice cubes chinking in the glass, and felt the smooth burn of alcohol in his throat. "Why are you back in uniform?"

Blake gazed contemplatively into his glass. "You heard about the death of the county assessor?"

Paul's eyes narrowed. "Wesley Durkin? It was ruled a suicide, wasn't it?" Paul knew little about the assessor other than what he had skimmed in the papers and couldn't even remember if he had voted for him. He did recall that Durkin had come out of nowhere running against far better known candidates to win the assessor's seat a few years back.

"That's what the police department says. And according to today's paper, so does the coroner." He paused and sipped his drink. "But I say it was murder."

"It was your case?"

"Me and my partner. I take it you know Mitch, right? Mitch Mitchell."

"Sure, I've worked on a few cases with him. He's a good guy, I thought."

His thick black sharp-cut brows furrowed and the permanent crease rising from his left brow deepened. He seemed to be choosing his words carefully. "He is. I'm not saying anything against him. He was comfortable with calling it a suicide, but there was something wrong with the scene. The place had been carefully searched. Somebody was looking very hard for something. And Wesley Durkin ended up slumped over his desk with a gun in his hand and a hole in his head."

"No one but you had a problem with the way it looked?"

"I got a sense the higher ups wanted this to go away. I don't think anybody wanted to make waves."

"Except you. How did you end up back on the beat?"

"Apparently I have anger problems." He took another sip and grinned sheepishly. "I punched my commanding officer in the mouth when he took me off the case because I was making too much trouble. Now they're sending me to a shrink as a condition for getting back on the Homicide table. But what they're really doing is waiting until the case is closed before letting me back."

Paul hadn't heard a word about any of this in the D.A.'s Office, and that bothered him. Somebody was keeping a tight lid on it. "That was it, just a feeling of yours that it wasn't suicide?"

"There was a young colored guy spotted running away from the scene, up the street behind Durkin's house."

Recalling the conversation between Blake and Mitchell in front of the theater earlier that evening, Paul said, "You think he was at the theater tonight? You think he tried to kill the man you were helping into the ambulance?"

"Had to be. He has a scar shaped like a horseshoe on his cheek. I mean, what are the chances? It can't be a coincidence." Blake went over to the scramble of blankets and picked up a book from the floor and brought it over to the column of light spreading from the kitchen doorway, gesturing for Paul to join him. He flipped through the pages. "I don't know if it's connected or not, but I found this next to the man who got garroted in the balcony. Ever heard of it?"

Paul took the book and glanced at the title and a line formed between his brows. *The Homosexual in American Society* by C. Aubrey Pruitt. He glanced at the copyright page. 1951. He had never read it, but knew the title. David had come across it years ago in college and raved about it. The author had stated the then extraordinary argument that homosexuals were an oppressed minority and demanded an end to their persecution. It was probably the first compassionate portrayal of the suffering routinely inflicted on homosexuals by oppressive laws and societal censure. It had become the bible of the fledgling homophile movement in the fifties, a rallying cry for a generation. David had told him he wept when he read it.

"I don't know what it was doing there, either, or if it has anything to do with the case, but I know this book means a lot to a lot of people."

"There's something written in the front."

Paul flipped to the inside of the front cover and read a note handwritten in ink with a long sloping scroll:

*You have awakened long dormant feelings in me and captured my heart. Couldn't you have warned me when we met that all I would want to do from that moment on is to touch you, caress you and whisper my love in your ear?*

A drop of water from Paul's wet hair fell on the page and he brushed it away. He looked up and realized Blake had taken a step closer and was reading over his shoulder. Their proximity brought a sudden burst of heat in Paul's face, and he wondered mortified if Blake could see his complexion turning red.

"I'm afraid I'm dripping on your floor, too."

"There's a towel in the bathroom. Just down the hall to the right. I can give you a dry shirt if you need it."

Paul handed him the book and his glass and went down the narrow hall and shut the bathroom door behind him.

He flipped the light switch and toweled his hair, then bent over the sink and splashed water in his face and gazed deep into his own eyes in the mirror. He told himself he shouldn't be doing this, that he shouldn't be here. That he could walk out now and forget the whole thing. Just abruptly excuse himself and go. He didn't owe Blake any explanation. Then he could drop by David's place and ask him for forgiveness for being such a bastard that evening and go back to the life he'd had all along.

But something deep in his gut told him that he wouldn't, that he had known all along what coming here would lead to, just as Blake had known it the moment the red

Thunderbird had pulled up in front of his house. He had gone down this road before and it had only come to grief, but he knew that wouldn't stop him, that the pull was like an ocean tide and resistance was a futile fight against unrelenting nature.

The door opened and Blake stood in the doorway, his shoulders wide as the frame. Frown lines cut deep grooves down from his mouth, but his eyes were hard and bright in the light glowing from sconces on both sides of the mirror. He held a shirt in his outstretched hand.

"I'm not sure if my size will fit you."

"I don't think I need it. I should go, anyway."

Blake watched him wordlessly as he finished with the towel and hung it on the rack. Paul felt heat prickle the back of his neck under Blake's gaze. As he turned toward Blake and they were face to face, Blake dropped the shirt and stepped into the bathroom, pressing his body heavily against him, pinning Paul against the porcelain sink. Paul could feel the protruding hardness between Blake's legs pressing through his blue uniform trousers.

"Don't go. I need you," Blake whispered. He leaned in close, their lips almost touching, and Paul could smell sweet whiskey on his breath. "I need this."

He held Paul's head in his big hands, gently at first, then with greater pressure, his thumbs pressing against Paul's temples, his fingers at the nape of his neck. He stared down at Paul with the strangest expression on his face. "Why couldn't I ever get you out of my head?" he asked softly. Then he bore down on him with a blistering kiss that made Paul gasp for air. Paul's head was swimming and he thought he heard a voice in the back of his mind tell him that this was a mistake, but no one knew better than Paul that this was inevitable, always had been, and he shut the voice out. Nothing could stop him from being drawn to

Blake's mouth again, first to taste his lips, and then his firm tongue.

Blake found the buttons on Paul's shirt and fumbled to release them, a cuff link falling and skittering across the checkered tile floor. He peeled the dress shirt off, still wet from the downpour, and tossed it aside, then slipped out of his own shirt. All the while they shared their tongues, playful and teasing, wide and soft, hard and darting, sometimes missing the other's mouth completely, landing on their noses, ears and chins, until Blake pulled himself away and bent down and flipped off Paul's shoes and roughly stripped him of his pants and underwear, leaving them all in a pile on the floor. As he rose again Paul reached down to loosen his belt, helping the blue wool slacks slide down Blake's legs until they lay in a jumble around his shiny black shoes and ankle socks.

Freeing his own underwear and pushing it down to his knees, Blake looked down at his cock, hard and erect, curving upward. He touched his index finger to the wetness at the end, taking up a dewy drop, then put his finger on Paul's waiting tongue, who closed his mouth around it.

Blake wrapped his arms tightly around Paul's waist, pulling him close, their hard cocks bobbing against each other, and lifted him up so his feet were no longer touching the throw rug on the floor. Then he set him down so Paul's butt was resting on the edge of the sink. The surface was cold and wet but Paul didn't care. He wrapped his arms around Blake's neck, caressing the cords of muscles in his back, his legs spread, knees tightening around Blake's hips.

With his eyes locked on Paul's, Blake spit in his hand, lathering up his own cock, spit again and reached down, first gripping Paul's rigid cock, then slipping his hand over his balls, cupping them, pulling at the hairs on his testicles. Then he reached farther and fingered his ass.

Paul flinched and Blake gave him a bruising kiss while he pressed his finger in deeper, as if to direct his attention elsewhere. They looked into one another's eyes and almost imperceptibly Paul nodded. He laid his palms flat on Blake's chest, as if bracing himself, fingers clutching the curls of hair around his hard nipples, listening to the quickened beat of his heart as Blake gripped Paul's buttocks, holding them tight, and pushed his way inside. A little sound came to Paul's throat.

"No," Paul whispered with urgency into Blake's ear, "wait."

But Blake wouldn't stop. Slowly, gently, he continued to push, driving himself deeper. At first Paul cried out, biting the lobe of Blake's ear, and then something happened in his head, and the pelvic rhythm, relentless as a piston, took over and Blake's cock was all he wanted, and he wrapped his legs more tightly around Blake's torso, slick with sweat now, pulling him in, opening himself to him, taking in all of him. Each bull thrust shook his body and he began to make little sounds in his throat with the tempo of Blake's thrusts.

Blake nuzzled his mouth in Paul's ear and breathed huskily, "I like it when you whimper." And then they were kissing again, softly then roughly, and then Paul's mouth traveled across the stubble of Blake's cheek and jaw to the sinewy muscles of his neck and downward to his chest, tasting the salt on his skin, his tongue lapping at the sweat forming in the hair, nipping cruelly at Blake's nipples. Paul licked at the thick tufts of hair peeking from Blake's armpits, wanted to bury himself in the intoxicating smell of him.

Stroking Paul's cock with a strong grip, Blake began to pound harder, as if the cadence of his pelvis had a life of its own and he could control it no more than the hammering of his heart. He shouted out loud then bore his mouth down on Paul's savagely as the muscles in his thighs went taut, trembling under the strain, and a spasm ripped through his body.

As they came together, the howls on their lips swallowed in each other's mouths, Blake gazed down at him sadistically and a wild thought passed through Paul's head that this was his punishment for staying away so long.

◇◇◇

Blake was still in the shower when Paul finished drying himself off and wrapped a towel around his waist, stepping out of the steamy bathroom into the hall.

He hesitated by the open doorway to the right, flipping the light switch inside, and glanced into the bedroom. All the furniture was gone. Even the curtains had been stripped from the window. Scratches on the hardwood floor revealed where the bed and bureau had been. The closet door was open, and Paul could see Blake's clothes hanging inside. His clean underwear and socks were piled in disarray on top of the only thing other than dust balls in the room, a squat black safe in the corner.

He heard the water shut off with a groan and a moment later there was a creak on the floorboards and he felt Blake's arms wrap around him from behind. Bending his neck, Blake grazed on Paul's shoulder with little kisses.

"Why don't you sleep in here?"

"The window has eastern exposure," Blake explained. "Even I don't like to get up that early. At least I have a bed ordered. It's supposed to arrive after the holidays."

"Now you tell me." Paul nodded at the safe. "You keep the family jewels in there?"

Blake stiffened slightly, and it struck Paul that the light tone of their conversation had just changed on a dime. Blake only said, "Something like that."

Paul wasn't sure what had just happened, but to rescue the moment he turned and mischievously cupped his hand around Blake's balls and nuzzled his face in the stubble on his neck. "These are the only family jewels I need."

Now Blake laughed. "You got 'em."

There was a closed door down the hallway, and Paul nodded at it. "What's in there?"

"That's Tommy's room. My boy." He pulled away from Paul. "It's hard for me to go in there now. It breaks me up too much."

"Where are they now?"

"Back in Wisconsin. I came home one day last week and they were gone."

Paul observed him for a moment. "How did you end up getting married?"

Blake shrugged. "I think I mentioned her to you once. She was a girl I dated for quite a while back in Wisconsin. When I moved here, I thought it was over. And then, a week or so after all the things that happened between you and me, she came out here on the train, and she wanted me back. I guess I kind of fell into it. I think I was pretty confused. And then she was pregnant and there wasn't anything else I could do." He went into the bathroom and came back with a wallet in his hand from the clothes strewn on the floor. "I've got a picture." He fished around in his wallet then handed Paul a black-and-white studio photo of an attractive blonde in her mid-thirties with sensitive eyes and a shy, enigmatic smile.

"She's beautiful."

"Yeah, she's a pretty girl." He took the picture back. "I've made one big mess out of my life. And I made a big mess out of hers. I don't blame her for hating me." He found another photo. "Here's a picture of my son, Tommy."

Paul smiled as he held the picture in his hands. "He looks like you."

"Well, he looks more like his mother. I mean he has her coloring. But he's a real handful, in that he takes after his dad."

Paul could hear the pride in his voice, and he looked into Blake's face and saw something he had never seen before.

"There isn't anything I wouldn't do to get him back."

In the living room they lay down, slipping between a puffy comforter spread on the floor and a twisted chaos of sheets and blankets. They were quiet for a while, comfortable in the silence, their bodies together, feeling the warmth of each other. Paul ran his finger along the profile of Blake's face, the prominent forehead, the worry line between his brows that never went away, the slight upturned curve of his nose, the cleft in his chin, the stubble along his jaw line, and found it hard to believe that he was with him again. A shiver ran through him.

"That lock of hair, you don't have it anymore." He remembered the unruly black curl that fell across Blake's forehead no matter how much Brylcreem he mussed into his hair.

"I finally figured out that if I got my hair cut shorter it wouldn't be falling in my face all the time."

Paul almost said he missed it, but he thought that would sound too sentimental, and he swept his hand up over Blake's forehead as if the curl was still there. The youthful beauty in his face had faded, and in its place a lived-in unvarnished masculinity had taken root that Paul found somehow even more appealing.

"Why wouldn't you talk to me all these years? Why did you stay away? I told you the things that happened back then, they didn't matter. I wanted us to be friends."

It was quite a while before Blake answered. "I couldn't after what I did to you." He gnawed on his lip. "Maybe I didn't know how to be your friend." He reached over and found a pack of cigarettes on the floor by their bed, and lit up. After he took a drag, blowing a plume of smoke in the air, Paul took it from him and set it on his own lips.

"I thought you quit."

Paul inhaled deeply and looked at Blake for a long time. Whatever elation he had felt earlier was gone and sadness settled over him as he thought about whose arms he was in, and in whose arms he wasn't.

"It's okay." He handed the cigarette back. It had tasted so good he didn't know how he'd ever been able to give it up. "It's only one time."

They fell asleep wrapped in each other's arms.

Paul woke in darkness and immediately sensed he was alone under the covers. He reached over anyway, feeling the rumpled blankets where Blake had fallen asleep. They still radiated his warmth. He raised his head and listened. The house was quiet except for the insistent patter of rain on the roof.

"Jim?" he called.

The kitchen was silent, so he padded across the floor down the hall. He hesitated there a moment, and then he heard the clink of glass against glass in the bedroom down the hall and noticed Tommy's door was open.

"Jim?"

As he entered he could see Blake in silhouette against the dark blue slab of a window.

"Hey," Paul said softly, "are you okay?"

"I couldn't sleep."

In the dimness Paul observed a whiskey bottle in one hand and a partially filled glass in the other.

"Geez, Jim. It's the middle of the night." He took the glass and bottle and set them on the window sill. He laid his hand on Blake's cheek, then pulled his palm away in surprise. His fingers were wet with tears.

"I miss him so much," Blake stammered.

And then Blake was in his arms holding him tightly, as if it were the only thing that could save him.

# Chapter 5

Paul drove the Thunderbird past a sun-bleached arcade filled with tiny shops a block from the beach, looking for the sign indicating where he should turn. Glimpses of the ocean and an almond ribbon of sand flashed at the ends of streets no wider than an alley, cramped with sagging yardless bungalows abutting the sidewalk. A pale blue expanse of sky scattered with gulls rose above the azure waves.

The street was dry as a bone. The only evidence of last night's downpour was the pristine air, cool and salty in the ocean breeze. On a corner several slender white boys with long shiny hair and silken tans, wearing nothing but shorts and sandals, sauntered without purpose past a black-skinned Negro with a fright of wild hair who sat on the curb in a fake fur jacket with a wine bottle in his hand.

Venice Beach had begun its existence as a popular resort and housing development at the beginning of the century, but the years of booms and busts had not been kind to the community. Its famous pier, a crazy-curl of rides, was now forlorn and bankrupt and the city had recently torn down hundreds of houses in favor of proposed expensive condominiums on the beach. The beat generation had found a home and cheap rents here a decade before, and recently a new breed had begun to proliferate, with long hair and colorful clothes, and the sounds of drum parties on the beach, mixed with the sweet smell of marijuana, beat long into the night.

"You're sure you want to pursue this?" Paul asked, glancing over at Blake, who was dressed in his uniform despite being off duty. They had both agreed it was necessary to look as legitimate as possible if they were going ahead with their plan.

Blake only said, "They kept him overnight for observation, then released him this morning. He should be at home."

They hadn't spoken about anything that had happened the night before, taking a late breakfast at a twenty-four hour diner on Sunset—one of the few open on New Year's Day. Blake had talked mostly about his son, just casual stuff, the fun they had going to Dodgers games and how Tommy would get sick eating hotdogs if his dad didn't stop him. His eyes lit up when he spoke of the boy's excitement when he'd joined the cub scouts, the little merit badges that meant so much to the nine-year-old. Watching Blake over breakfast, something stirred in Paul, and he felt moved by the gentleness in the big man's voice in a way he hadn't expected.

They had stopped by Paul's house so he could change his clothes. The Sunday *Times* was on the doorstep, and Paul had felt a mixture of disappointment that David hadn't come over to make up after their argument, and relief because he couldn't easily explain why he was arriving home in a rumpled tux with another man in his car. Whatever anger he'd held against David the evening before had largely dissipated, and he was left with churning and confused emotions about his tryst with Blake. He was totally broadsided by how good it had felt being with him again, overwhelming in fact—that startling electric charge of their bodies joined—and even as he changed his clothes he could still feel Blake deep inside him. He couldn't exactly say he felt guilty over what he had done, and yet he knew David would be devastated if he ever found out, and fighting the glow that radiated from within, he promised himself that it would never happen again.

Turning now down a narrow lane, Paul pulled the Thunderbird in front of a weathered shingled cottage with large paned windows and a crescent dormer peeking from the roof.

The woman who answered the door was brushing flour off her hands with a white dish towel. She was small, her graying hair parted on the side in a no-nonsense Ayn Rand style. Her checkered shirt rolled up to the elbows, faded denim pedal pushers and canvas shoes told Paul she didn't give a damn how she looked, and he liked her all the better for it.

She blinked hazel eyes at them. "You must be here about the mugging. I'm Leland's wife, Molly." She put a hand to her chin and left a flour smudge there. "Oh, I do think it's awful that you can't walk down the street anymore without having someone try to rob you. And to come up from behind you with a rope! Poor Leland. It's too terrible, isn't it?"

Paul exchanged a glance with Blake and wondered exactly how much Leland Serokin had admitted to his wife about the assault the night before in the balcony of a seedy downtown theater. It sounded like the motive and venue of the crime had been changed to avoid humiliating questions. Molly waved them inside and they followed her down a hallway past a cluttered living room and a kitchen where the makings of a pie were laid out on the countertop. Two small mutts who had been lounging on the linoleum floor joined them and scampered around their feet. She stopped briefly where rock music throbbed from behind a closed door.

"I wouldn't mind so much if he just didn't play it so loud," she told them, pounding on the door. "Gary, now could you please just turn that down a few decibels? The windows are rattling."

Continuing down the hall, the dogs nipping playfully at her heels, she confided, "I made the mistake of admitting I liked the Beatles, and that was the last time we heard the fab four in this house. At least *they* were clean. I guess I should have figured any band with parental approval would be off-limits for the kids. Now it's the Animals, and I tell you, those boys don't wash. I don't mind the long hair and the sandals, but really, you've got to wash."

They passed framed posters on the walls of CORE protests at the 1964 World's Fair and photographs of Martin Luther King leading freedom marches. She tapped on a door at the end of the hall. "Honey, you've got visitors." She pushed the door open and led them into a book-lined study. Leland Serokin, short, hunched, balding, sat behind a desk piled with papers, writing with a thick pen on a yellow pad. He had the sharp facial features of a rodent, but his eyes were kind, with dark heavy bags beneath them. Paul pegged him to be in his early fifties. A puffy white bandage circled his neck.

Hovering at the door, Molly asked, "Can I offer you something, some coffee or tea?"

Paul considered it less likely that they would get honest answers from Serokin with his wife present, and he didn't want her coming and going interrupting their interview, especially if her husband had embarrassing truths about his life to reveal. Both he and Blake shook their heads.

"And you, Leland?" She tsk-tsked with concern. "You haven't had a thing to eat all morning. At least let me bring you some toast and jam."

He winked fondly at her. "Perhaps later, dear," he said, his hand gently touching the bandage around his neck. "I'm fine, really."

Blake waited until she had left the room, then introduced himself. "I'm Jim Blake, LAPD. You may remember me from last night. This is Paul Winters from the District Attorney's Office."

Eyeing them warily, Serokin leaned back in his chair and let out a sigh. "A Sergeant Mitchell already visited me when I was in the hospital. I'm afraid I wasn't able to give him any more information about what happened last night than I can give you."

"Perhaps you could tell us what you were doing there."

"Why does anybody go to the movies?"

"Look, we're not here to make trouble for you," Blake said carefully. "You can tell your wife whatever you want. We're not here to reveal your secrets, but I don't think many people in that balcony were there to watch the movie."

Serokin arched an eyebrow and an amused curve came to his thin lips. "So you think I was there for a discreet assignation in the dark? Just so you know, Officer Blake, the activity I suspect you're referring to rarely occurs out in the open, even if it is dark. Oh, there may be a bit of petting and stroking, but generally the involved parties retire to the restroom downstairs for the act you're talking about. Sometimes a third party joins them as a lookout." He rose wearily and went to the bookshelf. As he searched the shelves, Paul noted the hunch on his back and determined he had been born with scoliosis. Serokin found the volumes he was looking for and brought them over to where they were standing. "Gentlemen, let me clarify this situation before we go any further. I'm a clinical psychologist and a professor of sociology and criminology at UCLA. These are some of my previously published works." His books all had long titles—*Ideology and Structure in an Association of Sexual Deviants: A Study* was one of them—and sounded like dissertations. "I was doing field work for my next book on deviant behavior, studying the anonymous mating rituals of homosexual males in public arenas—parks and movie theaters—when I was attacked."

"Why doesn't your wife know that?"

Serokin closed his eyes briefly in an expression of strained patience. "My wife is a lovely woman. Do I tell her everything about the work I do when I know it will only make her worry? Of course not. Don't you protect your wife from hearing about half the things that happen to you on the beat?" He went back to the shelf and replaced the books, then returned to his desk. "Is there anything else I can help you with?"

"Tell us what happened to you last night. Did you see who tried to strangle you?" Blake stepped closer to the desk, looking down on the professor, and Paul followed at his side, gazing at the paperwork on the desk.

Shaking his head, Serokin said, "It was dark. All of a sudden I felt something around my throat from behind. I struggled and I fought, but I couldn't breathe and I must have passed out. That's truly all I can tell you."

"There was a Negro seen running from the scene. A horseshoe shaped scar on his cheek. You see anybody like that?"

Something happened in Serokin's face at the mention of the Negro which Paul had seen many times in plea bargain meetings with accused criminals. Card players called it a tell. Serokin was about to lie.

"There were a number of people in the upper balcony, but it was dark and I'm afraid I didn't see any faces. I didn't notice a Negro."

"I found a book lying on the floor next to your seat," Blake said. "It was called—" He looked over to Paul for assistance.

"*The Homosexual in American Society* by C. Aubrey Pruitt."

A sly look came over Serokin's face. "I've heard of it before. I am of the same mind as the author of that book on many issues. He gives a forceful argument for the decriminalization of private consensual acts. In fact, I probably have a copy somewhere in my library. But it wasn't mine, if that's what you are asking." He rose from his seat as a gesture of dismissal. "Gentlemen, I'm quite busy writing a lecture for next week. I'm afraid I don't have anything to offer you."

Out on the porch a minute later, Paul squinted his eyes against the brightness of the day. The ocean glinted at the end of the street. "He was lying about the colored guy."

Blake nodded. "I caught that, too. Go Figure. Someone tried to kill him and he's not willing to help us find out who it was."

"We did learn one thing," Paul said as they got into the car. "I glanced at the lecture he was working on. I recognized that long slanted script. The handwriting of the love note in the front of the book, it was his."

Blake pondered a moment. "Then I guess the question is, who did he write it to?"

Up ahead the dilapidated Hollywood sign hung in the green brush-covered hills above Beachwood Drive. Paul turned off the palm-lined street after passing a little corner market onto a snaky road that curved into the hills.

"When I knew I was on my way out, I made a copy of the key," Blake said. "I figured it was the only way I would be able to get back inside if I needed to." He took another drag on his cigarette and tapped the ash out the open window into the breeze.

Wesley Durkin had lived in a vine-covered cottage with a mock-thatched roof that looked like something out of *Snow White*, a popular style in the neighborhood in the twenties and thirties until the original developers lost control of the area and builders with far different tastes imposed their mark on the landscape. Yesterday's quaint cottages and charming Spanish and Mediterranean designs now shared the hills with modern cantilevered structures which clung to the hillsides perched on stilts. The interlopers were a source of constant complaint from the old timers who remembered when Beachwood Canyon was a kind of hidden fairyland tucked into the folds of the city.

They left the car in the narrow driveway with a grass strip running down the center and went to the front door, which was curved on top and had a circular window. The police tape—if there had been one—had already been taken down, an indication that whatever evidence to be collected in the case was already in police custody.

The living room was tastefully furnished, with a vaulted ceiling, wide-planked hardwood floors, and a squat fireplace crowned with a rustic maple mantle.

"I could tell the moment I came inside something was wrong. Not just the smell of him, which permeated the place—he'd been dead in his study for two days. Look around, can you see it?"

Slowly Paul nodded. He hadn't noticed until it was pointed out, but everything in the room was slightly off kilter. The chairs a bit askew in relation to the coffee table, the pictures hanging at odd angles, drawers in cabinets not completely closed, knickknacks on the mantle clustered awkwardly.

66

"Somebody was looking for something. I'll show you where we found him."

Blake led him into a hallway then stopped abruptly, silently pulling his gun from its holster. Standing behind him, Paul tensed. A ladder stood in the middle of the hall and in the ceiling above a hatch door had been pushed aside, leaving a gaping dark hole into the attic. Paul didn't have to be told that the ladder hadn't been there when Blake had investigated the scene earlier.

"I'm going up," Blake whispered. "Check the rest of the place."

Paul nodded as Blake climbed the ladder, taking each step as quietly as he could. He headed down the hall, poking his head in what appeared to be a study. On the oak desk a blotter had a dark stain, and with a shudder Paul figured this must have been where Wesley Durkin allegedly committed suicide. He passed a bathroom and came to a bedroom with an adjoining bath. He stepped inside and stopped in his tracks.

A young Negro man lay naked on his side on the double bed hugging a fat pillow. Paul wasn't sure what startled him more, the fact that he was there at all, or the beautiful chestnut sheen of his skin in the light filtering in from the window. In his sleep he had pushed the covers aside and snuggled up to them, and they shared the shape of his slim body. At the far side of the bed, clothes were strewn on an upholstered chair and the night table. A tightly rolled sleeping bag sat beside a department store shopping bag on the floor.

Paul heard Blake's voice from the hall. "Looks like they're long gone." He was glancing down, holstering his pistol as he turned the corner into the room. "There's no floor in the attic. Just beams with insulation packed between. Some was torn up, though. I think something was hidden up there—" He froze next to Paul.

67

The young man woke, turned to them and blinked, his eyes widening. Then in a flash he jumped out of the bed and stared at them, fear filling his face. He snatched a pair of underwear that had been tossed on the nightstand, and quickly pulled them on, never taking his eyes off Paul and Blake. He was handsome, in his early twenties, with close-cropped wooly hair, a lithe, sinewy body and long finely muscled limbs. And on his right cheek, a scar in the shape of an upside-down U.

"Hold it," Blake ordered, reaching for his gun. "I want you to hold it right there."

The young man's eyes darted both ways, then he seized a pair of Levis hung over the chair, and grabbed the sleeping bag and the shopping bag. Paul spotted something falling out of the bag and tottering to the floor as the young man dove into the open doorway of the adjoining bathroom. The door slammed and the lock clicked. Paul could hear the young man breathlessly shimmying on his jeans behind the door.

Striding over to the door, Blake pounded on it. "Don't make me break this down. Just open up, *now*."

There was silence for a moment, and Blake put his ear to the door, listening. Suddenly he cried out, "Shit! He's going out the window." He charged past Paul out the bedroom doorway and down the hall.

Moving around the bed, Paul saw that the young man had left his shoes, socks and T-shirt behind. Paul bent down and picked up a bound file that lay on the carpet. He figured this was what had fallen out of the bag. The insignia of the Los Angeles Police Department was emblazoned on the cover. He flipped through it and frowned. Across the room by the window he found an upholstered chair and sank into it.

Opening the file, he leafed through a number of photos of Wesley Durkin. They were clearly taken on the sly without the subject knowing. A night shot showed him entering a bar. The establishment had no name, but Paul recognized the neon crown above the door and knew it was a gay bar downtown on Fifth. In another photo, Durkin was sitting at an outdoor café with a young Negro. Even though he couldn't see the young man's face, Paul had no doubt who it was. Another picture, taken at night, was a blurred shot of Durkin entering his own front door with the Negro. While there was nothing incriminating in any of the pictures, they left the impression of clandestine activity, a secret life lived in the shadows. Behind the pictures, there was a series of surveillance reports, detailing where Durkin had gone and when, and whom he had spoken to. Paul ran his finger quickly down one of the pages of one of the reports and stopped at a line stating that Durkin had returned home at midnight with a Negro and the Negro hadn't left until eight o'clock the next morning. Paul examined the dates of the reports. The LAPD had been spying on the county assessor around the time he had first begun his run for office. Paul cupped his chin with his fingers and puzzled over the significance of what he held in his hands.

Panting for breath, Blake came up the hall and stood in the doorway. "He got away. He ran around the back of a house up the street and into the hills."

"He can't go far. He isn't even wearing his shoes."

"I don't get it. Why did he come back? Why was he sleeping in Durkin's bed? If he killed the guy..."

"He didn't kill him." Paul looked over at the bed, remembering how the young man had hugged the pillows in his sleep. Paul could still see the sensual contours of his body in the twists of the sheets. "He was in love with him."

◇◇◇

69

Blake held the open file on his lap, gazing at its contents, as Paul took the entrance ramp to the freeway and headed toward downtown.

"Whoever killed Durkin searched his place at the time of the murder," Blake said, "but didn't find what they were looking for because it was in the attic hidden under the insulation."

Paul nodded. "But Durkin's boyfriend knew it was there. He waited until he was sure the police were gone then came back to get it."

"And decided to sleep over?"

"I have a feeling he didn't have anywhere else to go. Other than his jeans, the first thing he grabbed was a sleeping bag, which makes me think he hasn't had a place to stay since the murder and couldn't resist a warm bed, especially considering the downpour last night. You suspected him because he was spotted running away from the scene, right? Maybe he saw something and has reason to be afraid. Maybe he was a witness to the murder."

"So why would a surveillance report be so important to him... or to whoever killed Durkin?"

"There was something else in that shopping bag. Whatever it was, our guy was willing to risk going back to the crime scene to get it."

Thumbing through the pages in the file, Blake said, "The surveillance reports show that Durkin's relationship with the colored guy goes back more than two and a half years. But look at the dates of the reports. He was being watched during the six month period he ran for office. I don't see anything after that."

"You think they stopped spying on him after he got elected, or do you think the file is incomplete?"

"I think they got the dirt on him that they wanted. And whatever they wanted to use it for, it was enough."

"I didn't see anything incriminating. But it clearly implies Durkin had a homosexual relationship with a Negro half his age, and that's enough to destroy any career."

Blake was silent for a minute. He slapped the file shut and shook his head. "I wonder how Durkin was able to get a copy of this report. It's not the kind of thing the LAPD would give out."

"Unless," Paul countered, "they wanted to let him know exactly what they had on him."

New Year's Day traffic was thin on the 101, and they reached downtown a few minutes later, where Paul took the 110 south. "You know, there's someone I'd like to talk to about this." He glanced over at Blake, skeptically noting his blue uniform, and smiled crookedly. "But I think it's best if you stay in the car. Preferably with your head down."

"Oh," Blake said, noting their direction. "South Central?"

"You been down there before?"

"No. But I've heard the stories."

"You remember Jeff Dupuis? He used to be with the LAPD."

Blake shook his head.

"Then he got his law degree nine or ten years ago, and left the force. He has an office down there." Paul recalled how jarring it had been back then to overhear Jeff in conversations with other blacks, employing a jargon and tone utterly unlike what he used in his exchanges with white fellow officers. It had left Paul unsure of who the real Jeff was and if their friendly banter on the job was authentic or just a facade. Paul had given him pointers in law school, knowing Jeff dreamed of becoming a prosecutor. After passing the bar, the bitter disappointment Jeff had felt when no job in the D.A.'s Office materialized, despite Paul's strong recommendation, had changed him.

He'd opened a little storefront office in one of the worst neighborhoods in the city and took on cases nobody else would. He had changed in so many ways from the amiable young recruit Paul once knew it was hard to count them, but one thing stood out the most.

Now when Jeff Dupuis spoke, he spoke the same way to everybody.

They drove in silence for a while and Paul's thoughts drifted. He wondered what David was doing now. They would usually spend Sunday mornings reading the newspaper in bed, then meet up with friends for lunch at a sidewalk cafe. If David didn't call him, Paul decided, he'd drop by his place later. He knew David would still be mad at him for not intervening to help the men arrested at the bar the night before, but he would get over it. He always had before.

Leaving the freeway behind, Paul headed toward Avalon, where the year before the Watts riots had ignited over a routine traffic stop of a drunken Negro motorist by California Highway Patrol officers. As crowds gathered on the sweltering August night, an altercation between officers and the suspect triggered a melee which quickly escalated into the worst riot in U.S. history, a six-day nightmare leaving thirty-four dead, one thousand injured, over three thousand arrested and nearly one thousand buildings looted or burned. The violence of the insurrection—and the nightly news reports showing rampant looting and sniper attacks on firemen and the police—shook the city to its core, and left a citizenry more racially divided and fearful of its neighbors than it had ever been before.

The riot had come as a shock to most Angelenos who had convinced themselves the racial turmoil that had gripped other major cities could never happen here. The mainstream newspapers hadn't reported on growing unrest in the inner city, and whites knew little of the lives of blacks who lived there and the simmering resentments that were about to explode. But perhaps no one should have been surprised. Unemployment was sky high and young men aimlessly wandered the streets. Those lucky enough to have jobs faced other challenges. Many didn't have cars. The electric Big Red streetcars, which had taken most of the residents to their jobs for the greater part of the century, had been scrapped in favor of an inadequate bus system, which left riders stuck with multiple transfers and long commutes to get to and from work. Faces of frustration and quiet rage clustered at every bus stop. In the last few years dozens and dozens of young black men, often unarmed, had been killed by police, frequently shot in the back. The practice of redlining, which targeted areas with minority populations, meant no loans for home improvements, and whole neighborhoods were falling apart. Californians had recently voted overwhelmingly to maintain racial segregation in housing, overturning a law which would have banned the practice, greatly limiting where blacks could live. There were no hospitals in South Central, and medical emergencies meant long rides to other districts. A bond measure to provide a medical center in the area had been voted down by the city at large, showing just how little their lives mattered to the rest of the population. In the aftermath of the riot, Police Chief William Parker, in characteristic sensitivity toward the city's black community, had explained the upheaval to the press by saying, "One person threw a rock, and then, like monkeys in a zoo, others started throwing rocks."

Paul's red Thunderbird got cold assessing stares from old men at a shoeshine stand as he drove down Avalon and turned at a light. The rubble of burned buildings sprouted on every block like insidious charcoal-black flowers, the twisted remnants of plumbing reaching up like stems drawn to sunlight. Kids played the games kids play among the rubble, finding swords in charred sticks and battlements in piles of debris. On several unscathed buildings, Paul could see the words "Blood Brother" scrawled in now-faded spray paint to alert looters and arsonists during the riots to bypass these black-owned businesses. Palm trees that just didn't belong—not in this desert of gray concrete and crumbling one-story stucco shops with signs proclaiming "We Cash Checks"—swayed in the breeze, towering against a blue sky.

Jeff Dupuis' law office was a narrow storefront with a steel gate that rolled down over the door and window at night. Paul knew Jeff could be found in his office every Sunday. He parked down the block, figuring Jeff would prefer not having to explain to neighbors why a man in a blue uniform had been sitting in front of his office.

Blake, who had watched silently as they rode through the neighborhood, now slouched in his seat. "I see what you mean," he said quietly.

"I'll only be a few minutes."

# Chapter 6

An old woman in an African caftan with orange and black tribal designs and a matching scarf tied like a turban sat behind a desk tapping with long elegant fingers on an electric typewriter. She looked up when Paul entered. But it wasn't a woman. And he wasn't old.

"Hello, Alfred." Paul had first met Alfred Washington ten years before when the young man had been living on the street after tangling with the medical establishment, which had incarcerated him for his effeminate demeanor, fascination with women's clothes, and getting in a brawl with white Varsity boys who had taunted him with the epithet "dirty nigger queer" and thought he wouldn't fight back. "I can't believe Jeff has you working today. Is he available to see me?"

Alfred shook his head in a *nobody's seen the trouble I've seen* gesture. The Adam's apple in his scrawny neck bobbed when he talked. "After what happened last night at those bars over in Silver Lake, we're going to be busy all month long. The po-lice, they got no cause to do that." He wrapped his long arms across his chest, and Paul could see how thin he was under the loose colorful folds of the caftan.

He rose with a dancer's grace and opened a door behind his desk and spoke into the room. "The pretty white boy from the D.A.'s Office is here to see you."

"Hey, Paul, come on in," Jeff called, waving Paul in, obviously pleased to see him. He stood and reached over his desk to give Paul a handshake as he entered. Jeff looked him up and down and whistled. "Get a load of that suit. Do you even *own* anything casual? Hey, sit down, sit down."

Paul took a chair, noting Jeff was dressed as usual in his army-navy surplus garb. The perks of being self-employed. Alfred closed the inner office door to give them some privacy.

Jeff sat on the edge of his desk, one bell-bottomed leg swinging at the knee. "Tell me you've finally had enough working for The Man and you're going to come work with me."

Leaning back in his chair, Paul grinned widely. They'd had this conversation before. "Are you crazy? And get stuck working on New Year's Day? No thanks. At least I get paid vacation."

Jeff's smile faded. "You know we'd make a great team. There's a lot of important work to be done."

"Yeah, you want me to turn on, tune in and drop out, like all our friends? I can do more working within the system than I ever could out of it."

"You're wasting your time." Jeff shook his head and ran his fingers ruefully through the whiskers on his chin. His eyes were sad. "The revolution isn't going to come from the inside, I found that out."

"Last time I looked, the revolution wasn't coming, period." They could go on like this for hours, and some-times did. To change the subject, Paul asked, "How did it go last night?"

Because of the location of his practice, Jeff often defended young black men in trouble with the law, and went after cops in police brutality cases with a zeal that made Paul wonder if his years with the LAPD had left him

76

with a mission to utterly change how the department did business. He also took on entrapment cases and the harassment of gay bars, a problem throughout the state. The Alcohol Beverage Control Department sent plain-clothesmen into bars they wanted to close, entrapping men on sex solicitation charges, then used the accusation that lewd acts were being committed on the premises to shut the bars down. It was a brazen attempt to circumvent rulings by the California Supreme Court prohibiting bar closures on the sole basis that gays congregated there. The ABC would file a complaint against the bar, then the owner would have to show cause why their license shouldn't be revoked. It got very expensive, and mountains of legal fees alone shut down a lot of bars long before the cases ever went to trial. Fighting to keep those bars open kept Jeff very busy.

"At the Rampart Station? They arrested sixteen people. They're all out on bail. One is in County General Hospital in critical condition. Of course, the cops are claiming they were the ones who were attacked." Jeff returned to his seat and leveled an assessing gaze at Paul. "But you aren't here about that, are you? That's not what brought you down to my neighborhood, is it?"

"Okay, you caught me." Paul laughed and shook his head. "Look, I need your help on something. I'm trying to track down someone. A black guy, early twenties I'd say, with a big scar on his right cheek, like a horseshoe. Does he sound familiar to you?"

Leaning back in his chair, Jeff bit his lip and put on a show of thinking deeply. "Oh, that's right. All us black brothers know one another. All six hundred thousand of us in the county."

Paul was used to Jeff giving him a hard time. In fact, lately their relationship seemed to consist of taking little amiable jabs at each other. Only sometimes Paul wasn't exactly sure just how friendly the jabs were and if Jeff was joking or not. "Jeff," he said patiently, "he's black. He's gay. He's into white guys. Who better to ask than you?"

Finally Jeff cracked a smile. He raised his hands in surrender. "Okay, okay, I hear you. So what's this about?"

"He was seen running away from a couple of crime scenes. You heard about the death of the county assessor, right?"

Jeff's face puckered up. "Uh-huh. That's what this is about? I read in the paper he killed himself." He shook his head and whistled. "White guy commits suicide and the world says lynch a nigger."

"You know I hate it when you talk like that."

Jeff waved his hand dismissively. "What? Down here a nigger is just a man."

"And I didn't say he was a suspect." Paul thought again about how the young man had hugged the pillows in Wesley Durkin's bed, and puzzled over why Leland Serokin had denied seeing him at the theater. "We just want to talk to him."

"Oh. This is the first time you mentioned *we*."

Paul wondered if his cheeks had taken on color, and he was relieved he had asked Blake to stay in the car. Jeff was too sharp not to put two and two together. And he was in enough trouble with David as it was. "Yes, I'm working with the police on this, as I often do," Paul said with a show of strained patience. "It's not a conspiracy and I'm not out to hurt this guy. I just need to ask him some questions. I think he's alone and afraid and doesn't have any place to stay. Maybe if I find him he can stop running."

"All right. I'll put the word out. I've never heard of this cat, but maybe somebody else has." His face clouded over. "Hey wait—you think he was involved with Wesley Durkin? As in…"

"I think they were lovers and I know Wesley Durkin was being spied on by the LAPD."

"He ain't the only one," Jeff said under his breath. Before Paul could question what he meant, Jeff added, "I don't think too many folks around here will be mourning his passing."

"Wesley Durkin? Why is that?"

Jeff gave him his poker face. "They say it's become very expensive to be a Negro in South Central." He used the word "Negro" as if it had become a dirty word to him.

"Don't talk to me in riddles. What's that supposed to mean?"

"From what I've heard, property taxes in this area just keep going up." He began to rise from his chair and grabbed a pack of cigarettes on his desk. "Hey, I've been stuck behind this desk all morning. Let's go out for a smoke."

They passed through the outer office, where Alfred was typing up a storm, and stepped out onto the street. Jeff leaned against the brick wall of the next storefront and lit a cigarette. He didn't offer Paul one. He was well aware of David's campaign a few years back to get him to quit.

"How has Alfred been working out?" Paul asked.

"He's actually a good secretary. I think most people coming in believe he's a woman. And the ones who know better, they don't seem to mind." Jeff had slowly earned Alfred's trust back in the days when he'd lived on the street, and when he'd opened his office, he'd offered Alfred a job. Jeff inhaled deeply, savoring the taste, as if he had been waiting for this cigarette break all morning. "He doesn't seem to get the blackouts anymore. It's like his brain kind of repaired itself after all these years." Alfred's defiance toward his doctors in mental institutions while he was in his teens and his pronouncements that he was happy being homosexual and that the colored race was the most beautiful in the world had led to repeated cycles of shock therapy treatments and all the side effects that went with them. "He's actually taking classes. You know, before the psychiatrists got a hold of him, he was a ballet dancer, traveled all over the country. He's too old for that now, those years are lost, but I think he's interested in choreography."

Their conversation was interrupted by the shouts of four teenage boys running down Avalon at the far corner, followed by the shrill of a patrol car siren and flashing lights. They waited until the siren died out in the distance before continuing their conversation.

"More business for you."

"More of that kind of business I could do without."

They both gazed across the street, where shabby bungalows were surrounded by cyclone fences and guarded by wrought-iron bars on the windows. A little girl played by herself on a sagging porch. In the smoky aftermath of the uprising, Paul remembered the bleak pronouncement of a black woman to a TV cameraman: "We have one weapon... *babies*." Paul thought about how he almost never got down to this part of L.A. You could live your whole life in Los Angeles and never see South Central. He turned to Jeff. "How are things down here now?" Despite a well-publicized state commission to study the causes of the riot, some said nothing had changed, except more whites had fled and more businesses had moved elsewhere.

Jeff shrugged moodily. He blew out a stream of smoke. "Some people say there's going to be a race war in this country. I don't know. There's a group just formed up in Oakland, they carry shotguns. All I can say is, the thing that happened here last year, it's just going to happen again and again until things change."

Paul nodded. Their conversation seemed to have ground to a halt. "On that happy note..." he said grimly, preparing to take his leave. He gave Jeff a friendly pat on the shoulder. "Give me a buzz if you hear anything about the guy with the scar on his face, okay?" He was down the block before he heard Jeff call after him.

"I meant what I said. Come work with me! We'd be unstoppable."

Without answering or looking back, Paul waved his hand to acknowledge that he'd heard him. But as he went down the street to the car, he wasn't considering Jeff's offer. Instead he was thinking about a dead county assessor, a professor who was covering for someone who had tried to kill him, and something Jeff had said earlier about a property tax hike in South Central. It was time to give his reporter friend Marvin Botwinick a call.

Paul still hadn't heard from David by Sunday evening and he was beginning to get worried. He had called several times throughout the day and nobody answered. After dropping Blake off at his house in Hollywood, he'd gone by David's place, but he wasn't there. Finally he'd phoned Jeannie, who had been unusually subdued in their conversation. He guessed his falling-out with David was still making waves amongst their friends. She suggested he check out the Hub over in West Hollywood.

Dubbed in its ads as "The Grooviest Place in Town Where the Nicest People Meet," the bar had become the unofficial home for the political group that David had been spending most of his time with, PRIDE, which had been founded several months earlier by a landscape gardener named Steve Ginsberg.

It was getting dark by the time Paul crossed Fairfax and found a parking spot on Santa Monica a block from the bar. He walked quickly and looked both ways to see if anyone was watching before he entered. Hovering in the doorway, he saw about twenty-five men and women surrounding David, who was standing addressing the crowd like it was a pep rally.

"We're going to give them the biggest protest this city has ever seen, and I want to see you and all your friends there," he exhorted the gathering, his eyes shining. "We will not be alone. A coalition of our brothers and sisters, black, white and brown, will be with us, all over the city, in a mass demonstration against police brutality." He waited for the cheers to die down. "And we're going to be there in court to support our friends who are under arrest from the raid last night, and expose the fascist pigs for who they are and what they've been doing to our community for far too long."

Paul had never realized just how good David was in front of a crowd, his voice fierce and commanding. And he couldn't help noticing the admiring looks from the men in the crowd with a tinge of jealousy. Paul reminded himself that he sometimes forgot just how handsome David was, with his prominent nose, full lips, slim build and dark curly hair. It struck him that he still saw David as he had been when they'd met, at the time David was just graduating from creative arts school. He'd been a boy back then, but that was a decade ago, and he'd been a man for a long time. Why hadn't Paul seen it?

David ended his speech by asking everyone to join in and make picket signs. Paul was about to approach him, but hung back when he saw a good-looking shaggy-blond guy in jeans and a faded T-shirt go over and wrap his arm around David's waist. It was the flirty, friendly kind of behavior you saw all the time in bars—at least when vice cops weren't present—but Paul felt a frown forming on his face.

As Paul threaded through the crowd, he nodded to a couple of familiar faces, but it struck him how few of the people David associated with lately were known to him. He passed Steve Ginsberg, whom he'd met through David a few times, and nodded. In contrast to earlier gay organizers, who eschewed open sexuality and counseled protesters to dress conservatively—when David had joined picket lines in front of the White House, he'd been told to dress in a suit as if he were going to a job interview at the State Department—Ginsberg exuded a brash sexuality and liked to wear his leathers to meetings. It was a sign of the times.

Unlike earlier homophile groups from the fifties such as the Mattachine Society, that had settled into a timid approach to seeking acceptance for gays, soliciting the aid of sympathetic therapists, ministers and politicians to speak on behalf of homosexuals, a new, more confident and aggressive generation of activists had begun to sprout up in the early sixties. While their numbers remained small—one organization in New York actually boasted only one member—they had become increasingly adept at getting media coverage, appearing on talk shows, speaking on radio programs, and getting attention from newspapers who had had a near ban on the subject just a handful of years before. While some argued that a small membership of articulate professionals speaking for the community was preferable to a larger organization that included riffraff from the bars who might make a bad impression on the general public, PRIDE had burst on the scene with the revolutionary idea of mobilizing the kids in the bars to fight for social change in the way Negroes and farm workers, and even women, had started to in recent years. In fact, most of the men and women David knew in PRIDE had come from other movements, whether they had registered blacks to vote in the South, marched with Martin Luther

King, protested against the Viet Nam war, or unionized farm workers. A point had come when they had to ask themselves why they weren't fighting for their own liberation as well.

By the time Paul crossed the bar David was by himself on the floor crouched in a corner writing with a felt-tipped pen on a sheet of cardboard. He was concentrating on filling in the lettering for the words *BLUE FASCISM MUST GO!*

"Hi," Paul said, standing over him, his voice tentative. Now that he was in David's presence, he felt a sudden rush of guilt for what he had done with Jim Blake the night before. The irony that he felt jealous and possessive when he'd seen David moments before talking to another guy was not lost on him. He wanted to tell David right here and now that he loved him, but he couldn't bring himself to do it, not in this room full of people.

David looked up from the poster. "Oh, hi."

"How you doing?"

"Okay."

"How's your neck?"

"It's sore, I guess, but it's okay."

"Where were you today?" He hoped a tone of accusation hadn't crept into his voice. "I called you half a dozen times."

David's face hardened just a fraction, as if something had happened that was Paul's fault. "I was with Billy. He got hurt last night. He didn't get arrested, but some storm trooper clubbed him pretty bad. He has all these bruises on his chest and stomach. I told him he has to go to the doctor, but he won't listen to me. He's at home and he can't get out of bed."

"David, about the stuff last night—"

"Forget it," David said. He went back to filling in the letters on the picket sign. "Everybody's out on bail now, anyway. They have lawyers. They're getting arraigned this week, I think. The bartender at the New Faces bar was transferred to a hospital. The cops beat him so bad he's going to lose his spleen."

"I'm really sorry to hear that." They were silent for a moment, and Paul suddenly felt awkward and useless standing over him. He hated it when they talked but didn't communicate. His mind went blank and he didn't know what else to say, and then he recalled the book found in the theater and that he had wanted to question David about it. "David, there was something I wanted to ask you about."

David looked up at him hopefully and Paul realized immediately he had made a mistake phrasing his question that way. Especially considering the topic of their last conversation. They'd have to talk about it, the living together thing, before they could get back to normal, but he couldn't face it now.

"Uh, you remember that book by C. Aubrey Pruitt, *The Homosexual in American Society*?"

Disappointment creased David's face, and he hid it by going back to working on the sign. "Yeah, of course."

"Well, it's come up in a case I'm working on, and I wondered if you could tell me something about it. I mean, I remember how much it meant to you, but there was some kind of controversy somewhere along the line about the author, wasn't there? Do you remember that?"

David observed him thoughtfully for a moment, his pen hanging in the air. "You know, I actually met him. C. Aubrey Pruitt. When I went back east to protest at the United Nations that time. I wrote to him through his publisher and asked if we could meet. I knew his name was a pseudonym and his identity was this big mystery and everyone who read the book wondered who he really was. People in the movement worshiped him. I wrote this gushing fan letter telling him that I felt like my life had never been the same since I read his book in college. It was like he opened my eyes and articulated things I guess I'd thought about but never dared say. And here he was, with this lofty prose, standing up for us, saying that we deserved to be treated with dignity, too. That we were American citizens just like everybody else. That we needed to mobilize to change things just like the blacks are doing. It was like he turned a light on in my mind and changed how I look at the world."

"So, did you meet him?"

"Yeah," David said softly. He chewed his lip. "I met him. He agreed to get together in a bar in the Village. So, there I was, about as excited as I've ever been, going to meet my hero, this guy who had completely changed my life—" David stopped and let out a nervous little laugh, "—and I have to tell you, it was the biggest disappointment of my life. It turned out he was married and had a kid. He invited me over to his house but said that his family didn't know about this other life he had so I would have to play it straight. The whole thing was just kind of sad. And you know, just because of the forcefulness of his prose, I had expected him to be this big handsome masculine guy...." his voice trailed off. "Eventually I found out that he had created these two distinct personalities for himself, like Dr. Jekyll and Mr. Hyde. By day he was this family man who was working on his PhD in criminal sociology and by night he was involved—what?" David stopped in mid-sentence. "You should see the look on your face."

"Oh," Paul sighed, "this is beginning to sound very familiar."

"Well, by night he was involved in Mattachine over in New York. After I met him, there was this big stink when they were electing their officers. Pruitt ran on a conservative slate—you know, the prissy old schoolmarms of the older generation—and got trounced by younger, more aggressive activists. The older guys said we had to kowtow to the psychiatric establishment: if they say we're sick, then we're sick. The younger activists said *we* are the experts on who we are, not the bigoted shrinks who are making their living keeping us down."

Paul remembered a fiery activist in Washington, D.C. named Frank Kameny—who had relentlessly sued after losing his government job and security clearance—had argued that as long as homosexuals were labeled sick by the medical establishment the movement would never get anywhere because it was a blanket justification for firing people from their jobs regardless of what their profession was. And Paul recalled a time not so long ago when homophile groups were so desperate for any acknowledgement from the psychiatric profession they would invite hostile therapists to speak at their meetings, and sit passively and politely as they were denounced as psychotics and child molesters. Those days were coming to a close.

"It's sad that this guy went from being so far ahead of the rest of us to being so far behind in just over a decade. It was almost like since he was working on his PhD and wanted to be an academic that he felt he had to support the medical establishment's attitude toward us. After that election, I don't think anybody's heard of C. Aubrey Pruitt since. It's like he just disappeared from the scene." David paused a moment, adding, "Oh, one other thing. Pruitt was having an affair with this guy behind his wife's back...."

Paul shut his eyes momentarily as everything became clear. "Let me guess, the guy was half his age... and black."

David tilted his head. "Did I tell you this story before?"

"It was just an educated guess." At least now he knew who the love note in the book was written to. He just didn't understand why it was in the theater in the first place or what it had to do with the attempt on Serokin's life.

David got up and took a stick from a pile on the bar and came back and tacked it to the back of the sign. He set it aside, then started on a new one. "So, will I see you at the protest rally?"

"You know I can't, David." He watched him make up another sign in silence. Finally, he said, "Are you coming over to my place tonight?" He had almost asked, *are you coming home tonight?* but had stopped himself, knowing it would only create trouble. Would it really be so bad, he wondered, to give in and let David come live with him? Who would know? But as soon as the thought came to him he rejected it. He recalled the police photos of Durkin and his Negro boyfriend. There didn't need to be proof. There didn't need to be evidence of criminal activity. The mere whiff of impropriety would be enough to derail everything he'd worked his whole life for. In the end, the answer to the question *who would know?* was, everyone would.

"I don't think so."

Paul glanced over his shoulder, suddenly feeling self-conscious, as if everyone in the room was listening to their conversation, and he lowered his voice until it was barely audible. "Come on, David. Don't be like that. Tomorrow night, then?"

David looked up from the sign only long enough to make eye contact, then said, "I think I'm going to be pretty busy with this for quite a while."

"Why is it so hard with us," Paul asked, "when it should be so easy?"

There didn't seem to be anything left to say after that.

# Chapter 7

The shadows grew more prominent as light faded from the living room and Blake was left sitting in near darkness. Dusk had begun to settle over the city and outside his picture window the landscape changed from shades of yellow as the sun met the horizon to hues of blue. He leaned his back against the wall, his legs spread out on the hardwood floor. He had changed out of his uniform after Paul had dropped him off, and was wearing jeans and a button-down shirt that needed ironing.

The painful shock of seeing Paul Winters again outside the theater the night before, and the anxious churning in his stomach that accompanied every time he'd run into him over the last ten years, had all been turned upside down in what had come after, and he didn't know what to make of it. Would he see more of him, or was this just a one-night thing, like before, when they had come together in a thunder-clap, and then everything had broken into a million pieces that could never be fixed?

He gazed upon the swirl of blankets piled at the center of the floor where he had fallen asleep with Paul wrapped in his arms and the room didn't seem as lonely or as empty as it had before.

Blake got up restlessly and went to the kitchen, flipping the switch, and poured himself some whiskey. He looked down into the glass for a long time, as if reading his future inside, the ceiling light reflecting off the amber liquid.

He lifted the glass to his lips, but hesitated before the drink touched his tongue. He stared down into it again, his mouth tightening, then went to the sink and poured it down the drain.

Suddenly he didn't know what to do with himself and the evening seemed to stretch out interminably before him. He began to pace the empty house, and it spoke to him, as it had since he'd come home to find his family gone. Echoes of Tommy crying, "Daddy's home!" as a toddler still rang in his ears by the front door and the clipped silence between him and Cathy still loomed in the dining alcove. When he came to their bedroom, he could still hear her pleas to understand what was wrong between them and his cold rebuffs.

He stared at the spot where their bed had stood. The anger he felt for the way she had left and taken their son without a word couldn't shut out his guilt over the cruel manner in which he had denied her affection because she could never be what he wanted. The years of being with him had broken her confidence, taken her youth, and left her brittle. He had done that to her. He had done that to her because she loved him. Well, she didn't love him anymore. He'd called her parents' place in Wisconsin twice after she'd left and she had refused to come to the phone. He'd already been served with papers. He didn't know a thing about getting a lawyer and the intricacies of getting a divorce, but he figured he was about to learn.

He wondered if there could be some kind of forgiveness between them, or if it was too late even for that.

His eyes came to rest on the safe in the corner and he felt himself drawn into the room. It happened often when he was alone in the house. He would be passing by, occupied with some other matter, and then it would catch his eye and he would find himself pulled in.

Sitting down in front of it cross-legged, he laid his palm on the cool black steel.

He spun the dial idly but didn't attempt to open it. There were times when he could face it. Times when it gave him comfort. Times when it broke his heart and he couldn't take it.

He thought about Paul again. He wondered if starting over was possible. The warmth he felt being held by Paul the night before in Tommy's room came back to him. Standing in the darkness, holding tight.

He jumped up suddenly, brushing the dust balls from the floor off his jeans. He had to know, one way or the other. He quickly grabbed his jacket and his car keys and made his way to the front door.

Paul had forgotten to leave the porch light on, and in the shadows of the climbing wisteria a dark figure waited at the front door. He couldn't see his face, but the man's broad shoulders left no doubt as to who it was. What was Jim Blake doing here? he wondered. As Paul coasted the Thunderbird into the garage, he felt a rush of excitement in his chest, but it was mixed with a warning from deep inside. Doing it one time with Blake, that was one thing, he told himself. Maybe that was forgivable. If I do this again, it's something else.

He thought about how much he loved David and how impossible their relationship had always been. And yet it had survived a decade. How can you love someone so much and still be at such odds with him so much of the time? He knew this was the worst moment to betray David if he was to have any hope of reconciling with him. He resolved to tell Blake to go home, that he couldn't see him anymore. There was no reason he couldn't help Blake investigate the death of Wesley Durkin, but he reasoned even that would have to stop. The truth was, Paul knew in his heart he couldn't entirely trust himself around Jim Blake.

He took the path to the front porch where Blake was waiting for him. It was the first time Paul had seen him that weekend in street clothes.

"I thought it might be okay," Blake began. There was vulnerability in his face but the hint of a smile, too. "My mattress isn't supposed to arrive until Tuesday...."

"Look, Jim, about last night—"

Even in the darkness Paul could see Blake's gentle smile fade and that he understood nothing was going to happen between them tonight.

"It was wrong for me to come," Blake stammered apologetically. "I'm sorry, I didn't mean—" He looked down, embarrassed, avoiding Paul's eyes, and started for the porch stairs.

Paul felt a sudden twang of guilt. He didn't want to leave it this way and put his hand on Blake's shoulder to stop him. "You're here. I don't want you to go. Just—just come in for a minute and let's have a drink."

Once they were inside, Blake settled into an upholstered chair while Paul went to the liquor cabinet. "Whiskey?"

"Straight."

Paul poured two glasses. He only noticed how full they were when he brought one to Blake and had to walk carefully so it didn't spill. He sat across the room on the couch and they gazed at each other a long while without saying anything, sipping their drinks.

"I learned something this evening," Paul said finally. He explained what he had discovered about the authorship of the book Blake had found next to Leland Serokin in the theater, and his belief that the professor had written the love note in the front of the book to the young black witness they were searching for.

"So they were lovers."

"Yes, but years ago. Before our guy with the scarred face ever got involved with Wesley Durkin. Back when Serokin was living in New York."

"It doesn't sound like a coincidence they ran into each other in that theater."

"No, I'd say it was a planned meeting. With our suspect—witness, whatever you want to call him—desperate after Durkin's death and without a place to stay, maybe he reached out to an old flame and asked for help."

Blake nodded slowly. "I can understand why Serokin would deny knowing him. He's married with a kid. You think the professor wouldn't give our guy what he wanted, and so he got violent?"

Paul thought of the beautiful young man lying languidly on the bed and couldn't match the image with someone who would throttle an ex-lover in a sleazy theater. "We'll find out tomorrow when we go back and talk to Leland Serokin. This time we'll make sure he gives us some answers." Only after he'd said it did Paul realize he had just agreed to continue helping Blake with his investigation despite his earlier decision to end all contact with him.

They fell silent again and Paul was beginning to feel the effects of his drink. He looked down and saw his glass was nearly empty. He stood and he felt lightheaded. "Let me refresh your drink." He went over to the liquor cabinet and took the bottle of whiskey across the room and refilled Blake's glass. As he poured, they looked directly into one another's eyes, not saying anything, then looked away. He topped off his own, then set the bottle on the coffee table as he eased back into the couch.

"Mind if I light up?"

"No, go right ahead." His first thought was that David would think he'd gone back to smoking, or want to know who his visitor had been, but then he realized David wouldn't be coming over anyway, so why worry about it?

"Something happened at the party I went to last night at the Music Center," Paul said suddenly, "something I didn't tell you about." Bulgetti's announcement seemed like such a long time ago, after the last tumultuous twenty-four hours in his personal life. "The D.A. is going to resign. There's going to be an election in the spring. I'm going to be campaigning to be the next L.A. District Attorney."

Blake sat up and gazed at him in admiration. "Wow," he said. "Really? I mean, that's incredible. Geez, congratulations. I don't even know what to say."

Paul experienced such a surge of elation and pride at Blake's enthusiasm that he felt he had to tamp it down. "It's not like I'm going to be the only candidate," he explained quickly, "but with Bulgetti and his machine behind me, this could really happen." And in that moment Paul knew it would. It finally sank in. He was going to be the next District Attorney.

"I've always admired you," Blake said, observing him, taking a slow drag on his cigarette. "What you've done with your life."

This was how it was supposed to feel, Paul realized, a little drunkenly. This was how it was supposed to feel when you told the people you cared about that something great had happened to you, that you were on your way to achieving your lifetime dream. As he gazed at Blake, he thought about how cold David had been with him that evening and how little his lover was willing to see things from Paul's perspective. It would serve him right if Paul did as he damn well pleased until David came to his senses.

Something sad drifted across Blake's face, and he said wistfully, "You're so different from me. You've made so much of your life. I've totally fucked up mine."

"No," Paul said. "You and I, we're the same. We believe in the same things."

"I thought I had quite a bit once, but not now."

"You'll get your son back. I'll do whatever I can to help you. I'm not an expert in that area, but I can find someone who is."

Blake nodded gratefully and Paul saw that emotion in his eyes that surfaced only at the mention of his son.

"Well," Blake said, seeming to quickly swallow those feelings as if he were embarrassed to show them to anyone. He stubbed out his cigarette and slapped an open palm against the armrest. "I guess I'd better get going."

Suddenly Paul didn't want him to go. But he got up, a little shaky on his feet, and led Blake to the door. His head was light from the whiskey and he wasn't even sure who made the first move. All he knew was that they were in each other's arms. He wanted to explain that he couldn't do this, that he already had a lover, but before he could stop himself their mouths were locked in a kiss. Paul pulled himself away, telling himself to stop, but something about Blake's lips almost immediately drew him back, and he told himself he would only kiss him once more, and then he would send him home. But Blake's lips were so firm and his kiss so achingly tender, and Paul discovered he couldn't help himself. And then there was the scent of him, the bristle on his jaw, and Paul found himself fumbling with the buttons on Blake's shirt and resentfully telling himself this was David's fault, that he had been rejected one time too many this weekend, and whatever happened Paul was the last to blame.

In no time their clothes were off, strewn across the living room carpet, and Paul was leading Blake by the hand down the hallway to the bedroom. Paul slipped onto the bed and waited for Blake to follow.

Blake hesitated and Paul looked up at him expectantly.

"I'm not sure I can do this," Blake said doubtfully. Then he deadpanned, "I don't think we've ever had sex in a bed before."

"Get over here," Paul laughed, and Blake fell onto the bed beside him, chuckling.

"I like it when you smile," Paul said, running his fingers across Blake's cheek. He had never considered before how rare an occurrence that was. It felt so right lying next to him. Just being together, touching, looking into each other's eyes. As they made love, gentle this time, so gentle, Paul felt an ache that maybe he could never get enough of him, that even after a lifetime of this still he would want more.

After they were done, their breath slowing in unison, covered in a cooling sheen of sweat, they were quiet for a long while. Then Paul swallowed and said, "I have a lover. I should have told you."

The words seemed to hang in the air for a long time.

Blake's face grew thoughtful. "Is it... the same guy?"

"His name is David. Yes, it's the same guy from ten years ago."

"Why isn't he here with you?"

Paul hesitated. That was a long story. "We're kind of on the outs. It seems like we can't agree on anything any-more."

"I'm sorry," Blake said. He pulled Paul even closer. The warmth of skin touching skin was electric. "I'm sorry... and I'm not sorry." He covered Paul's mouth with his and then they started all over again.

◇◇◇

96

They had only been asleep a little while when Paul woke. He got up quietly, disengaging himself from Blake's arms, and padded down the hall to the bathroom.

Closing the bathroom door, he turned on the light and stood over the toilet. As he peed, Paul drowsily observed the framed image of a rather scruffy looking cat with big yellow eyes on a mustard-yellow and red background hanging on the wall. It was a cheap *Le Chat Noir* reproduction of the Steinlen poster from the late 19th Century Parisian cabaret.

On their trip to Europe a few years ago he and David had bought it for a few francs from a stand beside Sacré-Coeur then went to extraordinary lengths during the rest of their vacation not to bend or wrinkle it. It had become a running joke as they traipsed across Europe trying to keep the flimsy poster from harm's way on rattling metros and speeding trains. The cat found itself perched on head-boards and leaning on window panes in little *pensiones* from Marseilles to Barcelona to Venice. Once home, Paul had spent a ridiculous amount of money to have it professionally framed, and it had hung above the toilet, gazing enigmatically at them ever since.

His grogginess vanished and he became instantly alert when he thought he heard something at the front of the house, and went quickly down the hall to investigate. Was somebody trying to break in? When he reached the living room, David was coming through the front door, flipping on a light.

"Were you already asleep?" David shook his head apologetically. "I'm sorry I acted like that. I was just so mad about what happened at the bar last night, and I guess I took it out on..." his voice trailed off and he stopped in his tracks. "Why are your clothes all over the place?" He stared at the floor perplexed for what seemed like an eternity before the meaning of two sets of clothes strewn haphazardly across the carpet sunk in. His mouth seemed to fold into itself.

"David," Paul said quickly, crossing the room toward him, scrambling for an explanation, "I was angry at you and—"

"Oh, my God," David said under his breath, staring at him, his eyes taking on fire. But it was the hurt in his eyes that was hardest to take. He seemed to notice for the first time that Paul wasn't wearing anything, and Paul had never felt so naked standing before him. David took a wary step backwards, then another.

"David, please don't go," he pleaded. "Please—let me explain. I love you, you know I do, and—" He reached out for him but David recoiled from his touch. Before Paul could stop him he was out the door.

David hesitated a moment on the porch and when he spoke it came out as if he were being strangled. When Paul heard the anguish in his voice, he couldn't bear to look at him.

"I'll come by later to pick up my things." And then he was gone.

# Chapter 8

The campus was nearly deserted Monday morning as Paul and Blake crossed a grass expanse covered with brown and yellow leaves and took the main entrance into Haines Hall. The sociology department at UCLA was in one of the original four buildings of the university constructed in the late twenties, its patterned brick and limestone designed to evoke the warm climate and Romanesque style of twelfth-century Southern Italy. Leland Serokin's office was on the second floor.

A pretty blonde co-ed in a mini-skirt standing at a filing cabinet in the outer office pointed them in the direction of Serokin's office. As they passed, she smiled with freshman enthusiasm. "I can barely wait for his class this quarter. It's like he makes these connections that just blow you away. I changed my major because of him. Everybody scrambles to get in his class."

Serokin sat hunched behind his desk in a cluttered office filled with books. A new, less bulky bandage encircled his neck. He looked up as they entered and his thin lips became a fine line. "Gentlemen, I'm afraid what I told you yesterday is doubly true today. Classes start tomorrow and I'm far behind in preparing my lecture. I have nothing else to tell you about the incident Saturday night. So if you could please close the door as you go—"

Blake plopped heavily in a chair in front of the desk. "We wouldn't be here if you hadn't lied to us yesterday.

So why don't you put your lecture notes aside so we can have a little talk?"

Setting his pen down and interlacing his fingers on top of the yellow pad he had been scribbling on, Serokin breathed out heavily with resignation. "All right, how can I help you?"

"First, you can admit you wrote this book." Blake slapped the copy of *The Homosexual in American Society* on the desk.

"I didn't lie to you about that." The sly expression Paul remembered from Serokin's face the day before momentarily returned. "I simply told you the author of that book and I were of a like mind. I assumed as a policeman you would look between the lines. How much clearer could I have made it to you?"

Standing behind him, Paul saw Blake's shoulders stiffen and could tell this guy was rubbing him the wrong way.

"You could have told us the love note inside was written to your young black boyfriend," Blake charged. "You know, the one who you denied seeing in the theater, the one who tried to kill you and then ran away?"

From his experience in criminal negotiations, Paul knew it was a bad sign when interviews deteriorated this early in the proceedings. "Look," he said, trying to cool things off, "we're investigating a related crime and we need to track down the young man in question. We're not judging your personal life."

Serokin's heavily lidded, heavily bagged eyes traveled from Blake to Paul and back again in a cool, assessing stare, then an impish look of possessing a secret understanding about their relationship came over his face. "Of *course* you wouldn't," he smirked. "I'm sure we're all on the same page."

"I don't like your insinuation," Blake snarled, rising from his chair and waving his finger angrily. "You'd better watch your mouth, Professor."

Holding up his hands in amused surrender, Serokin said, "Point taken. I didn't mean to ruffle any feathers. I *appreciate* your discretion." Again the knowing smirk. "But anyway, Roland didn't try to kill me. At least I don't think he did."

"Roland...?" Paul asked. Blake had eased back into his chair, but Paul could see his shoulders were still tense. Paul was surprised at his angry gut-response to the professor's intimation. He decided he'd better take over. He figured the professor's suspicions could work to their advantage. He might open up to other gays in a way he never would with straights.

"Roland Mosley. He telephoned me out of the blue last week. I hadn't seen him in three years. I didn't even know he had moved to L.A. He told me he had to see me, that he had no one else to turn to."

"Wait a minute, how did you originally meet?"

"It was back in New York over three years ago when I was finishing my PhD." The sharp rodent features of the professor's face momentarily softened. "He had read my book and wrote me a letter. He was just a street kid, living in the Village..."

As Serokin spoke, his eyes drifting far away, his mind turning inward, Paul remembered the gentle filtered light on the smooth chestnut skin, the curves of the young man's body in the twisted sheets.

"...He was a beautiful boy with the loveliest body, despite the scar on his face, and old fool that I was, I fell head over heels in love with him, but I'm afraid it didn't last. You see, he had already fallen in love with the author of the book, as so many young men do. Every dream they've ever had becomes embodied in the name C. Aubrey

Pruitt and the words he wrote." Serokin's mouth took on a bitter twist and his eyes returned to the present. "But look at me. How could I possibly live up to that? How could someone like me ever fulfill all those dreams?"

"You said he was desperate when he called you, did he tell you what was wrong?"

"Not at first. He was upset and confused. Finally he told me a story, and whether it's true or not, I can't say. He claimed somebody had been murdered and he was afraid it would all be pinned on him. But he knew who was responsible—and soon he'd have proof—but for the time being he needed money."

"Did you agree to give it to him?"

The professor leaned back in his chair and crossed his arms. "I do not take kindly to former lovers hitting me up for cash, especially when it begins to sound like a demand."

"Was he trying to blackmail you?"

"Whether it was blackmail or not is a matter of interpretation. When I didn't immediately open my wallet, he told me he had something he assumed I would want, and he wanted to be paid for it."

"The book?"

"The book, and what I had written in it." Serokin sighed. "I wrote that note to him in the delirium of love, and like all impetuous acts, one learns to regret them. My penmanship may not be of the highest order, but it is distinctive, utterly recognizable. To have written a note like that in a book with that particular subject matter, well, it would not be easy to explain away."

"To your wife or your employer."

"My wife is a very understanding woman, but yes, it would be a problem. And my employer, well…"

Not only would he be fired from his job, Paul knew, but it would be unlikely he would find employment in his field elsewhere. The years he had worked for his PhD would come to nothing.

"He didn't ask for much," Serokin continued, "just enough to get by. There was something else, something very valuable, that he was going to retrieve. He just needed enough cash for a few days. He said after that he'd never have to worry about money again."

"So you agreed to meet with him downtown New Year's Eve. Money in exchange for the book."

"I suggested we meet at the theater because I'd done field work there before and I didn't think we'd be seen."

"What happened that night?"

"I arrived first. I waited for quite a while. I began to think he wasn't going to show. And then just when I was about to leave, he slid in the seat next to mine. He was really afraid. Out of breath. He kept looking around. He was sure someone had followed him into the theater."

"Did you give him the money?"

"I never got the chance. He handed me the book, and then he saw someone in the seats behind us and flipped out. He tore out of that theater like someone was out to kill him. Before I could look around, someone had come from behind and was throttling me with a rope. I remember the book dropping from my lap and then I passed out."

"We need to find him. Where do you think Roland is now?"

"He has no money. He has no place to go. He was on the street years ago when I met him, and he returned to the street when we broke up. But he's still young and beautiful. He'll find somebody else to take care of him. I can only hope he is more loyal to them than he ever was to me."

Blake leaned forward. His voice had calmed down, but there was a thread of insistence in it. "There was

103

something else, wasn't there? It wasn't just that note in the book. What else did he have on you?"

Serokin appraised them for a long time before he answered. "The dissertation I wrote for my PhD, *Ideology and Structure in an Association of Sexual Deviants: A Study*, was about my work with Mattachine in New York. I wrote it under my own name and neglected to mention my personal involvement as an activist in the group under my other identity. There would be those, I suppose, who might question the ethics of what I had done."

"Meaning your career would be over." Paul remembered what David had said the night before. "Your conservative slate was voted down in favor of a group of younger activists."

Color came to the professor's cheeks, revealing old emotional wounds on his face. "I swore to them that I would leave the movement forever if they went in that direction. Of course I want an end to discrimination and sodomy laws, but we must defer to science. Think of the arrogance of these young people, the unmitigated gall, that they're smarter than the medical establishment, that they're the experts on this malady just because they suffer from it. It's like a cancer victim claiming he knows more than his doctors! Do you know what they called me in New York? They called me the senile grandfather of the homophile movement. To be humored at best, ignored most of the time, and to be ridiculed at worst. *Me*, the man who created this movement, when they were all just frightened schoolboys bewildered because they liked to look at other boys in the locker room." The bitter twist returned to his lips. "C. Aubrey Pruitt died that night. And you know what? The same thing will happen to them, just you wait. Another wave of militants even more extreme than the last will come along and sweep them away."

Paul exchanged a glance with Blake. They had gotten as much as they were going to get; it was time to leave. Blake reached for the book on the desk, but Serokin laid his hand on the navy-blue cover.

"Could I keep this? I know it sounds silly, but..."

Blake looked over at Paul, who nodded almost imperceptibly.

"Go ahead."

Paul followed Blake out, but hesitated at the door, looking back. Serokin had opened the book and was gazing fixedly at the dedication he had inscribed years before. "Of all the people he could have gone to," Paul reminded him, "he remembered you when he was in trouble. Maybe you meant more to him than you think."

Serokin looked up at him pensively. "I wonder. Did Roland ever love me? I don't know. I'd like to think so. I do know one thing for sure." He gently ran his fingers over the loopy scrawl of his dedication. "He loved the man who wrote this book."

"I'm sorry I lost my cool," Blake said as they descended the stairs.

"Yeah, what was that all about?"

"I don't know. I don't usually do that. But something about that guy smirking at us really bent me out of shape."

Paul nodded but didn't say anything. He wondered just how comfortable Blake was in his own shoes, and what that meant for the both of them. He was still trying to filter through the events of the night before. Blake had slept soundly the entire night and was unaware of Paul's encounter with David. But after being confronted by his lover, Paul had slept only fitfully, trying to figure out why all the rough spots between him and Blake now seemed so smooth, and every encounter with David was prickly and perilous as the edge of a serrated knife. He had to admit he felt so good lying next to Blake, yet so lousy and ashamed of how he had treated David, and at a loss to know what he should do next.

"I have the day off," Blake said, "but I have to go to Hollywood this afternoon. I have an appointment with the police shrink at two. It'll just be an hour."

Paul nodded. "I'm getting together with a reporter friend of mine then. On Sunset. How about if I drop you off, then pick you up after?"

Dr. Socrates Stone sat behind his desk waiting for his next appointment. A Brahms concerto played on a classical music station in the background; a silent room always left him uneasy.

He cleaned his eyeglasses with a cloth, then fingered through his file notes as he always did, refreshing his memory in preparation for the session. The patient was a homicide detective who had been demoted after assaulting his commanding officer, but Dr. Stone wondered if there wasn't more to this case than initially met the eye. The cop's wife had left him about the same time as the assault, taking his son. Perhaps the stress of his home life had led to his aggressive behavior at work. And then there was the other issue, the one that hadn't been addressed at their meeting last week.

Stone only knew of it because of his encounter with Jim Blake a decade before. The officer had been caught in a compromising position and the doctor had aided his superiors in extracting a confession. And yet, from what Stone could garner about Blake's life since—marriage and a child—there was no evidence he had returned to the behavior that had gotten him in trouble in the first place. Which just proved what the psychiatrist had insisted all along, that Jim Blake never was, could never be, one of those people. He had just been confused and needed to be jolted in the right direction. Still, those tendencies needed to be considered in his overall assessment of the patient's antisocial behavior.

The doctor's thoughts drifted back to those days ten years ago, and the long way he had traveled since he'd first come to work for the LAPD. He had been a struggling therapist hard pressed to pay the rent on his office, and in desperate need of a job to support his growing family. His dream of opening a nation-wide network of therapy centers to treat homosexuals who had been arrested on sodomy and soliciting charges—at their own expense, in lieu of prison—had never come to pass. And yet, he had become quite influential, surprisingly influential, in fact, on the subject thanks to a book he'd published several years ago, *Curing Homosexuality in the Male*.

He had discovered all you had to do was get a book published, and once you did you were considered an expert in the field. Suddenly you were flooded with summonses to testify before Congress and invitations to address psychiatric symposiums. Perhaps most significant to building his reputation were the requests by the media for quotes in newspapers and guest spots on radio or television talk shows.

Stone had gone from being an obscure practitioner to perhaps the best known therapist in the world on the subject. He now divided his time between his thriving private practice, his professorial duties and his continued consulting work with the LAPD.

He had just recently been filmed lecturing before psychology students for an upcoming hour-long CBS Reports special, *The Homosexuals*, and was anxiously awaiting the air date. He had heard the episode had gone back for re-editing when the head of CBS News deemed the documentary too sympathetic to the homosexual. The editor had been ordered to re-cut the interviews with gay men in order to make them appear less happy with their lives. Even so, Stone had been annoyed to learn Mike Wallace would mention a minority of psychiatrists didn't consider homosexuality an illness at all. But at least he had been assured no psychiatrist with those beliefs would be invited to speak. He was relieved to know his word would hold sway. That's the way it was lately: a brief disclaimer that not all therapists agreed that homosexuality was an illness, then an in-depth interview with those who espoused the sickness model.

The doctor had little patience with therapists who disagreed with him on the matter. It was abundantly clear to anyone with half a brain that homosexuality was a serious mental illness that had reached epidemic pro-portions. If the trend continued unabated Dr. Stone feared that a majority of American's youth could be afflicted by the end of the next decade. He was especially steamed by that Hooker woman, the UCLA professor and social psychologist who had done a study that had rocked the psychiatric world a decade before revealing that homosexual males were as well adjusted as heterosexual males.

Dr. Stone had his suspicions about Evelyn Hooker. Oh, she had been married twice, that was true. But she was awfully tall for a woman, horsey in fact, with a booming voice. It was interesting to note—surprise, surprise—that she'd never had any children. Of course Dr. Stone couldn't point out this salient fact and all the implications it conjured without being pilloried by all the whiners and complainers and liberals who were beginning to pop up at every cocktail party.

And she was hardly alone. That upstart Judd Marmor, who was making such a name for himself in psychiatric circles, had recently edited a book expressing a wide variety of viewpoints on homosexuality—but had slyly used his introduction to poke holes in the theories of those promoting the sickness model.

Dr. Stone was quick to say he held no animosity toward the homosexual. In fact, he told audiences when he was interviewed on radio or television, he liked the homosexual. They are so charming, he would explain wistfully, but so sad, because they didn't fit in the natural man-woman design.

Yet there was little reason to feel sorry for the homosexual and his claims of persecution. On the contrary, Dr. Stone was only too aware that they were an aggressive and relentlessly persistent group. Their influence was everywhere. Thanks to a series of Supreme Court obscenity rulings reaching back to the late fifties, you couldn't walk down the street without being leered at by nude males in come-hither poses on the covers of pictorial magazines on every newsstand. It was a veritable flood tide of filth. Dr. Stone's biggest concern was the effect this smut had on the developing minds of young boys, whose natural curiosity about their developing bodies, coupled with the insatiable curiosity of youth, was being perverted into grotesque fantasies in which the male physique became an object to fetishize.

Just as startling, the male homosexual stranglehold on the fashion industry was neutering the sexes and de-feminizing women, shearing their hair and forcing them into boyish apparel that rejected their natural curves. This was not surprising, Dr. Stone reasoned, since the homosexual view of women was charged with hostile feelings caused by a smothering, overly intimate mother, and an ineffectual, emasculated father. No wonder they took out their rage by forcing the female into uncomfortable and increasingly ludicrous clothing. Worse, the bright colors of men's suits and slacks made even the most masculine male look like a pansy. It was getting harder by the day to find anything manly on the racks in department stores. Dr. Stone couldn't buy anything anymore without coming out looking like a peacock.

A knock on the door brought him out of his reverie. He sighed.

"Come in, Jim," he said.

"How are you feeling today?"

"I'm all right." Blake felt uncomfortable in the chair, despite its thick leather cushions. He disliked the doctor with a dark intensity for the way he had cruelly manipulated him in an LAPD interrogation room ten years ago, and yet it was important he not show it. Not if he wanted to get back to the Homicide table. Stone looked almost the same to him after all these years, tall and thin, with his calculated kind and thoughtful gaze behind glasses and his conservative suit, though his hair had thinned and was now being raked over a balding pate.

"You seem agitated."

"Oh, it was just a case I'm working. A witness wasn't cooperative." What was it that had irked him so in his conversation with Leland Serokin? That smug innuendo about his relationship with Paul had really set him off. Even Paul had noticed it. Why had he let that creepy little guy get to him? It had to be something about that knowing smirk. It did bother him, that some people could see it.

"Would you like to talk about it?"

"No, it was nothing. Actually I feel a lot better than last week."

"And why do you think that is?"

He did feel better, he realized, and he knew why. After years of shame and doubt Paul Winters had slammed back into his life and it was like a veil shrouding his existence had been pulled away. He couldn't get over that Paul really had forgiven him for the terrible thing he had done so long ago. Why had it taken him so long to believe it when Paul had assured him so many years before? He hadn't known that kind of love and forgiveness was possible.

"Is it because you've had time to accept your wife has left you?"

"I don't know," Blake lied. "Maybe that's it. Maybe I'm coming to terms with my wife leaving and taking Tommy."

"Have you thought about trying to get back together with her?"

"No."

Stone observed him. "Do you care to elaborate on that?"

"No." He was beginning to get annoyed. "This is about me socking my commanding officer, right? Isn't that why I'm here? I don't see what any of this has to do with that."

The hint of a smile played on the doctor's lips, and Blake wanted to belt him. "You don't think your personal life can impact your professional life?"

Blake shrugged. "Look, Captain Ridley made me mad because he was stonewalling my investigation and I decked him. I know it was wrong. I know you can't do that and get away with it. I know I have to kiss ass in order to get my detective's badge back. But I only did it because I care, and I thought the brass was looking for an easy solution to a case that looked to me a lot like murder. It doesn't have anything to do with my personal life."

Dr. Stone tapped his finger on the blotter on his desk. "I find it interesting you have no desire to reconcile with your wife."

Hadn't the doctor heard a word he'd said? "Why? It's over between us." He stared sullenly out the second-story office window. "There's nothing there. Nothing left to say."

"You sound certain about that." Dr. Stone angled his head. "Have you met someone?"

Blake swallowed and felt his Adam's apple jump. He wondered if the doctor had noticed it. Blake was sure he had. "No, I just don't think it's going to happen, me and her getting back together. All I care about is getting Tommy back."

"You really love him."

"That boy is everything to me." He was surprised his words came out fiercely.

"You do realize the fastest way to get your son back is to reconcile with your wife."

They stared at each other, not saying a word, as if playing chicken and not knowing why, daring the other to look away first, waiting for the other to blink. Blake held his gaze, the reflection on Dr. Stone's glasses rendering his hazel eyes unreadable. Finally Blake looked away.

Stone sighed. "I hope you understand now is not the time to start a new relationship."

He thought about that, about Paul. What was he getting himself into? Paul already had a lover, one he'd been with for ten years now. The fact that the pair were on rocky ground didn't change anything. He'd be a fool to open himself up to someone who wasn't even available. And yet, he had never felt so elated as when they were together. Even so he was filled with doubt. What would a man like Paul Winters, so smart, so educated, so successful, want with a guy like him?

It dawned on him that his life had come to a grinding halt in the last week. His demotion from Homicide, of course. But far worse, that terrible evening when he'd come home to find his wife and Tommy gone. The darkness that followed discovering the house empty still scared him, the crushing weight of it. It reminded him of so many years ago, just after the war, the pall that had descended over him after the death of his friend Jack Spenser. There were some kinds of darkness too deep to escape.

And then Paul Winters had come into his life and crowded out some of the pain. He felt equal parts hopeful and uncertain. Maybe he could get Tommy back, some-how. Maybe everything would work out. Maybe he and Paul had a future. He had known Paul only a few days a decade before, and yet somehow all these years he'd remained a seminal figure in his life. He wondered if he had loved him all along. But no matter what happened between them, he reminded himself, he had to keep his sights directed on what was most important. His son, Tommy.

The doctor launched into a series of questions about dealing with his anger, and Blake hardly paid attention, giving noncommittal replies until the clock read ten till three.

"It looks like our time is up." Dr. Stone glanced down at his appointment book, then back at him. "I'd like to see you more often. I think we should schedule our next session for later in the week."

# Chapter 9

Paul left his Thunderbird in the parking lot of a strip mall on the corner of Sunset and Crescent Heights. Here the lush Spanish-style mansion and hotel complex, the Garden of Allah, once stood. Its owner, the silent screen actress Alla Nazimova, had entertained Hollywood's most dazzling stars of the twenties and thirties and provided residences for F. Scott Fitzgerald and other celebrities. Now the parking lot lay hot and naked in the sun on the spot where palm-shaded Sunday afternoon poolside parties once catered to young girls eager to further their careers in the business—and powerful women like Nazimova eager to get to know them better.

Crossing the street against the light, Paul passed the shuttered teen nightclub Pandora's Box. It had been the site of a recent series of youth protests and riots against a ten p.m. curfew law directed at keeping young people off the Boulevard. Paul recalled the chuckles at the Music Center fundraiser over the comment about the boys who looked like girls and the girls who looked like boys now flocking to the strip. Business owners didn't like it. The City Council had voted to condemn the building—where bands like the Beach Boys had drawn in a young crowd—on the pretext its demolition was necessary to realign the street. Nobody was fooled.

Marvin Botwinick was sitting at a booth beside the deli's front window when Paul walked in. He was reading the newspaper, not surprisingly the *Times*, and a smoldering pipe hung from his mouth. His shirt sleeves were rolled up revealing maritime tattoos on his forearms. His clothes, as usual, were rumpled. He scratched his beard sheepishly.

"Sorry about my antics at the party Saturday night."

"I would have asked to see you yesterday but I figured you needed a day to sleep it off," Paul gently cajoled. "How does Julie put up with you?" He slid into the booth, noting that Marvin was reading the social section of the paper, with copious photographs of the Music Center party, the most prominent picture featuring a beaming Dorothy Chandler with the grinning new governor.

"With a weary smile and a sense of humor, I suppose." He folded the paper and set it beside him on the red vinyl seat. "You know those kinds of events always get to me. Beautiful people wearing beautiful clothes. And it irks me our friends the downtown business interests got their way, as they always do, and ten thousand people lost their homes." He sucked on his pipe. "All the reporters at the paper were gently pressured to buy tickets and put in an appearance. Never mind that the *Times* pushed hard to get the council to donate land to put Mama Dorothy's music center on that spot, knowing the value of their own land holdings in the area would skyrocket once the place was built."

"If I didn't know better, Marvin Botwinick, I might call you a cynic." Paul ordered a burger and a Coke and Botwinick did the same. When the waiter left, Paul placed the report on Wesley Durkin on the table. The LAPD insignia on the cover immediately caught the reporter's attention. "Do you know what this is?"

"If that is what I think it is, it's a dossier from the LAPD's Intelligence Division."

Botwinick reached across the table for the report, but Paul held it back. "Not so fast, Hemingway." He wanted more before he revealed the subject of the surveillance. "What else do you know?"

"The division gets millions in tax money, more than robbery-homicide, and has nearly a hundred employees. It was formed to investigate mobsters back in the day but quickly spread to the general population. It's rumored that they have over a million dossiers on tens of thousands of individuals and organizations. There are so many files detailing the political and private lives of people like you and me that they have to rent public storage to house them all." Botwinick reached for the file, but again Paul held it back.

"You've got more."

"Says who?"

"I know you. You always have more."

Marvin grinned conspiratorially and leaned across the table. He spoke in a whisper, puffing excitedly on his pipe. "Here's the scoop. When Sam Yorty ran for mayor, he held a press conference accusing the police chief of using the Intelligence Division to spy on him and promised to fire Chief Parker's ass if he got elected. You don't remember this?"

Paul shook his head. Local elections had been a nasty business for a long time, especially the mayor's race. Red-baiting smear campaigns and exploiting race fears ruled the day.

"It was five or six years ago. Yorty demanded the D.A. open an investigation into the department's illegal spying program." Botwinick leaned even closer. "So get this: Yorty wins the election and he and Parker have a private meeting. It was rumored that the Chief went to the meeting with a briefcase fat with surveillance files. Suddenly, they're best friends and jointly call on the D.A. to drop the investigation of LAPD spying."

"You think the Chief had something on him?"

"Shit, they have something on everybody, including the P.T.A. All I know is, Chief Parker kept his job until he dropped dead last summer. Information is power. So, whose file is it?"

Paul pushed the report across the table and Botwinick opened it. "Oh."

"What do you know about Wesley Durkin?"

"The one who committed suicide? Just that he was a nothing candidate going nowhere in a four-way race until Buck Chandler and the downtown powerbrokers got behind his campaign."

"Buck Chandler?" Paul vaguely remembered Agnes Chandler had mentioned her husband had supported Durkin's candidacy. Again Paul wondered why the LAPD had been spying on Durkin and who had ordered the surveillance. Suddenly he recalled what Jeff Dupuis had said about taxes in South Central. "Marvin, could you check something out for me? Have taxes gone up in South Central commensurate with the rest of the city?"

Botwinick blinked at him. "I can look. Why?"

"I'm not sure. It was just something I heard."

As Botwinick studied the surveillance photos, the nature of the pictures of the assessor and Roland Mosley seemed to sink in, and he said, "Paul, this looks like…"

Despite their friendship, Paul had never shared his personal life with Marvin, never mentioned his relationship with David, and he never would. If there was anyone in his professional life who wouldn't care, it was Marvin Botwinick; but after a decade of friendship and trust, he still felt he just couldn't risk it. He had become adept at turning any question about his private life on its head.

"I know what it looks like." Paul took the file back and closed the cover. "Marvin, I need you to keep a lid on this, just for a while, okay?"

Botwinick sat back and watched him for a moment. "What's going on, Paul? Do you have a story for me?"

"Maybe. I don't know. Just find out what you can for me about the tax thing, okay? Get back to me as soon as you can. And if I want to know more about the Intelligence Division, where should I go next?"

"Well, Dean Estes—who, by the way, is a real hard-ass bastard if there ever was one—is the head of the division."

"Dean Estes," Paul repeated, to remember the name.

Botwinick cocked his head. "You've met him already." When Paul gave him a puzzled look, Marvin added, "I saw you two together. At the party."

Off Paul's blank stare, Marvin laid his newspaper on the table and turned to the page featuring a photo-spread of the Music Center event. Marvin tapped his finger on a blurry figure in the background of a photo of Buck and Agnes Chandler. Paul immediately recognized the powerfully-built crew-cut man who he had presumed was a bodyguard for the Chandlers, the one who had brushed past him so aggressively at the phone booth.

"That's him," Botwinick said.

His patient had left only moments before when Dr. Stone's phone began to ring. It was on his personal line. He knew who it was before he answered and felt his blood pressure begin to rise. It was his ex-wife. Again. He strained himself to remain civil as she prattled on about this and that as if he had all the time in the world and they were the best of friends before coming to the point. Always the prattle, then the point. Could he take Michael for the evening?

She acknowledged he wasn't supposed to have the kids until the weekend in that breezy way of hers that implied she was a free spirit and if he didn't go along with every one of her whims and demands he was just an old stick in the mud. Their younger daughter wasn't a problem, she added, as if to lighten the load, because she was going to have dinner at a classmate's.

Michael was twelve now, a smart boy, not particularly interested in sports, but he was at the top of his class, on the debate team, with a precocious fascination with politics. His little sister had seemed withdrawn since the divorce, shy with her father, and that worried Dr. Stone, but he told himself it would pass.

Of course he would be glad to take Michael for the evening, he told her magnanimously. He had made it a point to show the world just how amicable a divorce could be though it made his blood boil how often Susan took advantage of his flexibility. Dr. Stone calculated that even though Michael would get to his house this evening before he did, the boy could be trusted to stay out of trouble.

As he hung up the phone, Dr. Stone realized he didn't have another patient for an hour, and decided to go for a walk. Taking the stairs to the street, he mused over how his ex-wife had reverted back to her old self after their marriage ended. Breezy before, whiny during, breezy after. Her physical transformation was also remarkable. She had gained weight every year they were married until she was fat as the Goodyear blimp, only to lose every ounce once they had separated, reclaiming the figure she had when they were dating.

Then he considered his present wife and his lips tightened. Jennifer. She had left a message with his answering service this afternoon. She had prepared dinner and put it in the fridge, to be warmed up later.  He shouldn't wait up—tonight she would be at a party in Malibu with people who were *finding* themselves.  Well, she would be *finding* herself in divorce court if she didn't grow up.  Why was it that these young women idolized and fawned over their professors, taking them to bed, insisting they were bored with male students their own age and longed for a mature man, only to find once the professor put a ring on their finger they couldn't wait to get out of the house and party with the very young men they had earlier spurned?

To the doctor's surprise, he noticed Jim Blake waiting on the corner, and Stone's ruminations about his wife were forgotten.  Something told him to step back into the shadows of a doorway.  His eyes fell upon a red Thunderbird pulling up to the curb, and he watched as Jim Blake got into the passenger seat.  But his attention was drawn to the person who was driving.  The truth hit him like a swift punch in the stomach.

Jim Blake had lied to him.  Had lied with the ease the doctor had seen in so many of the homosexuals he had treated.  It was amazing how easily the lie could slip off their tongue.  As if it came to them naturally.  Through the open window he recognized the man behind the wheel.  It was that prosecutor.  The one from ten years ago.  They were at it again.  Or maybe they had never stopped.

Dr. Stone watched silently as the red Thunderbird merged with traffic and disappeared down the street.  He could feel a vein throb in his forehead.

"That's his car," Paul announced, out of breath, slipping into the passenger seat.

A blue Chevrolet Impala emerged from the police department parking garage and headed down the street. Blake pulled into early rush hour traffic and began to follow. They had decided to use his car, a 1960 Ford station wagon he had bought new after trading in his Hudson Hornet, because it was less conspicuous than Paul's Thunderbird.

"Dean Estes carried a cardboard box from his office. I saw him put it in his trunk."

"Any idea what's in it?"

Paul shook his head.

"Did he see you?"

The Chevy turned on Fifth and Blake tailed it from two cars back.

"I don't think so."

"He's headed for the freeway."

They passed Pershing Square, stopping at a light, and Paul noted the decades-long crusade against plant life in the park appeared finally to be over, after wave upon wave of assaults by downtown business leaders. Once the most beautiful and lush park in the city, a tropical oasis retreat in the center of downtown—and a notorious gay cruising area since the turn of the century, prized for midnight rendezvous in its bamboo groves and banana tree thickets—each new renovation by city planners hacked away at its foliage to discourage amorous encounters between undesirables until the square had been finally reduced to a flat concrete and grass expanse with a handful of benches that roasted in the merciless afternoon sun. A few meager trees promised to provide shade in another twenty years.

But if city fathers had succeeded in driving gay cruising from the park—only a few stubborn drag queens and hustlers congregated there, valiantly refusing to give up the fight—they hadn't counted on a new enemy, the sudden influx of hippies and runaways pouring into Los Angeles from all over the country. Even the most recent paving and mutilation couldn't drive them away. A colony of long-haired squatters in love beads and tie-dyed T-shirts had found a permanent home, and Paul could hear guitars gently strumming and the patter of bongo drums in little groups that clustered on the ground amid vendors with blankets spread displaying their trinkets. It was a relatively laid back scene except for an occasional overdose, squabbles over public urination, overly aggressive panhandling, or when police sweeps prodded and bullied the latest residents away, only to have them migrate back as soon as the authorities were gone.

Paul jumped when there was a sharp rap on his window. A girl with long loose hair to her shoulders and a beaded band around her forehead held out a carnation. "Flowers for a dollar!"

Paul shook his head no.

"I love you!" She flirtatiously kissed the window, leaving a smear from her lips. When she went to the next car, Paul saw that she was barefoot.

"Christ," Blake muttered. "What the hell is the world coming to?"

The light changed, and in a few blocks they took the on-ramp, always trailing the Chevy a few car lengths behind. Soon they passed through Figueroa Street's four concrete Art Deco tunnels, then over the bridge spanning the Los Angeles River. Murky water flowed past the cement embankments on its long journey to the ocean. Saturday night's rain had engorged the river and tree branches caught on its banks caused swirls and eddies in the current. The water, in some seasons hardly more than a trickle, looked dark and deep and angry.

"He's heading for Pasadena," Paul said. "Did you find out where he lives?"

"Hollywood. He's not going home."

Traffic was sluggish, and it was easy to keep tabs on the Chevy from a couple of cars back.

Paul thought about what he had learned from Marvin Botwinick and glanced over at Blake. "What do you know about the Intelligence Division?"

"Not much, really. They were supposed to go after gangsters, I thought. I guess now it's radical groups, you know, the anti-war protesters and the Black Muslims."

And politicians, Paul thought. But who gave the order to go after Wesley Durkin?

By the time the Chevy exited the freeway and headed into one of the tonier neighborhoods in Pasadena, the sunlight slanted in the late afternoon sky, leaving harsh shadows in the yellow light. As Paul looked out, stately homes and impressive mansions passed by his window. After another ten minutes the Chevrolet took a hard left and pulled into a long driveway on a wide residential boulevard with towering shade trees. To avoid suspicion, Blake drove on past, but as he did, Paul got a glimpse of the house through open iron gates.

The sprawling Tudor structure with multiple pitched roofs was fronted by a circular drive with a fountain and pond in the center strewn with lazy lily pads. A thick tall hedge surrounded what must have been several acres of land.

"Somebody is living well," Blake said, pulling the station wagon to the curb. "Let's go find out who."

Approaching the hedge, they peered through thickly leafed branches to see Dean Estes trot up the wide stairs to the front door. He had left his car in the driveway. A moment later the door opened, and though Paul couldn't see the person's face, her uniform made it clear she was a maid. Estes appeared to be an expected guest, and was immediately shown in.

"I'd like to get a little closer," Blake said. "Let's try around the side."

They walked on a neighbor's lawn, staying near the hedge, until they were closer to the house. Paul thought he saw Estes talking to someone in the paned living room window, but reflection from the setting sun on the glass made certain identification impossible. They waited, and about forty-five minutes passed. Then, as the sun sank in the sky and the shadows grew longer, Estes exited the front door and went to his car. As he opened the trunk, the door to the built-in garage began to rumble upward.

Agnes Chandler stood inside next to a shiny Mercedes, waiting. She had let her bleached blonde hair down, softening her bony face, and held a cigarette in her hand, which rested on her hip. Her flower-print dress was simple but expertly coutured to accentuate what curves she had on her skinny figure.

She watched while Estes lifted the cardboard box from his trunk and carried it with squared shoulders toward the garage. As he walked, something slipped from the top of the box and slapped onto the pavement. Even in the growing dimness Paul could plainly see it was a bound surveillance file from the Intelligence Division. Hardly breaking his stride, Estes stooped and picked it up, replacing it in the box, and continued. By the time he had reached the garage, Agnes had opened the trunk to the Mercedes. He set the box inside and shut the lid.

"How many dossiers do you think he has in that box?" Blake whispered.

Paul shook his head. "I don't know. A dozen or more?" He wondered who the surveillance reports could be on, a growing unease descending upon him. Easily there could be one for every important politician in the city.

Estes pressed a button at the side of the door, and it began to descend. As it did, he put his arm around Agnes' narrow waist and pulled her close. She resisted, but apparently only on the unlikely possibility that they could be seen from the street. He gazed down the drive, the snake eyes in his pugilist face carefully surveying the expanse of yard. He seemed satisfied, then brought her deeper into the shadows of the garage. He kissed her hard on the lips, and one of her high-heeled shoes rose demurely in the air. A moment later the door closed.

Blake turned to him. "Should we get out of here?"

Paul nodded, more troubled than before. "I think we saw what we needed to see."

"Don't go in there."

Twelve-year-old Michael Stone followed his friend into his father's den.

"Why not?"

"My Dad doesn't like me going through his stuff. It's for adults." Michael looked back at the doorway anxiously as he came into the oak-paneled room lined with built-in book shelves. His father was probably going to be home any second. "C'mon," he whispered, "let's go."

Trey looked around curiously, languidly running his finger across the big desk piled with papers as he passed. He rolled a Life Saver on his tongue. "I like being here."

Michael thought he probably shouldn't have let Trey come home with him, but he'd tagged along, and the two of them did have fun together. And after those weird films they'd been shown in fifth period P.E. class, Michael felt like he wanted to talk to somebody. The first black-and-white short, *Boys Aware!*, had sputtered on a small screen the coach had set up in a corner of the gym. It was the story of a boy being befriended by a balding man who wore sunglasses and had a mustache. The narrator explained that this man was a Homosexual. The man talked the boy into getting together with him without telling his parents, and used dirty words that the boy didn't like but pretended he did because he wanted the man to think he was cool. The man showed him pornography, and the boy didn't like it but pretended to in order to please the man. And then the man brought him home... and suddenly they were at a police station and the man had been arrested for molestation. The film ended with the boy being led away from the police station by his parents while the narrator explained that this boy was lucky, he only got probation.

That seemed crazy to Michael. If the man had done something wrong to the boy, why was the boy in hot water?

The second film was even stranger. A Dade County cop lectured to an auditorium of high school students warning them to stay away from homosexuals, detailing the criminal penalties for such behavior, including those for teens of the same sex playing around with each other. Of those of you who experiment with homosexuality, the policeman grimly cautioned the wide-eyed assemblage, one third of you will turn queer.

After the films were over, Mr. Tanner the gym teacher had asked if there were any questions, but all the kids had remained stonily silent, as if they were being asked to snitch on a classmate. The whole experience had left Michael unsettled.

Trey picked up a book from the desk and held it up, laughing. Michael saw the word *homosexuality* in the title.

"It's just like those movies," Trey said, grinning.

Michael came over and took the book from him and set it back on the desk, hopefully in the same spot where his father had left it.

"Do you understand what a queer is?" Trey asked.

"It's a boy who kisses another boy."

126

Trey bent and kissed him on the lips. Michael blinked in surprise. Trey tasted of cherry Life Savers. Sweet like candy.

"Do you think that makes us queers?"

"No," Michael said firmly. "Because you have a crush on Cindy Tombarge and I have a crush on Patsy Blunt."

Trey shrugged and went over to a bookshelf, running his fingers over the spines of books.

"Maybe we should go," Michael said. Just then he heard his father come in the front door and his heart sank a little. In a moment his father was standing in the doorway to the den.

"Hello, boys," he said. He came in and set his briefcase on his desk.

"Dad, this is Trey."

Dr. Stone shook the boy's hand. "Good to meet you, young man."

"Good to meet *you*."

Trey and Dr. Stone smiled at each other for what seemed to Michael a long time.

"Well," Trey said, "I'd better get home for dinner."

After Michael showed him out, he returned to the den and stood tentatively in the doorway. His father was already seated at his big desk.

"I'm sorry we were in your den, Dad. I know I'm not supposed to."

"Oh, that's all right. I understand you're bound to be curious. I just want you to understand I have books here for adults. They're not for someone your age. But come, why don't you sit down for a minute so we can have a little talk?"

Michael sank deep into the leather chair that sat before the big desk. He liked the way it seemed to deflate under his weight.

127

"I don't suppose that it's such a good idea to cultivate a friendship with that boy, do you?"

"Why?"

Dr. Stone smiled as if he and his son shared a secret. "He isn't the kind of boy who *does* much, is he? I mean, playing ball, that sort of thing."

"Not really." Trey was usually the last to be picked for any team sport. But then, Michael was usually the second to the last.

"I bet he doesn't spend much time with his dad."

Michael shrugged, puzzled. He knew he was expected to agree, and yet that wasn't really true. "His dad owns a shoe repair shop. Trey works with him on weekends and sometimes after school. Trey showed me how they put a new heel on an old dress shoe."

"Well, perhaps that's the case, but what I meant was they probably aren't that close. Some fathers and sons have a good relationship, like you and me, and then some others... well, we don't need to talk about this now. Why don't you go ahead and do your homework? Your stepmother left us some dinner we can warm up later."

Michael got up and was about to head out of the den, when he noticed his father was already lost in deep thought. "Dad, are you okay?"

"Oh, it's nothing. I was just thinking about the power of a father's love for his son. It can be one of the strongest ties in the world."

Michael nodded, but he was unsure if his father was talking about the two of them, or Trey and his dad, or someone else. He was at the door when his father called out after him.

"Hey, I just had a great idea." Dr. Stone's eyes brightened behind his glasses. "You know, I think we should go up north for a little vacation some weekend together. Just us guys. What do you think about going white water rafting some weekend? I think we could use a little he-man adventure, don't you?"

"Cool, Dad, that would be really neat."

Michael went down the hallway and flopped on his bed. He didn't have any homework tonight and he'd just finished the Reader's Digest condensed books version of *Mutiny on the Bounty* and hadn't decided what to read next. His dad probably wouldn't be ready for dinner for at least an hour. He sat there bored for a few minutes, then his eyes drifted to the Sears & Roebuck catalogue he'd left on the bottom shelf of his lamp table. He opened it to page 174, which was the beginning of the men's underwear section. There was a man he liked to look at. He was tall and lean and there was something intriguing about him that made Michael come back to him again and again. He could look at his picture for long stretches at a time, and sometimes he liked to run his finger over the slick page. It was as if he could almost feel his smooth, cool skin.

He licked his lips. They still carried the sweet taste of Trey's cherry Life Savers on them.

# Chapter 10

"Okay," Blake said, taking the entrance ramp to the freeway, "what do we have so far?"

They had driven in silence, each with his own thoughts, since leaving the Chandler mansion and returning to the car.

"Well, in the first place," Paul said, "you were right about Wesley Durkin being murdered, even if we never can find any proof. Roland Mosley saw who did it and he's been on the run ever since."

"Roland *does* have the proof, though, whatever it is. That's why he came back to Durkin's house, right? He found it hidden in the attic and he had it in that shopping bag along with the surveillance file when we discovered him in bed."

Paul nodded. "But we're not the only ones looking for him. Someone else knows about him and they followed him Saturday night to that theater downtown."

Blake gazed in the rearview mirror for a moment, then back at the lanes ahead. "I think the attack on Leland Serokin was just tying up loose ends. Our murderer follows Roland into the theater. Maybe the plan is to do away with Roland, get rid of the only witness to Wesley Durkin's murder. But then Roland sits next to Serokin and they exchange something—it's dark, our bad guy doesn't know it's just a book and not the incriminating evidence. Roland gets spooked and runs off, but our killer throttles

Serokin because he's afraid Roland has passed the evidence off to him. The book just falls from his lap and our killer can't find it in the dark and skedaddles out of there."

Nodding slowly, Paul said, "But at the center of all this is the murder of Wesley Durkin. Now, we know he was under surveillance by the LAPD, and we know the head of the Intelligence Division is involved."

"How do we connect Dean Estes to Durkin? I mean, he runs the Intelligence Division, and they were spying on him *during* his campaign, but that was a couple of years ago."

"Agnes Chandler told me at the fundraiser Saturday night that her husband had supported Durkin's campaign... Durkin's run for assessor was going nowhere until Buck Chandler stepped in to support him. And now we find out the head of the Intelligence Division is having an affair with Agnes. The connections between them are there, even if we don't understand them yet."

They were quiet for a while then Paul noticed Blake's eyes were focused again on the rearview mirror. "What's wrong?"

"I think someone is following us. Since before we got on the freeway."

Paul turned and stared out the rear window. "You think it's Estes? Could he have spotted us at the house, and now he's on our tail?"

"I don't think so. He was still inside with Agnes when we left. It's hard to tell in this light, but it doesn't look like his car, either." Blake glanced over at him. "No, I think we've become of interest to somebody else."

Paul tried to think of who would have the resources to put a tail on them, and if they had made a mistake in their investigation by being too bold in asking about the information they were looking for.

Blake pressed on the gas, changing lanes, hopscotching between other cars, trying to get lost in the evening traffic.

"I think we've given them the slip," he said finally.

"If you could head for downtown," Paul said, reading his watch, "there's something I've got to do."

Paul had called David six times that afternoon but his phone had just continued to ring. Finally he'd put in a call to Jeannie, who spoke to him in a reserved tone that he was beginning to get used to. He could tell she had things on her mind but wasn't quite ready to spill them. He didn't look forward to what she'd have to say once she was ready. She had told him she didn't know where David was but Billy had checked himself into the hospital at the urging of several friends and suggested Paul drop by that evening. David was bound to show up.

After leaving Blake in the car in the parking lot, Paul ran into Jeff Dupuis coming out of the hospital entrance. Paul was clutching a bunch of flowers he'd picked up at a florist.

"Hey," Jeff said, grinning. "How's The Man?"

Paul grinned back. "Why can't you just say, *how's it hanging*, or something like that? I never know if The Man is me or somebody else." He observed Jeff a moment. "You look tired."

Jeff ran his fingers wearily across his forehead. "I told you I'm swamped. The arraignments are tomorrow for the guys arrested Saturday night. Other lawyers are involved, but I still got loads to do."

"You saw Billy upstairs? Is he all by himself?"

"Oh, no. You wish. They're all up there." Jeff eyed him slyly and shook his head, the hint of a rueful smile coming to his lips. "You old dog, what you been messing with? You got to learn to keep that dick of yours in your pants."

Paul sighed. "Everybody knows? And David is up there, too?"

Jeff nodded. "Have fun, now. I'm going to have a smoke. I left my pack in the glove box. But I'll stick around. Come and talk to me when you're done. I learned a few things about your friend with the scar."

Once Paul found the room on the second floor, he hesitated in the doorway before entering. Nobody noticed him at first. Billy lay in bed, clearly enjoying being surrounded by friends. His chest was bare but wrapped in cloth bandages. Pat was sitting on a red plastic contoured chair with Jeannie standing behind her. David leaned against the radiator by the window. Parker Huston, who was holding court, sat at the foot of the mattress, his hand resting affectionately on Billy's knee.

"I do find it telling," Parker was chattering on, "that your mystical Man in Black just happened to reappear to you on the night you got bonked on the head with a nightstick. Why is it that none of your other friends have ever seen this marvelous specimen of manhood? Why does he disappear for years at a time then suddenly pop up when you've had a swoon?"

"All I'm telling you is he was there," Billy said, grinning good-naturedly and shaking his blond bangs out of his eyes. "David, you saw him, didn't you?"

"Uh, there were a lot of guys packed in the bar that night...." David attempted diplomatically.

"I believe you, Billy," Jeannie put in earnestly.

Billy propped his hands behind his head, winced in pain at the sudden movement, and sighed contentedly. "He's the perfect man. And I don't care what you say, Parker. He's absolutely gorgeous, and someday he's going to be mine."

"Keep believing that, dear." Parker patted Billy's knee. "Sartre was right, it's our futile little hopes and dreams that keep us going in this dreary little journey we call life."

When Paul stepped into the room, every eye seemed to descend upon him. He couldn't be sure, but he thought everybody's lips tightened just a little. Pat positively glowered at him from her chair; tonight she was wearing an unbuttoned checkered shirt usually seen on lumberjacks over a loose T-shirt and jeans. Jeannie was back to her Twiggy cut; her cheeks colored and her eyes darted to the floor, and Paul knew she had it in for him. Parker and Billy just stared benignly, blinking. David looked out the window.

"I can only stay a minute, but I brought flowers...." Paul began, suddenly feeling awkward holding them up for everyone to see. His throat felt dry. "How are you, Billy? Are you doing okay?"

"Hi, Paul. I'm all right. They're keeping me overnight for observation. They took an x-ray of my chest, but I don't think anything's broken. Just black and blue."

"The exact colors you'll be if your Man in Black ever gets his hands on you," Parker remarked under his breath.

They all laughed, and that eased some of the tension in the room.

"Well, let me go hunt up a vase for these." Paul set the flowers on a table and went out. As he headed down the corridor a voice called out from behind him.

"Hey."

Paul turned. David was standing there, looking tall and handsome and forlorn. "Hey," Paul said back.

David didn't look him in the eye. Something on the wall seemed to draw his attention instead. "I thought I'd come by later this week to get my things. I'll leave the key then."

134

Paul took a tentative step toward him. He wanted to hold him but he was afraid how David would react. "We don't have to do this, David. We don't have to let it end this way. I'm sorry. I never meant to hurt you."

Shaking his head, David laughed mirthlessly. "I don't think I can have this conversation with you right now."

Now it was Paul's turn to look away. He stared at the shiny white linoleum tile floor as he tried to put his thoughts together. He felt himself choke up and sputtered, "You and I... we don't want the same things anymore." He hung his head. "Maybe we never did."

"How can you say that?" David's tone was sharp.

"You don't even respect what I do."

"How can I, when you're part of a system that hurts people?" The stridency that always irked Paul rose in David's voice. "Are you forgetting the fact that after the cops arrest us the D.A.'s Office prosecutes us? I know you're trying to do your best. I know you're one of the good guys. I know you try to do little things to make things better. But that isn't enough anymore, Paul. It hasn't been for a long time."

Paul threw his hands up and there was frustration in his voice. "I don't understand you and I don't understand any of your new friends. You think getting ten people together with picket signs is going to change the world? You think your little newspaper is going to make any difference?"

"It's better than doing nothing. It's better than being part of the status quo."

Paul brought his hand to his chest. "I need someone who believes in me. Someone who will cheer me on when good things happen. You live in a world where nobody has jobs and nobody cares about the future."

"It's because I *do* care about the future that I'm doing this. You care about *your* future. That isn't enough for me. And it shouldn't be enough for you."

David turned to go and Paul caught his wrist.

"I love you more than anybody. I always will."

Finally David looked him in the eye.

"You only loved me when no one else was looking," David said. Then he pulled away and went down the hall to the elevator.

Pat and Jeannie were saying their goodbyes and coming out the door of Billy's room when Paul came back from the nursing station with a vase filled with water.

"I'm so furious with you," Pat said, her eyes blazing with indignation, "I can't speak!" She brushed past him and stomped down the hall to the elevator.

Jeannie shook her head wearily and said, "Let me take that." She disappeared into the room for a moment to put the flowers in the vase, then returned to take Paul by the arm. She ushered him in the opposite direction of the elevator. "Paul, what's going on?"

He shook his head. "I screwed up and David caught me with another guy."

"I know all that. Why aren't you with David right now asking for his forgiveness?"

"I don't think he wants to see me at the moment, to be honest."

She stopped and stared at him and her features darkened. "You *do* want to make up with him, though, don't you?"

Paul's eyes dropped to the floor and he was stone silent.

Jeannie's fingers tightened on his arm and he knew she was upset. "How long have you known this other guy? One night? A couple of days? What are you thinking?"

"I can't explain it, Jeannie. All I can tell you is that he's everything I ever wanted. And David and me... I don't know, it's like nothing is ever right between us."

136

Jeannie let out an exasperated sigh. "Every relationship goes through good and bad times. You don't think Pat drives me crazy sometimes? That doesn't mean I run off with the first pretty girl who comes along! You and David have been together for *ten years*. There's something to be said for that. All those memories you share. All the things you've been through, the good and the bad. You two are beautiful together whether you know it or not. If you can't see that, I don't know what to tell you. Go after him *now*, before it's too late."

But Paul just stood there gazing at the floor like a shamed child.

An astonished expression came to her face. "You're going to throw it all away, aren't you?" Tears suddenly welled in her eyes and her palm rested on her cheek. "Oh, Paul, I don't even know what to say. After all these years, it's like I don't even know you." She shook her head, covering her mouth with her hand, and trotted down the hall to the elevator. She joined Pat, who was waiting inside still glaring at him, and the doors slid closed.

Feeling utterly worthless, Paul splashed some water in his face from a fountain jutting from the wall, then lumbered back down the corridor. He felt like sand bags were attached to his legs. Parker was waiting for him, leaning in the doorway of Billy's room with his arms crossed.

"Don't listen to the lesbians. Your dick will lead you in the direction you need to go." They waved their goodbyes to Billy, then Parker put his arm over Paul's shoulder and steered him toward the elevator.

"You know," Parker mused, "Chekhov said something interesting about being in love."

"Please, don't tell me you're going to quote Chekhov."

"It's the librarian in me. I can't help it. He once observed a rather interesting truth about love. Pardon me for paraphrasing." Parker cleared his throat. "He said love is a remnant of something which once has been immense, or it is a particle of what in the future will develop into something immense, but in the present is unsatisfying, it gives less than one expects."

"Thank you. That helps me absolutely not at all."

They rode the elevator down.

"Yes, profound ideas don't mean very much in the real world, do they?" Parker sighed. "Perhaps that's why I prefer porn. Pulp and porn. In pulp everybody suffers, and in porn everybody gets their rocks off. It seems closer to real life."

At the entrance to the hospital, Paul said, "I'm going to say 'goodnight' now, Parker."

Parker headed off toward his car. "Remember," he called out, "don't listen to the lesbians. Most of them don't even have penises! It's like sailing through life without a rudder."

Paul joined Jeff, who was leaning against his car in the parking lot, smoking a cigarette.

"What was that all about?"

Paul shook his head. "That was Parker being Parker. You said you learned something."

"Yeah. I put the word out about your friend with the scar. His name is Roland Mosley, and he has a bit of a reputation on the street."

All of which Paul had already learned after last speaking with Jeff, but he didn't let on. He appreciated Jeff's help, didn't want to dismiss his efforts, and hoped there would be more.

"He did a little bit of hustling when he first came to town a couple of years back. But then he got himself a regular boyfriend and disappeared from the scene. Until last week, that is. He's been seen around in the parks, trying to drum up some cash, no place to stay. I couldn't get any specific locations."

"In the bars, too?"

Jeff dropped his cigarette and crushed it under his foot. "Not that I heard. He seems to be lying low."

Paul bit his lip, thinking. "He had a sleeping bag with him when he was last seen...."

Jeff tilted his head, running his fingers through the hairs on his chin. "Wait a sec. You said he was spotted running from where Wesley Durkin was found dead, right?"

"Yeah, in Beachwood Canyon..." Suddenly it all fit together. A place where Roland Mosley could avoid the police and anyone else looking for him. A place where he could stay in contact with other gays and have a shot at finding a bed for the night. Paul took Jeff's head in both hands and kissed him on the forehead.

"What was that for?" Jeff laughed.

"I think I just figured out where he's been hiding."

Behind the wheel, Blake glanced over at Paul. "You've been awfully quiet since we left the hospital. You okay?"

Paul took a long time to answer. He couldn't get the last words David had spoken to him out of his head. "Yeah, I'm okay."

Blake observed him thoughtfully a moment, but didn't press. He turned north from Los Feliz Boulevard at Vermont and drove up the tree-lined boulevard in the neighborhood of oversized houses that led to Griffith Park. The sun was lost behind the horizon and blue light fell over the city.

"Why do you think he's in the park?"

"It makes sense," Paul said. "When you ran after him, he disappeared in the hills north of Durkin's house, right?

So he could have taken one of the trails in the hills above Beachwood Canyon into Griffith Park. The trails run all through these mountains. He had a sleeping bag. He could camp out in the park and avoid anyone who might be looking for him."

"But this park is huge, what, four thousand acres?"

"I think I have an idea where to find him." Paul peered out the windshield. "Turn right up ahead, after we pass the golf course."

Blake spun the wheel and the station wagon swung onto a potted blacktop lane, then slowed to a stop.

"What's wrong?"

"There was a car behind us. I'm not sure, but it might be the one that I thought was following us earlier."

Paul twisted in his seat and looked around. "Is it? Are we being followed?"

"I should have taken my gun," Blake muttered, his eyes fixed on the rearview mirror.

They waited for headlights to emerge from around the corner. None did. Finally Blake shook his head uncertainly. "Maybe I'm just getting paranoid." He pressed the gas pedal and they proceeded down the curving road as it snaked past the golf course and a tennis court. On their left the chaparral-covered hills rose steeply, dotted with red-berried Toyon and scattered with oaks, on their right twisting pines and parched wild grass spread over the sharp incline.

"Up ahead," Paul said. "On the left. The park trails are supposed to close at dusk." He glanced at his watch. "But I think some people linger."

Blake braked the Ford wagon on a sandy spit at the side of the road where four other cars were parked. They waited to see if anyone else came up the road, but no one did. Instead, a Buick wound down the road from above, the driver slowing to peer into the empty parked cars as he passed. He almost came to a stop when he spotted Blake and Paul, then continued on, never taking his eyes off them.

"What was that all about?" Blake asked.

"You'll see."

Blake reached over and got a flashlight from the glove box. They locked the car and started down a pine needle strewn path. Tinderbox-dry grass clutched the hillsides, and spiky brambles curling like razor wire grew shoulder-high around them. Occasionally they stepped over charcoal-covered logs flung across the path, and passed the pitch-black trunks of eucalyptus scorched in the last fire, their tortured branches reaching to the sky. In a few minutes they came to a clearing.

A man lay on his stomach on a beach towel, his shirt off, his underwear and jeans in a jumble at his ankles, as if he were trying to get a tan, only the sun had already drifted from the sky. Another man, blond and lean, stood in the distance languidly leaning against an outcropping of rock, and a third, with dark hair and a Varsity jacket, paused on the trail ahead. They were all young and handsome, athletic in appearance, and all had their assessing eyes riveted on Paul and Blake as they came into view through the brush. The college boy jerked his head at them, a clear invitation, then headed up the trail. He disappeared in a cave-like bramble of vines and dry branches hugging the side of a hill.

"Oh," Blake said. "I think I get it."

Paul glanced at Blake, grinning. "I think they like what they see. C'mon, tiger."

The man on the towel continued to stare, nodding approvingly as they passed and made their way along the trail. After they had gone by, the thin guy leaning against the rock let out a flirtatious whistle.

It was darker in the thicket, and they hesitated before going in, pushing aside overhanging dead branches. Blake went through the hollowed entry first with Paul close behind. A braiding of vines, dried leaves and branches created a roof overhead. In the cavernous dimness Blake suddenly stopped short.

The college boy was on his knees in front of him, his face in Blake's crotch, his hands eagerly working the zipper of Blake's pants. Blake pushed the groping hands away.

The young man wasn't more than twenty, a good looking big-boned jock with a square-cut face. He looked up at Blake, smiling, undeterred by the rebuff.

"Hey, man, why don't you let me? I know you'd like it. Your friend can be the lookout." As he tried again at Blake's fly, Blake pulled him up to his feet.

"All we want to know is if you've seen a colored guy around here, big scar like a horseshoe on his face."

The jock took a few steps back, fear growing in his face. "You're not a cop, are you?"

"Just answer the question."

"I ain't seen nothing!" He shook his head emphatically and darted past them out the entryway. They could hear the beat of his heels striding down the path, drifting into the distance, and then only the hum of insects in the dusk. Just as they were about to leave, a lilting voice with a Southern accent called out from the darkness behind them deep in the cave of brambles.

"You say you're looking for a colored man?"

A skinny young blond in a Hawaiian shirt open to the navel and shorts, his flip-flops snapping with each step, sauntered toward them, hips swaying.

"Step outside," Blake ordered, "into the light so we can see you."

Only it wasn't so light outside the thicket patch anymore; already the sky had developed into a deep blue, the path harder to make out in the growing dimness.

"Okay," Blake said, "have you seen him?"

142

Up close, Paul could see the young man's hair was bleached and he had bad teeth. And the young man wasn't so young.

The blond tilted his head coyly and placed an index finger on Blake's chest. "Wouldn't you like to know!"

"Better get that finger off my chest. I just might be a cop."

"If you were a cop, you would have arrested that guy."

"Look, have you seen a black guy around here or not?" Blake demanded gruffly.

"A pretty little boy with an ugly big scar?"

"That's him. A scar on the face. Shaped like a horseshoe. Where have you seen him? Has he been here today?"

Now the finger rested thoughtfully on the blond's chin. "Calm down, big boy. Don't get so excited." He observed Blake, an amused curve on his lips, and nodded to himself. "My, my, we like our chocolate hot and tasty, don't we?"

Blake grabbed him by the collar and shook him. "Stop fucking with me and tell me where you've seen him."

He put his hands up in mock surrender and Blake released him. "Please, I didn't know you liked it *rough*."

Paul stepped forward. "Tell us where you saw him."

The blond shrugged, straightening his shirt, his mouth petulant. "He's camping out up the hill. Comes down to bum cigarettes and to try to find someone to take him home for the night." He pointed a finger. "Just take the trail over there."

The path rose steeply into the hills, and Paul paused a moment as they climbed, looking back. The man who had been lying on the towel had put his clothes back on and stood watching them from below. Nearby another man Paul hadn't seen before stepped out from a scraggly bush and stared boldly at them, his hands digging into the pockets of his Levis.

143

"Let's get moving," Blake said. "It's getting dark."

A faint swath of stars was beginning to appear in the sky. The rolling hills of the golf course spread out below, and beyond, the lights of the city were starting to shimmer in the coming night. On a far promontory Paul could see the three domes of the observatory hugging the edge of a sharp drop-off. Under his feet the trail grew spongy with the mulch of decaying leaves.

They stopped to catch their breath halfway to the top. It was then that Paul spotted a man on a parallel trail across a ravine. The man stopped when they did, put his foot on an overhanging rock, and appeared to take in the panorama below.

"I think we're being watched."

"I should have taken my gun," Blake said again under his breath.

"He's probably just cruising us."

He was older than the men they'd seen so far, stocky. His clothes were dark and it was hard to make out what he was wearing. There was something about his demeanor, though, a certain swaggery confidence, a lack of hunger, that made Paul uneasy. It set him apart from the men cruising for sex they had encountered earlier. Paul wondered if he was a cop. Certainly there could be vice cops up here. He thought again of the headlights that had pursued them earlier. What, he wondered, was the individual following them supposed to look like?

As they continued on, haggard pines rose around them and the man and the trail across the ravine were lost from sight. They were almost at the top of the hill, their breath slow but heavy, when Blake halted. The stars were hardening in the black sky.

"Stop," Blake whispered. He gripped Paul's arm. "Do you hear someone? On the trail behind us?"

"What," Paul whispered back, "you think that guy…"

144

They stared down the trail but it was too dark to see anyone now. They waited a full minute, listening. Finally Paul shook his head. "I don't think so. Maybe it's just the wind in the leaves."

They didn't have much farther to go. They found him lying on his sleeping bag in a pile of leaves, surrounded by shaggy sage scrub, his shopping bag at his side. It was the second time they had come across Roland Mosley sleeping in two days. This time he didn't appear quite so angelic. His clothes were dirty and it looked like he had slept in them, and there were dried leaves in his wooly hair. He had come into possession of shoes, worn sneakers that looked two sizes too big. Blake took his flashlight from his back pocket and let the beam flicker in his face. This time, when Roland woke, he sat up straight, eyes wide.

"You're the guys who were at Wes's house."

"I'm Deputy D.A. Paul Winters. This is Jim Blake, LAPD."

Roland didn't even wait long enough to blink. He sprang up, tripped on his sneakers and clawed his way on all fours up the trail in a frantic attempt to get away from them. He quickly regained his footing and sprinted forward a few yards before Blake tackled him. They hit the ground hard and Paul could hear the air forced from Roland's lungs.

Blake got up and brushed dirt off his hands, breathing heavily. He picked Roland up by the scruff of his neck and steered him over to the sleeping bag, where he plopped him back down. "Don't try that again," he warned.

# Chapter 11

Roland Mosley's face looked haunted in the harsh beam from the flashlight.

"Can you get that out of my face?"

Blake lowered the beam to the ground.

Paul stepped forward. "We're not here to hurt you."

Looking up skeptically at Blake, who towered over him, Roland grunted. "How am I supposed to believe that?"

Blake grunted back. "You'd be dead already if we were. The other people looking for you might not be so nice."

"Look," Paul assured him, "we know you didn't kill Wesley Durkin. And we know you weren't responsible for anything that happened in the theater New Year's Eve. We just want to know exactly what you know and what you saw."

Roland leaned back on his elbows, watching them. "You got a cigarette? I haven't had any for days, except the ones I bummed off guys in the park."

Blake shuffled in his pocket and offered his pack. Roland took a Chesterfield then waited for Blake to light it for him; Paul sensed he enjoyed being taken care of, and he wondered about the relationship between this beautiful young man and the frumpy middle-aged Wesley Durkin. Roland inhaled deeply, still watching them.

"You can't imagine how good this tastes right now."

"Okay," Blake said. "Out with it. What happened the night Wesley Durkin was murdered?"

"I came home that evening—almost two weeks ago—and he wasn't alone. I came in the back door. That was my usual routine. It was just easier that way, no questions from the neighbors—and I could hear him with someone in his study."

"Do you know who it was?"

Roland shook his head. "He'd been to see Wes lots of times over the last few years, but I never got a peek at him. Whenever he came, Wes would always have me stay in the bedroom nice and quiet. All I know is he had a deep voice. Booming. You know, authoritarian like."

"Did you ever overhear what they talked about?"

"Well, at first it was always stuff about the campaign, and then once Wes was elected, it was like they were raising money for his next run. They were helping him, I guess, but Wes didn't like them. It was like they had a hold on him. And once they became involved in his campaign, he began to change. Before they came into the picture, he was way behind in the polls, but he was this idealistic, happy guy. They dumped lots of money into his campaign, and his numbers went up in the polls, but he wasn't happy anymore, he was totally turned off to politics. He would say things, cynical things. You know, about how corrupt stuff was in the government, all the back-room deals, what a sham it all was. It weighed on him. It was like something was churning in his gut, making him sick inside.

"And then one night—it was just a week before he was killed—we were in bed together, and he started to cry. He said how sorry he was for what he'd done."

At first Paul had pegged him as a callous hustler, but a wistful quality in the young man's tone made him believe Roland's feelings for his dead lover were genuine, and his hardened manner a result of his years on the street. He leaned in closer. "Did he say what it was? What he'd done?"

Exhaling a stream of smoke, Roland shook his head. "No, I think he was too ashamed. It was like he was afraid to tell me. That I'd never forgive him. All I know is he'd done something terribly wrong but he was going to fix it. He had a plan." He shook his head, remembering. "You know, something happened a month or so before he died that set this whole thing off. We had gone to visit my folks down South, Alabama. I mean, we didn't let on Wes was my lover. I introduced him as, you know, a friend of mine. His being white was probably about as much as my family could take, anyway. But something happened to Wes when we were there. He kept going out on his own, just wandering the streets, you know, in the black neighborhoods, looking at how people lived. It was like he'd never seen poverty like that before. After we got back, he started going to South Central. Just driving there for hours. I told him it was dangerous for a white guy, but he wouldn't listen. Something pulled him there."

He finished the cigarette, snuffed it in the dirt, and looked up at Blake expectantly. Blake pulled out his pack and lit him another.

"Sorry," Roland said. "I'm jumpy without 'em."

"Go on," Blake prodded. "The night he was murdered."

Roland's lip quivered before he spoke. "It seemed like all the other nights. Wes and this guy were talking in the study. I could hear the murmur of their voices. Then suddenly their voices were raised, like there was an argument." Remembering, his eyes filled with anxiety. "And then, just out of nowhere, this gunshot rang out. It felt like the whole house shook. I hid in the bedroom closet. But then, I heard someone going throughout the house, opening drawers, searching the place. I knew they'd eventually come into the bedroom and find me, so I slipped into the bathroom and climbed out the window." He

148

shuddered. "The same escape route I took when you two showed up."

"You have any idea what they were looking for?" Paul asked.

Roland glanced over at the shopping bag beside him. A tell. "No."

Blake gave him a quick firm kick on his too-large sneakers. "Wrong answer. What about what you took from the attic?"

Angling his head as he coolly observed them, Roland blew out smoke and drawled, "That might be worth a lot of money if I can figure out what to do with it."

"Not to you," Blake shot back. "Not if you're dead. You have no idea who you're dealing with here. But you do know they murdered your lover. And if you looked over your shoulder when you were scrambling out of the theater Saturday night, you would have seen your ex-boyfriend the professor getting throttled within an inch of his life with a garrote. You have no money and you have nowhere to go. It's just a matter of time before they catch up with you. And when they do, you're done."

"We can protect you," Paul said. "Come with us. Give us the evidence we need and we'll make sure these people are behind bars forever."

"We already have the LAPD surveillance file that dropped out of your bag," Blake said. "What do you know about that?"

"Nothing. I had no idea we had been watched. I found that file with—" He stopped himself.

"With this?" Paul snatched up the shopping bag and groped inside. He felt the cool plastic of an eight-inch reel for a tape recorder. Blake flashed his light inside the bag to confirm what it was.

"What's on it?" Blake demanded.

"How should I know? You think I keep a tape player up here?"

"How did you know where it was hidden?"

Roland sighed and sat up straight. "He told me a few days before he died that he wanted me to go out for the evening, that he had called an important meeting and he didn't want me in the house. He had some kind of a plan, but I don't know what it was. I came home earlier than I was supposed to, and there were several cars parked on the street. Ritzy cars. When I came in the back door, I could hear them talking. I couldn't hear what they were saying, but there were a lot of people, maybe a dozen. Later, after they left, I heard Wes up in the attic. He was hiding something up there. He told me he was going to blow the whole thing wide open and a lot of powerful people were going to get burned. I don't know what's on this tape, but it's important. There's got to be somebody out there who will pay good money for—"

A piercing shot rang through the night and Paul and Blake both ducked for cover. Roland continued to sit upright for a moment as if he hadn't heard a sound, then his head and torso fell heavily backward onto the sleeping bag. He didn't move again.

"Stay down!" Blake hissed into Paul's ear. He reached for the flashlight, which had fallen to the ground, and switched it off. Then he crawled over to Roland, cupping the bulb, clicking it on just long enough to shine the beam for a moment in his face.

There was a small dark hole in the middle of Roland Mosley's forehead.

150

"C'mon," Blake whispered, gripping Paul's hand and pulling him up from where he lay on the ground. "We've got to get out of here. Stay low."

They crouched as they went, ducking their heads, trotting down the trail as fast as they could, waiting for the next shot in the darkness. The only light came from a sliver of moon and a band of stars above them. Paul clutched the tape reel in the bag to his chest, trying to quiet his ragged breath, hoping their footfalls couldn't be heard in the distance.

"Let's get off the trail," Paul said. "It might be safer if he tries to follow us. The only way to go is down, anyway. No matter how we go, we should hit the road."

Pushing through pines and brush, they scrambled down the rough hillside, branches whipping at their faces, tearing at their sleeves, sometimes tripping, sometimes falling until the ground began to level off and they found themselves in the clearing where they had originally encountered the men cruising the park. No one was there now, the surrounding trees and bushes still, the leaves of branches tipped with silver from the faint light of the moon and stars.

Blake looked over his shoulder one last time before they made their way down the trail lined with brambles to the wedge of sand where the Ford was parked. The other cars were gone, and there was a ticket pinched beneath the windshield wipers of the station wagon. Paul figured the park rangers must have been by earlier, rousting people out of the park, citing vehicles left after dark. As Paul tucked the bag with the tape reel under his seat, Blake pulled onto the blacktop road and gunned the Ford. Speeding down the curving lane, they flashed past a car parked in darkness by the side of the road. Only after it had disappeared from view did Paul realize he should have gotten the license number.

Blake seemed to read his mind. "That was an Imperial Crown, 1963."

"You get the license plate?"

"Just the first three letters. AJN. We went by too fast, I didn't catch the numbers. Too late to go back now." Blake turned into the residential neighborhood and headed toward Los Feliz Boulevard. He glanced in the rearview mirror. "The quicker we get to the freeway and out of here the better."

In a few minutes they were on the northbound entrance ramp to the 5 and merging with late rush-hour traffic. The serrated blue hills of the Valley stretched out in the distance ahead. Hugging the east side of the freeway, the L.A. River snaked along beside them. The concrete-slab embankment sloping down to restless black water was constructed years before to tame the river and protect the city from periodic catastrophic floods when the waterway became engorged.

"Let's go to my place," Paul said. "We can alert the police about Roland Mosley then." He shook his head grimly. "He's dead because of us. We led them straight to him."

"No, if he'd gone to the police in the first place this never would have—" Blake countered, then stopped himself. "Yeah," he said finally, "I guess you're right. It's on us."

Paul's eyes gravitated to the rearview mirror the same moment Blake's did. A vehicle was coming up fast in the lane behind them.

"That's the Imperial that was parked beside the road." Paul sat up straight, alarm in his voice.

Blake studied the mirror. He floored the gas pedal, cutting off a car in the next lane, and swerved across the freeway to the far left lane, tailgating when he had to, in order to lose the Imperial behind them. He changed lanes again, forcing his way into any space he could find. "We can outrun him."

But just as he said it, the traffic ahead began to slow, and Blake had to press on the brakes.

"Shit!" Blake slammed his hand against the steering wheel. All around them cars began to grind to a halt.

Paul turned and gazed out the back window, trying to spot their tail in the sea of vehicles coming to a stop, their headlights blazing.

He couldn't see the Imperial but in the lane to their right several cars back a door opened and a dark figure emerged and began to stride toward them. His right hand was stiffly at his side, hugging his thigh, as if he were holding something he didn't want others to see.

"He's coming after us," Paul shouted. "Get out of the car, now!" Before he could make a move, the back window shattered in pellets of glass. He threw the door open and dove down onto the pavement, scrambling on all fours for cover behind the front of the next car, a shiny Buick. He caught only a glimpse of the dark-clad figure coming toward them, now at a quick trot. Paul looked around frantically to see if Blake had gotten out of the car. He could see the driver's door was gaping open but Blake had disappeared. Had he even gotten out of the car? He crouched down to try to spot Blake's feet from under the stopped vehicles, but he couldn't see him.

When he raised his head above the hood of the Buick, a shot rang out over his head and Paul ducked down, hugging the car's front grille. He could hear their assailant's footsteps coming closer. Paul crawled on all fours over to a long produce truck that was stalled in the slow lane, hoping it would provide the best cover. As he rounded the back of the vehicle, he spied Blake crouched by the truck's cab, peering under it to try to catch a glimpse of their pursuer's feet.

The look of relief on Blake's face when he saw Paul approaching tugged at Paul's heart. Blake grabbed him hard and hugged him tight. "There you are!" he whispered in his ear.

Paul let himself be held for only a moment, then pulled back. "C'mon, the river's our best chance."

A low wall rose along the shoulder of the freeway; the rush of the river hissed in the darkness below. They hopped onto the wall then moved down the concrete-slab embankment sloping toward the water. The surface of the churning waves rippled with reflected silver highlights from the night sky. Paul pondered if they should follow the river or risk trying to cross.

"Wait," Blake said, slowing down behind him. "The cars on the freeway are beginning to move. Where is he?"

Paul turned back. Cars had begun to creep tentatively forward; the obstruction up ahead had apparently dissipated. He saw Blake take a few steps farther up the incline.

"That's him! That's the Imperial. He's driving away!"

When they were sure he was gone, Blake and Paul returned to the roadway, crossing the lanes on foot, dodging oncoming traffic. A car sped by blaring its horn at them. An obscenity was shouted out an open window. A moment later they reached the Ford; other vehicles streamed around it like currents circumnavigating an island, tapping their horns gently to warn Paul and Blake to get out of the way. They quickly slid inside and Blake started the engine and they were off. The back window was gone and nuggets of glass were spread throughout the interior, but the windshield was intact.

Blake bit his lip. "I don't get it. He probably could have gotten us if he'd kept following after us. Instead, he just left."

Paul poked his head down under the seat. His hands patted the carpet but found nothing. The shopping bag with the tape reel was gone.

"Of course he did," Paul said with disgust. "He got what he wanted."

◇◇◇

Paul ran the bath while Blake spoke on the phone down the hall in the bedroom. Hot water splashed into the tub and he hoped it would soak up some of the aches and pains from their frantic flight down the trail and hillside in Griffith Park. When Paul returned to the bedroom, Blake looked up from where he sat on the bed and nodded at him.

Into the phone, he said, "If you could run a check on the car... yeah... a dark blue '63 Imperial Crown... first three letters on the plate, AJN... no, that's all I got. There's one other thing that might help. The car may have been issued a parking ticket this evening in Griffith Park. That should narrow it down. I need to know who it's registered to, and any info you might get on this guy beyond that. We know already he's packing a gun." He hesitated, then added, "I hate to say it, but we could be looking for someone in law enforcement. Thanks, I'll file my report in the morning. Call me as soon as you can."

He hung up the phone and addressed Paul. "Homicide is sending a team to Griffith Park. I requested my old partner, Mitch Mitchell, but I don't know if he's available."

Paul came over and began to unbutton Blake's shirt.

"The tub is ready."

They undressed each other then headed down the hall. Paul got in first, and after the initial sting of the hot water, steam rising off the surface, the heat felt good. He sat down, his back at the end of the tub, and Blake climbed in after him.

155

"Ah," Blake moaned as the water enveloped him and Paul wrapped his arms around Blake's waist. "I need this." He leaned back against Paul's chest and let himself be held. He was way too tall for the tub and his bent knees jutted up from the water.

"Your fingers are all cut up," Paul said, observing Blake's hands. He kissed Blake's neck. "And you have scratches on your neck."

"You're all scraped up, too." Blake brought Paul's hands to his mouth and kissed them. "That's what happens when you drag me through a cruising ground at night. I got all of the pain and none of the fun."

"Oh, I can show you some fun."

Blake suddenly tensed. "Shit, I forgot my cigarettes in the bedroom."

He began to lift himself out of the tub but Paul firmly pulled him back down.

"I need them to relax," Blake protested.

"I have ways to make you relax." Paul clasped his arms around him tighter.

"Oh, yeah?"

"Yeah."

Paul felt arousal between his legs and could see Blake hanging long and low in the water, but he knew they were both too exhausted to do anything about it. It felt good just being wrapped together in a warm package.

"You were awfully quiet after you came out of the hospital this evening. Anything you want to talk about?"

"I spoke with David. He's coming by later this week to pick up his things."

Blake was silent for a long while.

"I've got to know something," he said finally. "Does this mean anything to you... I mean... you and me... us?"

"Yeah, it means something to me."

156

Blake turned his head and kissed Paul, clasping Paul's arms tighter. They lay there together for a while, and then, Blake's breathing slowed and his grip lessened, and his head fell to the side on Paul's chest and he began to snore softly. The water was beginning to cool but the heat radiating from Blake's body kept Paul warm. All he knew was he didn't ever want to move from this spot or stop feeling the way he felt right now.

Paul had never considered what a long-term relationship with Blake would look like. They had only connected in short bursts of time, never more than enough to dazzle with promise. But he knew this kind of feeling didn't come along often, and the depth of it, the feeling of being lost in it, attracted and elated him as much as it scared him.

He wasn't sure why, but he found his eyes resting on the *Chat Noir* poster above the toilet. He knew he loved David more. He would always love David more. David was his first great love, and nothing could diminish that. They had shared experiences together that formed who they were, not just as a couple, but as individuals as well. It was David who had been there for him when Paul's mother had died, David who plucked the random hairs that grew on his back in a monthly ritual in front of the bathroom sink, David who had always been there in the morning to tell him when his tie didn't match his suit, David who had fought with him, kidded with him, made him laugh and loved him like nobody had ever loved him before. David was the one person in his life who always tried to make him a better man. And yet his life with David had become impossible.

He looked down at Blake, and let his lips brush the dark bristles of hair on the crown of his head. He felt such a rush of tenderness that he didn't know what to do with it and tears came to his eyes.

"I love you," he whispered.

He wasn't sure how it sounded in his own ears or how it would be received if Blake had heard him. He was surprised how tentatively the words came out, how charged with electricity, as if in the history of the world they had never been uttered before.

If Blake had heard, he didn't let on. He just breathed softly in Paul's arms.

<><><>

The call came at dawn.

Blake jumped up from the bed and had the phone in his hand on the second ring. Dim light filtered through drawn curtains; the room was covered in a blanket of shadows. Paul sat up in bed, immediately wide awake, and waited.

"Yeah, it's me. No, no, I'm glad you called." Blake rubbed his fist in his eyes with his free hand. "What do you got?" He listened for a moment. "Okay, hold it for a sec." He switched on the lamp, squinted, and found a pen and pad on the bedside table and began to jot down notes.

"All right, so the car is registered to a man named Clayton Biggs?" He listened for another minute or two, asked a few questions, then thanked the caller and hung up. He had a troubled look on his face when he sat back on the bed next to Paul.

"It turned out I was right, there was a parking ticket issued last night in Griffith Park to a '63 Imperial Crown. The license number fits the partial we had. The name on the registration sounded familiar, so my pal in the department dug a little deeper. Clayton Biggs was a cop until he got booted off the force two years ago."

"For what?"

"Extortion. Apparently he had a little blackmail business on the side."

"Blackmail?" Paul said, pondering that a moment. "You say he was a cop. What department?"

"The Intelligence Division."

Paul let that sink in before he asked, "Has the LAPD put out an APB on him?"

Blake hesitated. "They found the Imperial abandoned on Ocean Avenue at the Palisades Park in Santa Monica."

That was just a few miles from Paul's house. A quick ride down San Vicente Boulevard to the ocean. They could be there in ten minutes.

"Well," Paul said, throwing off the covers, "we'd better get dressed and get over there." He caught the expression on Blake's face and knew there was more. "What is it? What else did he tell you?"

"That's not all they found."

# Chapter 12

Far off, a haze of early morning mist obscured the bright horizon, the sea and sky merging in subtle shades of blue. Waves crashed and receded, and fingers of current capped with white foam nearly reached the soles of their shoes in the sand. In the distance to the east, following the long stretch of beach, a sharp cliff, still bathed in morning shadow, rose monolithic. The Pacific Coast Highway lay at its feet, quiet in the minutes just after dawn. At the top of the cliff, the pencil-thin Palisades Park ran along its edge, palm trees swaying in the breeze, and beyond, the silhouettes of bungalows and newly constructed apartment buildings jutted up to touch the rising sun.

The body lay in a heap where the surf met the sand. Beach strollers at dawn might have mistaken it for a sack of old waterlogged rags. The crime scene photographer had taken his pictures, and the Medical Examiner had looked over the body and placed the victim back in his original position, on his stomach with his face buried in the sand.

"They beat him pretty bad," the M.E. explained. From previous cases, Blake knew his name was Brandower. He couldn't have been more than thirty, but looked older, with no hair to speak of and eyebrows so pale they seemed to fade into his skin. His black plastic framed glasses glinted in the sunlight as he spoke. "His nose was broken. And his chest was caved in. Several broken ribs. Massive hemorrhaging in the chest area."

"With what?" Paul asked. "Some kind of truncheon? Or just the perp's fists?"

Brandower shrugged, squinting his eyes, looking away from the body and staring out to the horizon. "Wait for the autopsy. I'll know better then. But I don't think you could have done this with fists, even if you were a boxer. They really crushed him."

Sergeant Mitch Mitchell stood tall and thin with his hands on his hips, his trench coat billowing in the breeze. The brim of his hat threw shadow on his face. "We didn't find anything around the body. Whatever they used, they could have thrown it in the ocean, or taken it with them."

"What about all those abrasions on his hands?" Paul asked doubtfully. "And his torn clothes?"

"Well, it looks like they dragged him," the M.E. said. "That might account for the abrasions and the ragged clothes. And he was in the water for a while. They must have hoped the body would drift out with the tide, but instead, as you can see, it washed up on shore."

An errant wave rolled farther than the rest and lapped at their feet and the group took quick steps to keep from getting wet.

"All right," Mitchell said. "You can take the body away." He put his arm on Blake's shoulder, pulling him aside. "Let's go for a little walk, just you and me."

They strolled aimlessly down the coastline until they were out of earshot of the others. The Santa Monica Pier stretched endlessly into the water to the south. The bleak caw of seagulls echoed from above.

"This isn't our turf," Blake said. "How did you catch the case?"

"The Santa Monica police called us in when they realized Clayton Biggs was one of our own." Considered the dirtiest cops in Southern California in the thirties and forties, even putting the LAPD's bad apples to shame in

161

their brazen corruption, the Santa Monica Police Department had cleaned up its force in recent years. "Well," Sgt. Mitchell corrected himself, "one of our own until he got kicked out of the department a few years ago. When I heard his name mentioned as the victim I came over."

"So it's ours?"

"If we want it."

"You're going to want it."

Mitchell stopped in his tracks. "Jim, what's your part in this? I get a call last night because of you and suddenly I find myself in the hills of Griffith Park investigating a dead Negro with a bullet in his forehead."

Blake chose his words carefully. "We came out on different sides of the Wesley Durkin thing, but I trust you. I'm not sure how many other people I can say that about in the department."

Mitchell's eyes narrowed. "So the scar on the guy in Griffith Park wasn't a coincidence. The dead guy last night, he was the same one reportedly running from Wesley Durkin's house..."

"And the same one running from the theater New Year's Eve."

"Hold on," Mitchell said, anger coming to his face. "What have you gotten yourself into? Didn't I say just keep your nose clean and do your time on the beat and you'd be back in Homicide in no time? Didn't I tell you to stay the hell away from the Durkin investigation?"

"Listen to me. If Durkin wasn't murdered—if he committed suicide like you and the coroner and the brass say—then why did Roland Mosley have to be killed? He was the witness. He was the one who knew Durkin didn't commit suicide. And he had proof."

Blake could see he was beginning to win the sergeant over.

"What proof?"

"A tape recording."

"Of what?"

Blake shook his head and knew he was losing him again. "I don't know," he admitted.

"You've got to be kidding me."

"Look, Mitch, Clayton Biggs killed Roland Mosley last night for that tape. He nearly gunned Deputy D.A. Paul Winters and me down on the 5 freeway to get it. That's proof to me that whatever's on that tape is enough to incriminate whoever is behind this."

They headed back up the beach. The coroner's men were bending over the corpse and putting it in a body bag. In the distance they looked like black crows pecking at carrion.

"So where is it, this tape?" Mitchell asked. "I had my men check his car. There was nothing in it." He was silent for a while. Then he said, "You had me called last night for a reason. You want me messed up in this. This is going to drag me down, too."

"Not if we do our job. Not if we find out who's behind this." Blake held back on the connection with Dean Estes and the Intelligence Division and the Chandlers even though he trusted Mitchell; he knew the sergeant had integrity. He just wasn't sure he could trust the people Mitchell reported to. "I don't expect you to stick your neck out for me."

Mitchell studied his shoes as they shuffled through the sand. "You were my partner. I should have fought for you," he conceded gravely. "I should have stuck with you no matter what."

"Forget it."

Paul was waiting for them, watching as they approached. The breeze was lapping in his hair.

"I want to see the car," Paul said.

"It's already been searched," Sgt. Mitchell replied, glancing up to the top of the cliff. "We didn't find anything. But have a look if you want. The driver's door was unlocked, but no keys were found on the body. That could mean the killer took the keys to search the car, or it could mean they were lost when the body was in the water. But you'd better be quick if you want to see it. I have an officer stationed up there. The impound truck is on its way."

They each shook Sgt. Mitchell's hand, then trudged across the sand toward where Paul's Thunderbird was parked in the empty lot of a private pool club on the beach side of the Pacific Coast Highway. Traffic had increased as the morning progressed, and a long line of vehicles waited at the light for the steep road winding from the highway to the crest of the cliff.

As they walked Blake gazed at the cliff in the distance, easily a few football field lengths away. "So, how did he get from there to here? He left his car up there, but ended up in the ocean." On their drive over, he and Paul had passed Clayton Biggs' Imperial parked on the street; he couldn't see it now, but Blake knew the car was close to the cluster of six-foot aloe that perched on the edge of the precipice. Below, on the sheer hundred foot drop-off, scrub clung tenaciously to the wind-swept raw sandstone surface.

"Clayton Biggs has a meeting in the middle of the night in the park with whoever hired him," Paul began, putting the pieces together. "He has what they want, the tape reel."

"All right, so how does he get down here?"

Paul considered for a moment. "They walk, they talk. Maybe they take the road that slopes down from the bluffs to the Pacific Coast Highway. They cross the highway and start walking down the beach."

"Uh-huh," Blake agreed. "But maybe Biggs isn't quite ready to give up the tape."

164

"You think he could have gotten greedy?"

"Maybe he realized whatever they were paying him wasn't enough. He's killed at least one man for them, we know that for sure. Maybe he killed Wesley Durkin, too. And he came after a deputy district attorney and a cop and endangered a lot of people on the freeway last night. That makes Clayton Biggs an endangered species in this city. Maybe he wanted more money so he could just disappear. He holds out for more, they don't like it, and so they kill him."

"Like that? Smash his face and his rib cage? He must have made them very angry."

"It sends a message. Don't mess with them."

"The tape, you think maybe he didn't bring it?"

Blake shook his head. "I guess he could have hidden it somewhere. We'll have his place searched, but I don't think we'll find it there. I bet he brought it with him. I think they have it now. Otherwise, do you think they would have killed him with it still floating around?"

They reached the Thunderbird, and Paul pulled onto the highway then took the steep road cut in the cliff leading to the top.

"Who's the 'they' we keep talking about?" Paul asked. "Do you think Clayton Biggs was still working for Dean Estes?"

Blake nodded. "It fits. Clayton Biggs gets caught with his fingers in the cookie jar and gets fired from the Intelligence Division a few years back. I mean, working in that department means he had access to the goods on a whole lot of people. On a policeman's salary, I can see why he was tempted to use it to his own advantage. It could be that once he was cut loose Dean Estes kept in contact with Biggs to do dirty jobs for him."

"It would explain what happened last night. Estes spots us tailing him over to Pasadena—or maybe he saw us peeking through the hedge at Agnes Chandler's place—so he calls up his toady to get over there quick to tail us."

"And we brought him right to Roland Mosley."

"Who he was searching for anyway. Biggs must have been the one who followed Mosley into the theater New Year's Eve. He probably planned to kill him then, but Mosley got skittish and ran and Biggs went after Leland Serokin instead, thinking erroneously that the professor had been handed the tape." Paul suddenly remembered his strange altercation with Estes at the phone booth at the Music Center Saturday night. The head of the Intelligence Division had been spitting invective into the phone when Paul had approached. Could Estes have been learning from Clayton Biggs that Roland Mosley had escaped his grasp in the theater and Biggs had failed to get the tape?

A uniform was leaning against the Imperial when they pulled up and climbed out. Biggs had parked his car on Ocean, the wide street that ran parallel to the park. Paths curled along the long narrow park through manicured lawn and towering palms. A low protective fence rose at the cliff's edge. The highway was hidden far below, and only the sound of traffic let on it was there at all. From where they were standing, even the beach couldn't be seen, only a strip of shimmering ocean and rich blue sky. A snarl of monstrous aloe, tall as a man, reached up at the edge of the bluff, and other scrub and succulents peeked from their precarious spots clinging to the sheer slope.

"I did a thorough search," the officer in blue explained to them. "Top to bottom. Under the hood. Underneath the chassis. Nothing hidden there. Trunk was empty except for a spare tire. Nothing in the wheel wells. Nothing under the seats. Just ordinary junk in the glove box. The registration, some pens and a pad."

"Take off the hubcaps," Paul ordered. "We've got to be sure."

The uniform sighed and went for the tire iron in the trunk. He plucked them off one by one, and each clattered to the pavement and wobbled before coming to a rest. "Satisfied?"

Blake and Paul left him without answering and headed back toward the Thunderbird.

"So you think they have it?" Paul asked.

Blake opened the car door. "It wasn't on his body and it's not in the car. They have it. I'm sure of it. It's gone for good."

Paul slid in the driver's side and slammed the door. "So we've got nothing."

Paul had been thinking a lot about the dossiers in the trunk of Agnes Wingate Chandler's Mercedes and how he was going to get a peek at them. On the drive back to his house, he and Blake kicked out a plan and agreed to meet that evening. The party hosted by Agnes Chandler in Paul's honor, to introduce him to potential contributors for his bid to become the next District Attorney, was to be held at eight that night in West Hollywood.

In the meantime, with the holidays over, they both had to go back to work. Blake headed for his own place in the hills above Hollywood to put on his uniform for his shift that morning. He'd just have time to fill out his report on the murder of Roland Mosley before going on patrol. He hoped to find time during the day to get the back window of his station wagon replaced. Paul dressed in a crisp suit, one of dozens in his closet, and headed for downtown.

In his office, Paul went through the cases he would be handling over the next few months. While the courts came to a grinding halt around the holidays, he had a busy schedule in the new year and his docket was full.

It struck him suddenly that today was the day the men arrested in the bar raid Saturday night were going to be arraigned. He pondered about that for a while, and the sting of David's accusations came back to him. *I know you try to do little things to make things better. But that isn't enough anymore, Paul. It hasn't been for a long time.* Maybe, Paul thought, he could use his influence to get the charges dropped. He picked up his phone and held it a moment listening to the dial tone. He wondered who was prosecuting the case. Whoever it was, they probably owed him a favor or two. He put his finger on the dial but hesitated. If he intervened, there would be questions. Why was he getting involved? Why did he care about a routine fag bar bust? Questions he wouldn't be able to answer.

He sighed heavily and put the phone back in its cradle.

He received three important phone calls that day.

The first came in the morning. It was David. Whatever tears he might have shed were not evident from his voice, which sounded measured and almost impersonal, his tone pleasant but businesslike. The conversation came across to Paul like the culmination of a legal transaction. It made Paul feel far worse than anger or recrimination possibly could.

"I wanted to come by and pick up my things on Friday. The afghan over the couch that my grandma knitted, and there's some Tupperware bowls in the kitchen. The ones with the yellow lids. And I left my tape recorder there too." He had brought it over so he could record music from Paul's own recorder onto his. "I thought I'd come over during the day."

That meant he didn't want to run into Paul when he came by.

168

"I'll leave the key under the door mat for you," he added.

Paul was silent for a long moment. He was cognizant of a grinding movement in his jaw.

"Anything else?" Paul was surprised by the cold hard edge in his voice. Suddenly he felt anger and hurt and he had to steady his hand holding the phone.

David hesitated. "If it's okay, I'd like to have the picture in the bathroom. You know, the *Chat Noir* poster."

"You mean the one of the cat?"

"Yeah, I'd like to have that, if it's okay. I know you paid for the frame."

Paul swallowed and his throat felt thick. A jarring image of the two of them lying together in a small French hotel came to him and his hand began to tremble uncontrollably. "Of course," he said slowly. "Sure, if you want it."

"All right then. Goodbye, Paul."

The phone went dead and Paul was left staring at the receiver in his hand. Just like that. It was over. Paul felt a dull headache coming on. He would go home one day at the end of the week and every indication that he and David had had a life together would be gone. He felt as if a smooth, sharp blade had just been planted in his gut.

After lunch, his secretary told him Agnes Chandler was on the line.

"Mrs. Chandler, it's good to hear from you."

"I just wanted to remind you of the little soiree I'm hosting for you tonight," she purred.

Nothing in her tone let on if she was aware he and Blake had been spying on her and knew about her affair with Dean Estes.

169

"I wouldn't miss it for the world."

She laughed that throaty laugh of hers. Whiskey and cigarettes. "Eight o'clock, then. Chasen's." She paused. "Everybody will be there."

"I look forward to meeting your friends."

◇◇◇

The call from Marvin Botwinick came late in the day.

"You asked me to look into tax increases in South Central."

"What did you find out?" Paul could hear him sucking on his pipe on the other end of the line.

"The tax base has remained pretty constant in the last few years. I mean, there's been an increase in population, of course, but nothing unexpected. The little town of L.A. just keeps getting bigger and bigger."

"Okay," Paul said, wondering where Marvin was heading with this.

"If you look at the city at large, property taxes have gone up slightly across the board since Wesley Durkin took office."

He had thought Jeff Dupuis' comment that the assessor was unpopular in Watts because of rising taxes might point to some kind of corruption, but from what Botwinick had to say, it didn't sound like it. He let out a disappointed sigh. "So everybody's taxes have gone up, in South Central and everywhere else?"

"Yes, but there's a bit more to it than that."

Paul could almost see Botwinick raking his fingers through his beard and grinning. He'd found something.

"Taxes have gone up *more* in areas like Watts and Compton, less so elsewhere."

"But surely someone would have noticed this by now." As soon as he said it, Paul realized that people *had* noticed,

170

the people of South Central. But no one had been listening. "How could they do this and not get caught?"

"The rise in taxes was so slight, it wouldn't be noticed unless you were looking very closely. According to my sampling, taxes went up on average five bucks in Brentwood, but ten or twenty in Compton. The poor people in South Central would notice, because they were struggling to pay their taxes in the first place, but it was lost in the fact that everybody's taxes were rising. Everybody grouses when their taxes go up, but who compares what's happening in their own neighborhood versus other areas of the city? And there were enough examples where taxes in the inner city didn't go up at all to throw off anyone looking for a pattern. But there definitely *is* a pattern."

Paul contemplated for a moment. Again he was disappointed. "Ten or twenty bucks? That's not going to amount to anything." He was looking for a scandal big enough to justify murder.

"Paul, we're talking ten or twenty bucks multiplied by tens of thousands, no hundreds of thousands if you count black neighborhoods across the city."

Leaning back in his chair, Paul whistled, finally understanding the implications. "I get what you're saying. We're talking millions of dollars."

"You're not asking me the important question, Paul. Who benefits?"

"Well, the city would, I guess. More revenue. But what do you mean, *who* benefits? You said taxes were going up across the board..."

"Yes, in general. Taxes went up in every neighborhood in the city. But not on all *individuals*."

"Out with it, Marvin."

"Remember how I said Durkin was in a four-way race for the assessor's office and going nowhere until Buck Chandler stepped in to back his campaign? Well, I checked the records. The list of his contributors is a roll call for the downtown business interests. You remember Charlie Barnes from the California Real Estate Association? He was at the party Saturday night. Red-headed guy? He's the one who led that campaign a few years back to repeal the law banning racial discrimination in housing. He was a big contributor, too. The list is a who's who of the power-brokers who razed Bunker Hill and are rebuilding down-town. Since Durkin was elected, their individual taxes have gone down, and so have the taxes of the companies they own."

Paul ran the sequence of events through his mind in chronological order. The LAPD spies on a trailing can-didate for the assessor's office and gets compromising goods on him. Enter Buck Chandler and his cohorts with the money to push this guy into the winner's circle. The taxes of Durkin's contributors go down, and the least powerful members of the community carry the burden of rising taxes to make up the difference. That about said it. Except that Wesley Durkin decided to fight back and ended up dead.

And something else didn't quite fit. Why go after a specific minority—who might raise a ruckus if it came out they were being unfairly targeted—rather than just take a few dollars from everybody across the board? Why go after blacks in South Central?

"Marvin, I want you to hold off on writing about any of this until I know the whole story."

"They killed Wesley Durkin, didn't they, Paul? That's what this is all about, isn't it?"

Paul hesitated before he spoke. "Yes," he said finally. "Wesley Durkin, and at least two others. But I don't have a case yet, and I'm still not sure how all the pieces fall together. There's something else I haven't told you. Dean Estes is feeding Intelligence Division dossiers to the

Chandlers. I witnessed him delivering easily a dozen of them to Agnes Chandler yesterday."

Botwinick whistled. "You think they're using that information to control dozens of politicians in the city?"

"I'll find out for sure tonight. I have a plan to get my hands on those surveillance reports at a party Agnes Chandler is throwing for me this evening."

Botwinick gave a little staccato laugh. "Agnes Chandler is giving a party for you?"

Paul let out a sigh. "Look, it was set up before I had any inkling what she and her husband might be involved in. It hasn't been announced yet, but Bulgetti is taking a position in Washington. I'm going to be running for District Attorney in the spring. When I met her Saturday night Agnes Chandler offered to host a party to introduce me to potential contributors." Paul hadn't had time to consider the implications of the likely possibility that the people who had backed Wesley Durkin's campaign were probably the same folks who were going to be at the get-together tonight.

"Well, first, congratulations. That's incredible news—"

"And completely off the record until Bulgetti makes a formal announcement, okay?"

"All right, Paul, that's the good news. But do you know who you're dealing with here? Do you know about the politics of Buck and Agnes Chandler?"

"I have a feeling you're going to tell me."

"Their political views are slightly to the right of Attila the Hun. You do know about the big blow-up in the Chandler family after Otis came on board as the editor of the *Times*, right?"

"Yes, yes," Paul replied wearily, "you told me this already. Dorothy Chandler got her husband to name their son Otis Chandler as publisher, passing over Buck. The rest of the family was furious."

"No, it's what happened *after* Otis became publisher of the paper that I'm talking about. This was in the early days of his tenure, when he was struggling to wrest control of the editorial board from the red-baiting lunatics who were in charge, back in 1961."

"I'm listening."

"Otis okayed a series of exposés on the John Birch Society. You know who I'm talking about, right? This is the crazy nut group that sees communists in every woodshed. They even accused President Eisenhower of being a communist dupe. They claim water fluoridation and the Civil Rights movement are commie plots. Exposing these hate-mongering wackos was a pretty courageous move on Otis's part that cost the paper easily fifteen thousand of their right-wing subscribers. But it was an utter slap in the face to the conservative wing of the Chandler family, especially Buck and his wife Agnes, both of whom were purportedly card-carrying John Birch members. They demanded a retraction but Otis instead wrote a front-page editorial backing the exposé and standing behind everything it said."

Despite everything he'd heard, Paul suddenly had second thoughts. "Okay, they have a screw loose when it comes to politics, but am I out of my mind to think they could be involved in the murders of three people? I mean, they're pillars of high society in L.A., right?"

"Remember what Balzac said. *Behind every great fortune there is a crime.* You can multiply that maxim tenfold for some of the Chandlers, going back three generations. Nobody makes that much money without getting a little blood on their hands." He took a puff on his pipe. "Are you sure you want to go to that party?"

Paul thought about the carton filled with Intelligence Division reports in the back of Agnes Chandler's Mercedes, and the plan he and Blake had concocted to get at them. "At this point," he muttered, "I don't think I have a choice."

"Paul," Marvin said, "just be careful."

# Chapter 13

Chasen's had begun its life as a chili shack with borrowed silverware in the thirties, but those days were long gone. Now the governor had a booth named in his honor there—where he had proposed to Nancy—and Hollywood luminaries such as Frank Sinatra and Alfred Hitchcock were devoted fans of the restaurant with its dark wood paneling and high-backed blood-red leather upholstered booths.

A green awning stretched from the front entrance to the street to protect patrons being dropped off from the unlikely occurrence of rain.

"There's her Mercedes," Blake said as they trolled past down Beverly Boulevard. He hadn't taken off his uniform after his shift ended; looking official was part of their plan. "See it, near the front of the lot? It's close enough to the street that there'll be plenty of light. You shouldn't have any problem seeing what's in those reports, but people will be able to spot you from the street. Just act like it's your car and they shouldn't be suspicious."

"How far will you park down the street?"

"Say half a block. I'll keep the valets busy while you check out what's in the trunk." He patted a book of mug shots on the seat beside him. "I can give you a good ten minutes, maybe more."

"It won't take that long. I just want to know the names in those dossiers. The other politicians they have control over. Eight-thirty, then?"

"Eight-thirty."

"You can let me off up the block."

A moment later Blake pulled the Ford wagon to the curb along a palm tree lined parking strip. His car was complete again; Blake had found a garage to replace the back window after work.

Before Paul could get out, Blake angled his head at him. "Wait a second." He reached over and straightened Paul's tie. "There. You look good."

There was something familiar in the gesture. At first Paul couldn't place it, then he realized it was because David had been doing the same thing for him for so long.

Blake hesitated before continuing. "If something goes wrong—"

"Nothing will go wrong."

Agnes Chandler, dressed in a pink satin dress with matching lipstick, gloves and a pillbox hat, her hair done up in a high stiff blonde coif, came toward him with her tight but friendly smile as he walked in the door.

"Come, come," she said, taking Paul's arm. "There are so many people I'd like you to meet."

"Thank you for having me, Mrs. Chandler. And thank you for all of this."

"It's my pleasure. I'm afraid you have quite a few fans here, especially among the ladies, who've followed your career and your cases over the years in the papers. I bet you've got quite a few stories to tell."

Including one unfolding right now, Paul thought, as he was led through the gathering. As promised, the party was a small, intimate affair of a few dozen friends of the Chandlers who "wanted to get to know" the next aspiring candidate for District Attorney. Paul recognized some of the faces from social columns, others seemed familiar yet he couldn't place them. Maybe he had seen their pictures in the business section of the *Times*. He and Agnes came upon Buck Chandler in a small group who were well on their way to their next cocktail.

"There's the man of the hour," Buck Chandler announced amiably in his folksy booming voice, extending his hand. Again the bone-crushing handshake.

"Good to see you again, Mr. Chandler."

"Buck, everybody calls me Buck. We're all friends here. Good to have you. Of course you've been to Chasen's before."

"No, I can't say I've had the pleasure."

"Well, you really must try the chili. The story goes that..." he faltered and his snow-drift eyebrows came together, his pale blue eyes registering confusion, "uh, what is that woman's name..." he looked to Agnes in an appeal for help, "you know, the actress, the beautiful one... the one in that movie... the one who wanted the chili..."

Others surrounding him kept frozen, expectant smiles plastered on their faces.

Agnes placed an affectionate gloved hand on her husband's forearm. "I think you're talking about Elizabeth Taylor, aren't you, dear?"

"Elizabeth Taylor! Yes, she was on the set of that movie... that movie they were filming in..."

"In Rome, dear? Do you mean *Cleopatra*?"

"Yes, yes, that's it. She was on the set of *Cleopatra* and she got a yen for Chasen's chili and had it shipped all the way to her in Rome."

Everybody chuckled dutifully, while Paul began to suspect Buck Chandler was far less lucid than their previous meeting let on, and he started to doubt the old man had a meaningful part in the conspiracy after all.

Charlie Barnes, the balding red-head Paul had met at the Music Center fundraiser stepped forward and offered his hand. Paul recalled he was the president of the California Real Estate Association and had been on the list of Durkin's contributors.

"Good to see you again, Paul. We were just discussing the new governor. I was saying without Goldwater there would have been no Reagan. That speech he gave before the '64 election put him on the map."

Others nodded in agreement, sipping their drinks.

Paul tilted his head and smiled. "But Goldwater lost by a landslide."

Agnes produced her brittle smile. She placed her hand on Paul's arm as if it were her job to take him under her wing. "But *we* didn't lose. Goldwater was a stepping stone. Conservatives control the Republican Party now. And because of Johnson and his civil rights bill, the South is ours. Next time we'll win."

A drink was put in Paul's hand and he found himself glad-handing around the room until all the introductions were made, all the while wondering how much each of them knew and which politicians they owned.

Once he'd made the rounds he glanced at his watch. It was already eight-twenty-eight. According to their plan, at eight-thirty Blake would present his badge to the three valets on staff and usher them to his car parked down the street, purportedly to look at photos of a suspected burglar working the area. While the valets were engaged, Paul would slip away from the gathering and get the key to Agnes Chandler's Mercedes and pop the trunk. After gleaning the names of the politicians under surveillance, he'd return to the party. No one would even know he had been inside the car.

He was looking for the best way to make a discreet exit when he noticed Dean Estes, sharply dressed in a tailored suit, watching him from across the room. Paul made small talk with a couple standing next to him, hoping Estes would lose interest, but when he looked back the Intelligence Division head was still observing him. Paul read his watch. It was eight-thirty-three. A sheen of sweat was beginning to form on his forehead. Every minute wasted here in the restaurant was a minute he wouldn't have to examine the surveillance reports in the trunk of the Mercedes. He imagined Blake was walking the valets down the block to his car right now.

He tried to lose himself in the crowd, but Estes' eyes remained on him. Wherever he went, the focus of the crew cut cop with ramrod military posture unabashedly followed. Finally Paul ducked down a hallway into the restroom. He dabbed his forehead with a towel. He checked the window next to the stalls. Too small to climb out of, and painted shut. Eight-thirty-nine. *Dammit.*

When Paul exited the men's room, Dean Estes was waiting for him at the entrance to the hallway.

Paul decided only a bold move would get him off his back. He strode up to Estes with a big smile and an outstretched hand. "I recognize you! Aren't you Dean Estes, the head of the LAPD Intelligence Division?"

"I'm here in a private capacity tonight," Estes replied stiffly, his lips hardly moving as he spoke. His hands remained at his sides.

Paul's eyes drifted meaningfully to Agnes Chandler, who was standing next to her husband by a booth with a wine glass in her hand.

"I bet."

Estes' expression didn't change, but suddenly his features seemed cast in stone. Color began to flood his cheeks. Not embarrassment, but steely anger. He turned on his heel and walked away. Paul knew he would only have a moment before Estes recovered and he took the opportunity to slip through the swinging kitchen door.

As he made his way through the busy clanging kitchen, a waiter approached with a polite but puzzled look on his face. "Sir? Can I help you?"

Paul grinned sheepishly. "I was just headed out back for a smoke. The wife, she seems to think I've quit."

The waiter grinned back conspiratorially. "Women. We guys gotta stick together. Just step out back." He winked. "No one will see you."

Outside the night air had turned cool. Paul walked stealthily in quick strides to the valet station in the back of the lot. No one was there. Even so, Paul worked fast. He knew Blake couldn't keep them down the street forever. He scanned the board and grabbed the key with the number corresponding to the one on the space where Agnes Chandler's car was parked, then threaded through the maze of automobiles to the Mercedes.

As he raised the trunk lid, he had a sudden fear that this had all been for nothing, that the box had been removed already and he would never discover which politicians had been compromised. But to his relief, it was there.

Before he could look in the carton, he heard voices coming up the street. Standing on his toes, he could see the valets in their red jackets ambling back to the lot. He read his watch. Eight-forty-five. Blake had kept them for fifteen minutes, as long as he could. He knew he had to think fast. He wouldn't have time to look through the dossiers before the valets returned, but maybe he could get the information he wanted right under their noses.

Leaving the trunk unlatched, he scurried back to the key board and hung the key where he had found it, then, keeping out of sight he crouched down between the other parked vehicles and sneaked back to the Mercedes. He hid there until the valets had returned to their station, then he sat behind the car and slowly inched the trunk lid up so there was room enough for him to reach in and take the top intelligence report in the box.

Sitting cross-legged on the blacktop, he opened the cover emblazoned with the LAPD insignia and gazed down at the first page. He gave a little start. It was a photograph of him and David sitting at a booth in a restaurant. He quickly flipped the page and a coiled snake seemed to be unwinding in his gut and working its way up his throat. The next photo showed him and David in swim suits lying on lounge chairs around a friend's pool in Bel-Air. All the other guests at the pool party were male. The implication was obvious and Paul felt heat suddenly stinging his cheeks. Another picture taken through his front window revealed him and David sitting close together on his couch, Paul's arm over his lover's shoulder. He flipped through the text of the surveillance reports. He had been followed; the times, the places, the dates all logged. The many nights David stayed at his place were noted, when David arrived in the evening, and when he left in the morning. Paul felt his hands begin to shake, and he wasn't sure if it was from cold rage or the terror that gripped him at the thought that everything he'd worked for could be stripped away in an instant.

He didn't see anything specifically incriminating, but the data in the report was damning enough to derail his life. He suddenly recalled the aggressive, contemptuous manner in which Dean Estes had brushed past him at the telephone booth at the Music Center. No wonder, he'd seen Paul's Intelligence Division file, and all it implied.

His throat was dry and his tongue felt thick as he reached into the trunk and took out the next dossier in the box. He blinked, puzzled as he flipped through it. He had assumed it would be another public servant or politician targeted for blackmail, but it wasn't. It was another copy of the file on him he had just seen. He pulled out another and another, and they were all the same. Every dossier was on him, and he tried to fathom what it meant. And then he understood. His file had been copied a dozen times for distribution.

Before it could all sink in, the icy chill of cold steel prodded the back of his neck.

"Put those all back very quietly," a voice said from behind him.

Paul didn't have to look over his shoulder to know who it was. He slipped the reports back in the trunk and shut the lid.

"Now, you're going to get up and you and I are going to casually walk straight to the sidewalk. You're not going to look back. You're going to cross the street and when a car pulls up on the other side you're going to get in the back seat."

Paul rose and he and Estes walked side by side to the street. He felt a barrel jabbing his ribs. Paul realized if the valets even noticed the two men walking out of the lot, they'd only see them from behind and wouldn't be able to identify them.

As they crossed the street, a blue Chevy Impala pulled to the curb. Paul slid in the back seat and Estes went around to the front passenger door and got in. Agnes was behind the wheel. She pressed the gas as soon as they were inside. The scent of Estes' cheap cologne permeated the car thick as fog. This is what I'm going to die smelling? Paul asked himself grimly. They drove past Blake's parked Ford wagon and Paul could only wonder if Blake had seen him get in the car.

At a stoplight Agnes looked at him darkly in the rearview mirror. She had taken off her pillbox hat and gloves.

"You could have had a successful career, you could have gone far, and we would have helped you, but you had to ruin it all."

"I'm not sure the kind of career you're talking about. You mean like Wesley Durkin?" Paul leaned back in his seat. "The lifespan of those receiving your largess seems a bit short. I think I'm better off taking a pass."

"Too bad. You're good-looking enough, with that strong jaw of yours. You would have cut quite a dashing figure as the next District Attorney."

"You two make an attractive couple as well. It's awkward you already have a husband, but you clearly haven't let that get in the way. Until tonight I thought Buck Chandler might be the mastermind behind all this. What is he, senile?"

"His mind comes and goes, poor dear. Sometimes he's still sharp as a tack."

"But not sharp enough to see what's going on right in front of his nose. How did you two lovebirds get together?"

"It was at a benefit for the Policemen's Benevolent Association. The moment we laid eyes on each other we knew. I convinced Buck we needed a bodyguard for public events and that Dean was willing to moonlight. The first night we spent together—" she reached over and placed a bony hand on Estes' shoulder, and her middle-aged face seemed to glow like a girl's, "—Dean mentioned all the files his department had on politicians, and the plan just came to me in an instant. I got Buck and our friends to put their weight behind Wesley Durkin and everything would have been fine if he hadn't decided to betray us."

Three people dead and tens of thousands cheated out of their hard-earned wages, Paul thought, and it all started with a little adulterous pillow talk. "Whoever said adultery is a victimless crime?" he muttered under his breath.

"What did you say?" Estes demanded, turning back toward him, waving his gun over the seat.

"Forget it." Paul tried to determine where they were going. His captors seemed to be meandering around the city before deciding on their destination. "I still don't understand why you went after the people of South Central. Why burden them with your little scheme? Why not spread your corruption evenly across the board?"

At a light Agnes looked back at him. "The niggers burned this city down. They did forty million in damages during their riot in Watts last year. Forty million. Good hardworking people had their businesses snuffed out. Their whole lives up in smoke. The niggers burned this city down, and the niggers should pay to rebuild it."

"With you and your friends conveniently being the beneficiaries."

"Call it reparations for all my taxes that go to food stamps so they can sit at home and have more babies," she replied tartly. "If things keep going the way they're going, by 1970 half the population of this city will be black and then God have pity on the white man."

"Enough of all this." Estes leveled his gun at Paul. "Before we go any farther you're going to tell us where that tape is."

Paul stared. Now he was baffled and a line formed between his brows. "But you have it."

Estes half climbed over the seat, slamming the gun in his hand against Paul's face. Paul's head was thrown back with the impact and he felt a stinging laceration open on his cheek. He tasted blood in his mouth. He put up his hands defensively to ward off further blows.

"I'm going to hurt you very badly if you're not more forthcoming," Estes warned.

"I don't have any idea where it is," Paul protested, sucking the blood off his lip. "Maybe you should have

185

gotten it from Clayton Biggs before you killed him on the beach in Santa Monica if you wanted it so badly."

An expression came over Estes' broken boxer's face that made Paul realize he and Blake had gotten the scenario of how Biggs died all wrong. They had envisioned Biggs and—most likely—Dean Estes meeting at the park and walking down to the beach, negotiating the exchange of the tape. But it would have been crazy to kill Biggs without first getting possession of the tape. What had he and Blake missed?

"What's on this tape that you're so afraid of?" Paul remembered what Roland Mosley had told them the night before in the park. "Wesley Durkin called a meeting of all his big contributors, didn't he?" It was the night Roland had come home early and seen a lot of fancy cars parked in front of the house. "He secretly tape recorded it, incriminating the very people who had paid good money to put him in office. What did he tell you the night you shot him in the head, that he was going to expose you all?"

"He was an ungrateful little queer," Estes growled. "He threatened to ruin us all. You don't do that to the people I represent. You don't even think about it."

"So when he wouldn't turn over the tape you killed him and made it look like suicide, then you searched the place but you never did find that reel. But that wasn't your only problem. There was that other loose end. When you were searching the place, you heard someone in the bedroom. But Roland Mosley jumped out the window before you could get to him."

"I had access to the police report on Durkin's death. Neighbors in the area spotted a Negro with a facial scar running from the scene. Clayton Biggs nearly tracked him down on New Year's Eve in a theater downtown, but he got away. I have to say, maybe we never would have found him if you hadn't led us right to him."

186

"If he doesn't have the tape," Agnes said in a barely audible voice, glancing over at Estes, "then we don't need him anymore."

Estes silently nodded and Agnes headed southward. A few minutes later the Chevy took a curved entrance ramp onto the freeway. Paul wondered what had become of Blake. He took a quick glance out of the back window but couldn't recognize any of the cars behind them.

"Where are you taking me?"

"Nigger town," Estes said.

Paul didn't doubt what neighborhood he was referring to. Several minutes later they were on surface streets again. He didn't recognize any of the buildings or the names of streets, but he knew they were traveling through Watts. At a red light, a gleam of headlights appeared in the back window. From what Paul could gather looking in the rearview mirror, it looked like a station wagon and his spirits soared. But in the glare of the car's front lights, he couldn't make out who the driver was. He didn't dare look over his shoulder and bring attention to it.

"Look around," Agnes said as she turned on a main drag and they passed buildings gutted by fire. "Look what these people did to their own neighborhoods. They were too lazy and good for nothing to even shuffle to someone else's neighborhood to throw their Molotov cocktails. These people shit where they eat. And now we're supposed to rebuild their neighborhoods with our tax dollars? No wonder new businesses don't want to open here."

"If you say so." Paul gazed fixedly out the window.

The deterioration of the inner city had been exacerbated by the proliferation of freeways throughout Los Angeles in the previous decade. Wealthier whites fled to the San Fernando Valley, eroding the tax base, and the Valley's racially restrictive housing covenants kept blacks from following. As more and more businesses left, mixed neighborhoods turned black, were redlined by banks and deteriorated into squalor. In a final bitter irony, during the Watts riots, police had been stationed at underpasses of freeways dividing white and black areas. The very thoroughfares that had allowed the flight of whites from the inner city were used as barricades to keep marauding blacks from entering wealthy white neighborhoods to the north.

Paul looked over his shoulder but he couldn't see any car headlights in the distance, and what hope he'd had that Blake was trailing them began to fade and he knew he had to get out of this on his own. The neighborhood began to change, fewer low ramshackle houses, more boxy warehouses.

After several minutes of silence Estes spoke.

"Pull over here."

Agnes curbed the car on a dim deserted street. A lone stark streetlight down the road cast pale silver light on the industrial area. Through a high chain-link fence outside his window, Paul could see the inky water of the L.A. River, the smooth surface of the sloping concrete embankment obstructed occasionally by renegade weeds forcing themselves up through the pavement. In the distance to the south, the only thing lit was a shadowy art deco bridge that spanned the river to the other side, where silent factories lay still in the night. Across the street dilapidated structures that looked like warehouses loomed in the darkness. There wasn't a soul in sight, but Paul could hear muffled barks, probably from watch dogs guarding the factories and warehouses after business hours.

Estes climbed out and came around and swung open the back door, waving his gun at Paul. "All right, get out."

Paul did as he was told, but his mind was clicking. Standing between the car and the fence, they took stock of each other for a moment while Agnes stepped out from behind the wheel, straightening her dress and hanging a pink spaghetti-strap purse over her shoulder. Paul decided Estes was too powerfully built for him to grapple with even if he wasn't holding a gun. Better to bide his time and look for any means of escape that might present itself. At first he couldn't fathom the next piece of their plan. Shoot him here, on the street and leave his body beside the fence? That would be reckless, risking witnesses if a stray car happened to pass by. Maybe take him behind one of the nearby warehouses and do it there? Then Paul noticed a long slit in the chain-link fence, undoubtedly where kids in the area slipped through to access the river for dangerous games of wading and swimming in the turbulent runoff, and he understood why they had parked in this spot.

Estes nodded at Agnes. "If he tries to run, shoot him."

Agnes produced a small pistol from her purse that fit snugly in her hand and she observed Paul with a gleam in her eye. "Don't think I won't. And if you believe I can't handle a gun, you should be aware I belong to the Pasadena Rifle Club and I've won three shooting tournaments. I'm considered to be a rather good shot for a lady."

Estes grinned. "She can nail your ass at two hundred yards." He slid through the hole to the other side of the fence while Agnes trained her pistol on Paul.

"You next," she said.

Paul squeezed through the opening, and a moment later, Agnes followed.

"You wait here," Estes told her. "Watch for anyone coming. I'm going to take a little stroll by the river with our new friend."

Agnes looked at her watch, petite and diamond encrusted, on her bony wrist. "Hurry up. We haven't got all night."

"What I have to do won't take long."

189

The two men walked together down the embankment toward the sound of rushing water. The flat concrete expanse stretched into darkness in both directions, offering no protection if Paul should dart away from his captor and attempt to escape. He wondered how many moments he had left as they approached the bank of the river. Keep him talking, Paul decided, and look for a way out.

"She's going to throw you away when she's through using you," Paul prodded.

Estes chuckled. "No, she's going to marry me."

"Yeah, right. How many men have you killed for her and what have you gotten out of it?"

The still snake eyes glinted in the dim light. "The old man has cancer. Buck's days are numbered. It isn't just his mind that's going. He won't last out the year. And then, after a suitable length of mourning, I'll be the master of that big house in Pasadena."

"Not when the bodies start being traced to you. Watch how fast she turns her back. When the cops come ringing her doorbell, she won't even know your name."

Estes raised his gun toward Paul's chest. "Shuddup about her. Just shut up."

The screech of tires echoed from the street, and they turned their heads.

"Someone's coming!" Agnes hissed, alarm rising in her voice. She took several steps back from the fence, raising her pistol.

As Paul looked in the direction of the street, a car swung around the corner at a rapid pace, its headlights blazing at them head-on. Illuminated in the harsh beams of light, Agnes froze, her pink outfit glowing, and a long sticklike shadow crawled down the cement slope from her skinny figure. Holding her arms out straight in locked position, knees bent in firing stance, she squeezed off a few rounds. A spider web of cracks appeared on the car's windshield.

Paul was momentarily blinded by the brightness, and only the sound of the engine racing warned him that the car was coming at them at full speed.

The station wagon seemed to rise up as it hit the fence, then the chain link came crashing down beneath it, and the car jounced against the cement embankment as it landed back on the ground. As the driver regained control of the careening vehicle and directed it toward her, Agnes held her stance and repeatedly fired into the windshield. A series of webs spread across the glass, but it kept coming.

She screamed as the car struck her and her body sailed through the air. For a moment it seemed to hang there, nightmarish, then her broken body hit the concrete ten feet away with a hollow thud.

Estes let out a guttural cry of anguish and Paul lunged for his gun. Paul wrestled for control of it as Estes kept pulling the trigger. A bullet shied off the concrete, letting off a sharp twang, then something hot and piercing burned in Paul's thigh and he knew he'd been hit. Out of the corner of his eye he saw the station wagon swerve and lurch to a halt, the passenger side facing them, and the driver's door flew open. Blake tumbled out and crouched behind the hood, using the car for cover.

"Paul, get back," Blake shouted. "I have a clean shot."

Paul head-butted Estes to stun him, released his grip on the gun, and stumbled a few feet backward toward the water. Estes blindly shot off a round in the direction of the car, then pivoted toward Paul and fired wildly. As Paul dove into the river a bullet whizzed past his ear. For a moment the shock of frigid water swirling around him, deep and tumultuous, made him forget everything else except the instinct to survive. Submerged, he gulped the brackish stew and something struck him hard in the foot, then slipped away, and he was reminded that branches and other debris could move with fatal speed when the river was engorged with runoff.

He came up for air, breaking the roiling surface, coughing and choking and spitting. His eyes stung but he could see Estes crouched in firing stance unloading his gun in a barrage of fire at the station wagon. And then the fusillade was over and his gun went click, click, click.

"You're done, Estes," Blake called from behind the hood of the station wagon. "Drop it and put up your hands."

Estes let his gun fall and it clattered to the pavement. Blake rose from behind the car, and came around the front, pointing his gun. "You heard me, hands up."

Slowly Estes raised his hands, still crouching, watching Blake approach, then in one swift move snatched a pistol holstered at his ankle.

A spit of fire erupted from Blake's gun, and Estes flinched as the pistol jumped from his hand and fell, skidding a foot on the ground.

Blake moved in closer in quick strides. "Step away from it, Estes."

At first Estes didn't move. He seemed to focus on the dirty pink form that might have passed for refuse not far from the car. Something twisted in his face and he lunged for the pistol and came up firing. Blake commenced to empty his gun into him and Estes tripped backward, clutching his chest as his weapon dropped to the ground. He teetered for a moment, then another bullet ripped through him, and he staggered a few feet to the river, spun around by the force of another round and fell face first into the water. Current splashed around him, and his head bobbed on the surface for only a moment, then he was pulled under and swept away downstream.

Paul paddled to the river's edge and climbed on the concrete bank. Water streamed off him. He winced as he tried to stand and collapsed to the ground. Blake came rushing up.

"I can't walk," Paul croaked, panting for breath.

Blake bent down beside him and examined his leg gravely.

"My ankle hurts like hell."

"It's all puffed up. It might be broken. But you're bleeding on your thigh."

"He got me. I think it went clear through."

"Can you keep the pressure on it until I get back? There's got to be a phone somewhere around here where I can call for help."

Paul pressed his palms firmly against the dark red spots on the front and back of his thigh. "I'll be okay. Go ahead." His teeth started to chatter and his whole body began to shiver uncontrollably.

Blake got up, hesitated, then bent down and cupped Paul's cheeks in his hands and kissed him on the lips. "I love you," he said.

Then he headed at a fast clip up the slope.

# Chapter 14

Blake stayed with him until he was out of surgery, then left to make out his report at Parker Center downtown. Paul's ankle was badly sprained but at least it wasn't broken and he wouldn't need a cast, although he would be walking with a crutch for the next few weeks. The doctors had sewed up the holes in his leg and a dull pain emanated from his thigh.

The hospital had turned quiet in the late evening and Paul had dozed off by the time a nurse flipped the lamp in his room off. He woke sometime later to find Marvin Botwinick poking his head in the doorway, standing in the carpet of light from the hall, scratching his beard.

"I warned you to watch out for the Chandlers."

Paul grinned sleepily. "You and Balzac."

Botwinick came in and plopped into a chair by the bed. He didn't turn on the light and they spoke in the dimness. "So I understand you have quite a story to tell me." He took his pipe out, seemed to think better of it, and tucked it back in his jacket pocket. He had a pad in his hand and opened it to a clean page.

Paul told him everything that had happened that night, filling in all the details he knew about the case, with Marvin often interrupting with questions, all in the deprecating banter that had developed between the two of them over the years.

After Paul was done, Botwinick just nodded. "You know that Agnes Chandler is dead. They should find Estes' body in the river once the sun rises. Bodies usually snag on something on their way to the ocean. He'll be found. I have another question for you, though. Did Estes name any of the downtown businessmen in the conspiracy?"

Paul shook his head. "Marvin, I don't think we're ever going to be able to touch those people. Without that tape, we have no proof of their involvement." He sighed. "Even if we had it, I'm not sure what it would prove."

"So it ends here."

Paul could hear the disappointment in the reporter's voice.

"But you have evidence they contributed to Durkin's campaign, right? And you have records to show their taxes went down."

"Enough to raise questions, not enough to put them behind bars," Botwinick said. "It doesn't prove *they* did anything wrong. We need evidence there was an exchange, campaign donations for tax breaks. We need that tape."

"You can still say there was a conspiracy of downtown business interests even if you can't name names."

"No," Botwinick said. "The *Times* won't print it. Not until I have unassailable proof. Even Otis and Dorothy, who didn't particularly have any love for Buck and Agnes, won't be happy about the family being dragged through the mud. Anything that taints the new Music Center is going to have a hard time seeing the light of day. At least I understand why Agnes talked Buck into donating to the Music Center at the last minute."

Paul's eyes narrowed. "Why?"

"It was insurance. Agnes figured if the conspiracy was ever exposed Otis Chandler would have a very hard time allowing coverage of it in the newspaper if some of the money gained in the tax scam had gone directly to his mother's dream project." He shook his head wearily, took out his pipe, looked at it absently, then stuffed it back in his pocket. "No, Paul, I have to be very careful on this one, I've got to dot every i and cross every t before I submit anything to my editor. No specific proof the big boys downtown were involved, no conspiracy story."

Paul abruptly sat up straight in bed. The mention of the tape moments before suddenly brought a shard of memory back to him. He recalled the strange look on Estes' face when Paul had accused him of killing Clayton Biggs on the beach. He had gotten something wrong in his theory of the murder, but he couldn't figure out what. If he could, he realized, maybe it would lead him to the tape.

Marvin tilted his head at him. "What? You look like you just saw a ghost."

Easing back onto a pile of stuffed pillows, Paul shook his head. "Nothing. I'm just trying to figure out where that tape could be."

"Well," Botwinick said, getting up. "I guess I've got a story to write. At least part of one. I'd better get to it." He went to the door, then hesitated there, silhouetted against the light from the hall. He took a step back into the room.

"You know, we've known each other, what, ten years now? I really like you, you know that, but I feel like I don't know you very well. It's like you keep a part of yourself at a distance." He glanced at the floor for a moment, as if he was trying to fit together what he had to say, then looked back at Paul. "I've always thought a person's personal life is his own business, you know? I wouldn't bring it up, but, well, it's just something I want you to know."

"Sure," Paul said stiffly, suddenly tense. He was glad the dimness of the room provided cover. He was glad there wasn't enough light for Marvin to see the expression on his face. "I guess I'd better try to get some rest," he said finally. "Good night, Marvin."

Botwinick stood there, as if he wanted to say something more, then took a step back, his eyes dropping again to the floor. "I'll stop by tomorrow." At the door he hesitated one more time before he disappeared down the hall. "You'll make a great D.A., Paul."

David stood in the doorway to Paul's room for a long time, listening to the slow familiar cadence of his breath. It was a sound he had lain awake listening to for as long as he could remember. Even when Paul snored, as he did sometimes in the moments just after he fell asleep, David had never roused him so he could get to sleep himself; it had always been a comfort, just knowing that Paul was there in the darkness by his side.

He came into the room, closing the door so only a crack of light shone on the floor, and went over to the bed. He stood looking down as Paul slept. There was a bandage on his cheek. An IV pole with a hanging bag towered nearby, a tube slipping under the covers beside Paul's arm. David gently put his palm on Paul's forehead. Warm to the touch, with beads of sweat. He saw a bowl of water with a wash cloth on the nightstand, dipped the towel and wrung it out. He placed the cool towel on Paul's forehead, then pulled up a chair and sat beside him, holding his hand. A little later he took the cloth off and felt Paul's forehead. Whatever fever he might have had was gone.

He heard a nurse walk by down the hall, her heels echoing, and then it was quiet again. Somehow holding Paul's hand and sitting beside his bed wasn't enough. Soundlessly David slipped onto the bed and curled next to him, snuggling at his side, draping Paul's arm around him. His head rested on the hospital gown covering Paul's chest.

He lay there a long while before he raised his head and looked at Paul, the contours of his face barely visible, pale highlights painting his features in the darkness. David wondered if this was the last time they would ever lie together and the thought made his body shake in a convulsive sob and tears came to his eyes. He gripped his hand hard over his mouth to stifle the sound, and fought to control the emotions welling up from within. Soon he felt calm returning and he trusted himself enough to take his hand from his mouth. He felt a lump form in his throat but he had to say it. He had to say it out loud even though he knew no one would hear.

"You're the only man I ever loved," he whispered, his voice coming out ragged. "The only one."

As if in response Paul shifted in his sleep, breathing slowly and regularly next to him.

Then David laid his head back down on Paul's chest, the beat of his heart softly pounding in his ear. He felt peaceful there, as he always had, in the crook of Paul's arm. In no time he was fast asleep.

Paul woke just after dawn. Groggy with sleep, his bearings still rooted in dreams, he felt David's warmth next to him, as he had more mornings than he could count. Because it was second nature to him, he reached over to pull him closer, only to realize with a start he was alone in a strange bed. He blinked, disoriented, and patted the rumpled covers at his side. Only a patch of warmth remained there, as if a ghost had come to visit him in the night, and a pervasive sense of loss settled over him.

He became aware of the IV tube in his arm and the ache in his thigh, and the events of the previous night came flooding back to him, reassembling quickly in his mind, and his confusion began to lift.

His throat was dry and he felt the lethargy of someone who has slept too long or too little. But more than anything, a nagging thought kept pecking in his head, and a plague of dreams that had troubled his sleep returned to him in bits and pieces. None of them had made any sense, a jumble of thoughts and memories and people, but in every one he was on the beach, yet somehow far from it. He had that sinking feeling again of unfinished business, that he and Blake had gotten it all wrong when they'd theorized about where Clayton Biggs had been killed.

He was sure of one thing. Clayton Biggs hadn't died on the beach. The expression on Dean Estes' face the night before when Paul had brought up his death had convinced him of that. But if not the beach...

Paul sat up in bed. Suddenly he understood. The tape. It was there. It had been there all along. He winced at the pain in his leg as he turned toward the nightstand and grabbed for the phone.

Fog rolled in thick and moist from the ocean and behind the mist the sun shown as a luminescent white pearl in the sky. A chill morning breeze swept in off the water and Paul shivered. He could hear the lapping waves but the ocean was lost in the enveloping shroud.

"What are we looking for?" Blake scuffed his shoe in the dirt on the shoulder of the Pacific Coast Highway. Northbound traffic whizzed past them too close for comfort and it was hard to say if drivers just didn't see the two men at the roadside or if they took a certain glee whipping by in such proximity.

"Blood." He had been advised against leaving the hospital, but Paul was far too excited at the moment to follow doctor's orders. He leaned on the crutch, and tried to keep his swollen foot in the air.

"You think they beat Clayton Biggs here, then dragged him over to the water?"

Paul walked farther down the highway, hobbling along on his crutch.

"They didn't beat him. He fell. From the top of the cliff. That's why his nose was broken and his chest was crushed. That's why he had lacerations on his hands and face and his clothes were torn." He stopped. "This could be the spot."

Dark stains soiled the rocky landscape. Squinting his eyes, Paul scanned the rough sandstone surface of the cliff. There was something different in the area just above them, a barely discernible path where scrub was bent and plants hung from their roots. It was hard to tell, but they looked like possible skid marks made on the way down.

"When he fell, his body must have hit several times as he tumbled down. Maybe he tried to grab on to plants but nothing broke the fall until he hit bottom."

Blake picked up a sharp stone on the ground and observed it carefully.

"Yeah, that's blood."

Paul gazed straight up to where the man-sized aloe perched on the edge of the cliff, now covered in a silky mist of fog. "That's about the point where he parked his car, right?"

"Yeah. So how do you think it all went down?"

Paul tried to put the pieces of his theory together in his mind starting from the beginning. "After he got the tape from us on the freeway he called Dean Estes with the good news. They agreed to meet late at night at the park, when no one else was around."

Blake nodded. "Undoubtedly Estes expected Biggs to turn over the tape. But that's not the way it played out."

"I think it finally dawned on Biggs just what he had gotten his hands on. No more petty blackmail stuff. No more little payoffs from husbands caught going to hookers or old men caught buying dirty pictures. He had the attention of the movers and shakers who run this city."

"So what happened between the time he parked his car and ended up down here?"

"I guess we'll never know for sure. But I figure Biggs realized at the last minute bringing the tape to the meeting wasn't such a good idea. He tucked the tape inside his jacket or in the back of his pants so Estes didn't know he had it on him."

Blake continued the thought. "Estes didn't like being double-crossed and he wasn't about to pay more money. They fight and Biggs goes over the edge."

Nodding, Paul said, "Estes races to the bottom of the cliff, but doesn't find the tape on Biggs' body. He disposes of the corpse in the ocean, figuring it will wash out to sea, then checks the car but doesn't find the tape there either. It never occurs to him that Biggs had it on him until he went over the edge and the tape fell somewhere on the cliff when he went down. It's been waiting there for someone to find it."

"Only thing that bothers me about this theory is that I don't think Estes would have deliberately killed him without getting his hands on the tape first."

"What, you think killing Biggs was an accident?"

Blake shrugged. "Let's go up and have a look."

They walked back to the pool club parking lot across the highway.

"How is your leg?"

"My thigh is fine. They patched me up pretty good. I guess I'll have a couple of scars. But it's my ankle that really hurts. I don't need a cast, but they wrapped it up tight with bandages."

Blake slid into the driver's seat of a bright new Buick he'd rented while his Ford wagon was in the shop for repairs, while Paul maneuvered into the passenger side, angling his crutch from the foot well into the back. Fog swirled around the windows and it seemed like they were the only people left in the world. Blake sat for a moment before starting the car. Something seemed to be on his mind. He didn't look at Paul when he spoke.

"That thing I said last night, before I went for help. I meant it."

Paul didn't say anything as Blake turned the key and pulled the car onto the highway, but something akin to fireworks exploded in his chest. He put his hand on Blake's knee and squeezed.

They parked at the top of the cliff in the spot where Biggs had left his car and walked across the narrow strip of palm-laden park to the edge of the bluff.

"Unless we find that tape," Paul said, "the trail ends with Dean Estes and Agnes Chandler. The rest of them will get away with it." He leaned against the cement fence, fashioned in a split-rail design. Next to them giant aloe rose up above their heads.

"Are we really sure the rest of them had anything to do with the murders?" Blake asked. "I mean, it's clear they went along with the whole tax scam, but I'm thinking Estes was such a hot-head he probably took it into his own hands to knock off Wesley Durkin and then order Biggs to hunt down Roland Mosley. I have a feeling the big guys didn't want to know any of the details, they just wanted the results."

"We'll let a jury figure that out. If we can find the tape, at least we can get them on the graft, even if we can't pin them to the murders."

Blake climbed over the cement fence and stood on the precipice, gazing down into the misty abyss.

"I can't even see the Pacific Coast Highway down there, the fog is so thick."

"The tape is probably still in the shopping bag. Look for something white, caught in the branches of scrub or the cactus plants growing out of the cliff."

Crouching down, Blake ran his hand across the ground. "Look here, the earth has recently fallen away at the edge."

"You think Estes held him there, threatening to toss him over if he didn't tell him where the tape was, and the ground gave way?"

"It would explain things."

Blake tested the strength of the branches of a bush overhanging the cliff, then gripped tight and began to lower himself down. In a moment his head disappeared and Paul could hear his progress as Blake kicked at the side of the cliff to gain footholds in the sandstone as he went down.

"Be careful," Paul called after him. He waited nervously at the fence counting the seconds.

"I see something," Blake exclaimed a few minutes later. "If I can just..."

Paul leaned as far as he could over the fence but couldn't see anything but layers of fog. He could hear rustling in the branches of a bush.

"I found it!" Blake shouted.

It was an eerie experience listening to the voice of Wesley Durkin. Paul had possibly heard him speak once or twice before on television, although county assessors were rarely quoted for the evening news. Durkin was better known since his reported suicide than he ever had been during his tenure in office. But hearing him now, knowing he was deliberately recording himself in an attempt to break free from the people who had shackled him with a LAPD surveillance report and bought and paid for his political success, added poignancy to every word he spoke. Paul remembered Roland Mosley recounting the evening when Durkin had confided he had a plan to blow the whole thing wide open and a lot of powerful people were going to get burned. But all it had brought was untimely death for both of them.

"Listen to him," Paul said in a low voice. "Listen to what he's doing."

As the reel whined on the tape recorder, they heard the dead man speak.

"But look, Mr. Barnes—Charlie—you know a lot about this kind of thing—you're the president of the California Real Estate Association, for God's sakes. We simply can't sustain this overtaxing of certain areas of the city in order to give you all personal and business tax breaks without getting caught...."

Blake nodded. "He's making sure every person at that meeting he called in his house is specifically identified, both first name and last. He's even slipping in the names of their companies or the positions they hold, and that they financially benefitted from their contributions to his campaign by getting tax breaks."

They listened to Charlie Barnes' reply, who insisted the group's tax cuts continue, that they had donated big money for the assessor's consideration, and Paul knew that Durkin had utterly nailed him on tape. Then Durkin went after another, and another, always speaking naturally, but fitting in the pertinent information needed for a conviction.

"...and Mr. Holder—I was able to cut taxes for your company, Holder Enterprises, last year, but Jack, don't you see how it's too much to expect me to do it year after year, even with all the money you contributed to my campaign...."

"So what's next?" Blake asked.

"It's time to hand this over to the D.A.," Paul said.

Paul met with District Attorney Bulgetti in his office late Wednesday morning and gave him the tape.

"Take good care of it. It's the only proof we have to nail these bastards."

"We'll get them, Paul, don't worry."

"Without Wesley Durkin able to testify to its authenticity, we could still have problems using the tape in court. Their defense attorneys will do everything they can to quash it. I think our best bet is trying to get one of the defendants to turn on the others and corroborate everything Durkin recorded that night."

Paul agreed reluctantly that his involvement in the case and the fact that he would undoubtedly be called as a witness precluded him from prosecuting the members of the conspiracy.

Bulgetti walked him to the door, one hand resting on his protruding belly, the other lightly on Paul's shoulder. "How's the leg?"

He leaned on his crutch. "It'll heal."

"Take as much time off as you need. I want you fresh for next Wednesday."

Paul paused by the door. "Next Wednesday?"

"The day I announce my resignation. The day you announce your candidacy for Los Angeles District Attorney."

◇◇◇

Paul had looked forward to taking the rest of the week off, but as he lounged around his house that afternoon, he found himself restless and unsettled. After the driven life he had led since law school, playing the invalid even for a few days wore thin fast. Blake was down at Parker Center being grilled again, this time by higher-ups: the violent deaths of a member of one of the city's most influential families and the high-ranking head of a police division required careful public relations management. Paul didn't envy Blake, but he knew he could handle it. They had the law on their side.

He had slept off and on, which never quite relieved his exhaustion, and the ache in his thigh had come back. But the worst part of his convalescence was not knowing what to do with the time he had off. Nothing seemed to be on television except soap operas. He had always depended on David to recommend books for him to read, and he couldn't find anything on his shelf that piqued his interest. Finally he spotted several magazines David subscribed to, sometimes delivered in plain brown wrapping, in a rack by the console.

He lay on the couch, his leg raised and resting on a cushion, and flipped absently through the pages of a copy of *ONE Magazine*. David had stopped volunteering at the periodical years ago, deeming it too conservative for his evolving politics, but he'd kept his subscription. Paul recalled how the magazine had been seized by postal inspectors on obscenity charges in 1954, and the case had wound all the way to the Supreme Court, which ruled in 1958 that merely having homosexual subject matter did not make a publication obscene, and such periodicals could legally be sent through the mail. While homophile activists hailed the ruling as a great victory and predicted a proliferation of gay publications, in the ensuing years journalistic magazines with gay subject matter remained few, with limited circulation.

He picked up a copy of *Tangents*, which had been founded by L.A. activists dissatisfied with the timid direction of *ONE*. Paul read an article, "Raid!," detailing the bust at the Black Cat on Saturday night, and he felt his ire began to rise. He had never pictured the level of police brutality that night and what David had been through. The wildness in David's eyes and his disheveled hair and the bruise on his neck after the police raid came back to him; the night everything between them had begun to fall apart.

Next he read a copy of the newsletter David was involved in, *PRIDE*. It seemed amateurish in comparison with the others, which were professionally printed, but far more dynamic. It could be mimeographed quickly, and distributed immediately whenever the community needed to be informed. It spoke in a voice seldom heard before, radical and aggressive. Unapologetic. Still, at a few pages, it didn't seem like much. But then, Paul thought for the first time—who knew?—maybe this little rag would amount to something some day.

He grew drowsy again and his eyes drifted to the afghan draped over the back of the couch that David's grandmother had knitted. When he remembered that David planned to come by at the end of the week to pick it up, a veil of melancholy descended over him. He idly fingered the intricate pattern. He wondered if David had heard what had happened to him last night. The story of his kidnapping and the shootout at the L.A. River had been emblazoned in banner headlines in all the morning papers. You couldn't miss it. He must know. Paul knew it wasn't fair to expect anything from him, but it hurt that he hadn't called. Even after everything that had happened between them. Everybody else had. But then, maybe David just didn't care anymore. Why should he? Paul had to admit he had treated his lover shabbily, probably the worst he'd treated anybody in his entire life, when David had never done anything but love him.

When he closed his eyes to take a nap he discovered his lashes were wet with tears.

# Chapter 15

Paul was relieved when he got a call from D.A. Bulgetti Thursday morning asking him to drop by his office at noon. At least it would get him out of the house.

He wondered if the conspirators caught on the tape had been arrested already; he had agreed with the D.A. to withhold their names from reporters—and in Paul's case, that included Marvin Botwinick, even though Bulgetti wasn't privy to their relationship. If the identities of the conspirators broke in the press before they were rounded up and in police custody, it might allow some of them to slip out of the country. Botwinick was a friend and Paul trusted him, but being ahead of the crowd on a story like this might prove too much of a temptation.

Blake had cooked him dinner the night before and Paul had been genuinely surprised at how good it was.

"I can only cook two things," Blake had said with a grin as he was cleaning up the mess he'd made in the kitchen. "Be warned."

"Well," Paul had countered, leaning on his crutch and giving Blake a kiss, "There are probably five dishes I can cook, so we can last at least a week."

Blake had already left by the time Paul got dressed for his visit with the D.A.; he had another appointment with the police shrink, but promised to meet Paul in front of the D.A.'s Office for lunch after they were both done.

It was very quiet in the D.A.'s inner sanctum when his secretary ushered Paul inside. He stood before Bulgetti leaning on his crutch, wondering why he had been called in. The District Attorney, immersed in paperwork, didn't seem to notice him at first, and he didn't look up from his mammoth desk when he finally spoke.

"Why don't you go to the conference room down the hall? Room 306. I'll meet you there in a few minutes."

"Tony, what's going on?"

Bulgetti's eyes rose from his desk to Paul's. He pushed his reading glasses down his nose. "I said I would be there in a few minutes."

Paul sensed immediately that something was wrong as he went through the outer office and down the wide echoing corridor to the conference room. His first thought was that politics had somehow intervened and Blake might be in trouble for what had occurred at the L.A. River. He had taken down a powerful commander in the LAPD and killed a well-connected society matron. But Paul was sure everything he had done was clean. The perpetrators had kidnapped a deputy district attorney in order to execute him and hide their previous crimes of blackmail and murder. Blake had acted in self-defense and to stop the brutal killing of a public servant. Undoubtedly Blake wouldn't be popular with the brass in the department who had called Estes a friend and colleague for years, and unquestionably there would be pressure from powerful forces like Buck Chandler claiming his wife's innocence and laying the blame for everything that had happened at Blake's feet. But whether it was naïve to think so or not, the D.A.'s Office was supposed to be a bastion against such political pressure.

When Paul stepped in the doorway of the conference room all his previous anxiety about Blake being made the fall guy in all this vanished. He just stood there for a long moment letting what he saw in front of him sink in. Twelve men sat at an extended table looking at him, as if they had been waiting for him to arrive before they began.

They were the men behind the voices on the tape.

At the center of the table sat Charlie Barnes, with his balding red hair and scattered freckles. He seemed to be the one in charge. Paul recognized other movers and shakers from downtown that he had met at the party at Chasen's. But the smiles and the friendly handshakes and the cocktail glasses were gone.

"What's going on?" Paul demanded. He began to match the voices on the tape with the faces in front of him.

"Sit down, Mr. Winters."

Paul stepped farther into the room but remained leaning on his crutch. "What are you doing here? Do you have the arrogance to think you can negotiate with me and this will all go away?"

"It's time we had a serious talk."

Paul's eyes scanned the group. "Everybody is here but Buck Chandler."

"I'm afraid Buck isn't feeling too well."

"You won't be, either, when I'm finished with you."

None of them said a word in response, instead they just watched him and to his bafflement Paul couldn't discern any emotion in their faces. Whatever they were experiencing, it didn't look like fear.

It was only then that he noticed each of the men had a folder lying in front of them at the table. Each folder carried the insignia of the LAPD. Barnes opened the file first and Paul could see the photograph of him and David on the first page, and his entire body involuntarily jolted and he almost lost his bearings. His fingers clutched tighter to his crutch to maintain his balance. The others at the table followed suit a moment later, and he remembered what he had suspected when he had opened the trunk of

Agnes Chandler's Mercedes and examined the dossiers inside. They had been copied for distribution.

There was no animosity in Charlie Barnes' voice when he continued. Paul had to hand it to him, he was a businessman first and foremost.

"I think we can come to some kind of understanding, don't you?"

Without a word Paul turned on his heel and hobbled out of the conference room and down the corridor. His mind was racing and his cheeks burned as he maneuvered around employees of the D.A.'s Office who were streaming out of their cubicles to go to lunch. He pushed his way through the door to Bulgetti's outer office.

The blonde secretary looked up and smiled. "The D.A. is on an important call, Mr. Winters, if you could just wait—"

Paul stormed past her, working his crutch like a piston, and threw open the inner office door.

The secretary scrambled up from her desk and came in after him, eyes wide and flustered. "I'm sorry, Mr. Bulgetti," she began, "I know you didn't want to be disturbed, but—"

From behind his desk Bulgetti said a few words into his phone then hung up. He took off his reading glasses and set them on his desk. His lips became a fine line.

"I'll take care of this, Patty. If you could just close the door behind you."

When she was gone Paul pointed his finger angrily at the door.

"What are those people doing in there? Why haven't they been arrested? Why aren't they in a holding cell right now? You heard what's on that tape, right?"

Bulgetti blinked.

"What tape?"

Paul gaped at him stupidly before the meaning of the District Attorney's words sank in. A sledgehammer blow to the chest couldn't have affected him more. The image of his mentor seemed to deteriorate before Paul's eyes and the man he had revered his entire professional life appeared to him as lower than a common criminal.

Paul briefly shut his eyes in dismay and a darkness like night came over him. Of course. It was Anthony Bulgetti who had introduced him to the Chandlers in the first place. It had all been carefully planned. They had searched for the individual they could control once Bulgetti left office, and they hadn't had to look far. Paul was the obvious candidate to run for District Attorney, and the information provided by the Intelligence Division showed that he fit perfectly the profile of the candidate they wanted to back.

"You bastard." Paul spit the words out. "What do they have on you?"

"What difference could that possibly make to you?"

"At least I would know what it took for you to sell me out."

Bulgetti leaned back in his upholstered leather chair. "I have a bit of a predilection for girls. I like them young. Not too young, understand. But one or two might have been underage."

Paul's mind scanned over what he recalled of the surveillance data they had on him. The photographs. The dates and times. David's regular overnight stays. If the file got out, he wondered if he would be disbarred. No, there wasn't enough evidence against him in the file. At least he was safe there. But he would be tarnished. Word would spread. Running for office would be out of the question. Even without proof of criminal sexual activity, his career in the big leagues would effectively be over. The prestigious law firms that would have vied for his attention if he chose to leave the prosecutor's office would turn their backs on him now.

"Go back to the conference room, Paul. I want you to take a long and hard look at your career and where you want to be in another year. It's not so bad working with these people. In fact, you can't do it alone. Not in today's political climate. You can have it all, if you want it. Or you can have nothing. When you get right down to it, I guess there isn't that much to think over after all, is there?"

Something exploded in Paul's head and when he spoke his voice came out a growl.

"I don't care what it costs me. I'm going to bring you all down."

The District Attorney sighed. He put his glasses back on and went back to the work on his desk. "You have no proof of anything, remember? And I'm afraid you'll find the personal cost of going against us to be rather high. You always had a melodramatic touch, even in your pros- ecutions. I used to find your final arguments rather em- barrassing. Effective, of course, considering the jury pool, I'll give you that. But you do have a weakness for emotion. If you'll just stick to the cold hard facts, I think you'll find there's a way everybody can be happy."

Paul turned to leave. The physical punishment he had endured at the L.A. River earlier seemed to hit him all at once and he felt like a defeated old man. His face was drained of color. It took all his concentration just to make his way to the door. He placed his hand on the knob.

"Paul?"

Paul slowly turned back to face him, his hand still on the doorknob. He could feel it tremble. Bulgetti pushed his glasses down his nose. His face was sympathetic.

"Have you thought about marrying your girl?"

Paul heard his voice come out dully as if someone else was speaking.

"No."

"You should, you know. Jeannie would make a very nice addition to your campaign. An important contribution. Sometimes having all the right components is more important in running for office than what you say in a stump speech. My wife has been an invaluable addition to my career."

"I don't think Jeannie swings the way you think she does."

Bulgetti's eyes met his and held. "All the better. Then you would understand one another. This can all work out Paul, if you let it."

Without saying another word Paul went out the door and closed it behind him. He passed through the D.A.'s outer office like an automaton. The secretary rose from behind her desk. "Mr. Winters, are you okay? Can I get you something?"

Paul walked on without hearing her. Once he reached the main corridor, he leaned against a wall and felt weak in the knees. His hand gripped his crutch tighter. He felt numb. He found himself looking down the hallway both ways, to the right and then to the left.

The conference room lay in one direction, the elevators in the other.

Dr. Stone observed him from behind his desk with a benevolent expression on his face.

"I'm surprised you showed up for your appointment considering what I've read about you in the papers. Are you all right?"

After crushing a cigarette in an ash tray beside his chair, Blake sank back into the thick leather cushions and lit up another Chesterfield. "They've put me on leave pending an investigation. But I have every reason to believe I'll be cleared of any wrongdoing."

"Still, if you don't feel up to it…."

Blake blew a plume of smoke toward the ceiling. "I just want to get this over with and get back on the Homicide table."

"Very well. Now, if I can recall how we left it at our last session…"

Blake felt his stomach tense and he wondered what the doctor was up to. He had seen Stone studying his file when he came in; the doctor knew precisely what they had discussed. "I think you were suggesting ways I could manage my anger."

"Was that what we were talking about? Funny, that's not how I remember it. I seem to recall discussing how you don't believe your personal life reflects on your job performance."

"Well, I guess we may have. I already said this is about me punching my commanding officer and that's it. I'll apologize to him, if that's what it takes. It would be hard for them to justify not bringing me back when I was right about Wesley Durkin's death and everybody else was wrong."

Dr. Stone watched him without saying anything and an uncomfortable silence developed between them. Finally the doctor spoke.

"In regards to your private life I think you said all you cared about was getting your son back."

Blake was becoming annoyed. Dr. Stone was like a broken record, always coming back to the same spot. "That's right."

"I believe you said your son means everything to you."

"Yes."

"And we concluded the quickest way to get your boy back was to reconcile with your wife."

"That's what you concluded. I told you Cathy and me are finished." He threw up his hands in exasperation. "Why don't we just move on? I got nothing to say about this."

Dr. Stone's eyes seemed to beam into his.

"And you told me you weren't in a new relationship."

Blake didn't answer, but he felt his Adam's apple jump. He averted his gaze, fixing his sights on the cigarette in his hand.

Stone leaned back in his chair. "You've been lying to me all along, haven't you?"

"I don't know what you mean."

"Yes you do. The prosecutor. From before. From ten years ago."

Blake said nothing but he felt his face grow warm.

"Has this been going on all along? Have you been seeing him all this time?"

Blake shook his head but continued to stare at his cigarette. "What, you mean ten years? No, of course not. I met up with him again last Saturday."

"Last Saturday. Do you believe your behavior has been conducive to getting your son back?"

Blake's eyes narrowed. Finally he met the doctor's gaze. "I don't understand."

"Do you think family court will give you visitation rights to see your boy if you keep doing what you're doing?"

It was an issue he hadn't even considered, and it hit him with a wave of anxiety.

"It's none of their goddamned business."

"They may think differently. What about your wife? You think she'll ever let you see your son if you carry on like that?"

He thought about Cathy. She wouldn't understand. If anything, it would just make things worse between them.

She could make trouble. She was mad enough at him to make trouble.

Dr. Stone studied him. "Under the present circumstances, what kind of a father do you think you could be to him?"

"I'm a good father," Blake replied defensively, sitting up straight.

"I wonder. I wonder how you could be a good role model for your son."

"I'm a good dad," Blake said, his voice rising. "I always have been."

"Perhaps. Perhaps when you and your wife were together and a family." Stone looked doubtful. "And you'd toss it all aside for someone you've known less than a week."

They didn't have anything to say to each other for several minutes. Blake stared out the window, anger stirring within, but there was a kernel of fear, too, and he knew it would only grow. He wished the hour would pass.

Finally the doctor sighed wistfully. "It's always a sad thing when a family breaks apart. I bet she loves you more than anything in the world."

"That's how little you know."

"I can help you," Stone said. "I can help you fight it. You're not like them, don't you know that in your heart? You never could be one of them. I've helped countless men like you, lost and confused men who just needed to be shown the way." He leaned forward in his chair and behind his glasses zeal flickered in his hazel eyes. "I guarantee you in six months you won't even be thinking of him. It will all be forgotten like a bad dream from long ago."

"You don't get it, do you?" Blake blurted out. "I'm in love with him. I'm going to love him until the day I die."

The doctor seemed taken aback, as if Blake had gotten up and slapped him across the mouth. "Don't say that. You know it isn't true. You know it can't be true."

"I'm in love with him," Blake said forcefully, jabbing his cigarette in the air, "and I'm going to be with him. I've thrown away years of my life and I'm not going to do it anymore. And I've hurt people. I hurt Cathy. I hurt her in a way no one should ever be hurt."

Stone's lip twisted. "You don't even know what love is. How could you? You think what you do with him, you think *that* is love?"

Blake mashed his cigarette in the tray. "I don't have to put up with this. Go fuck yourself, Doctor. I'm getting back on the Homicide table whether you recommend it or not. I'm done here." He began to rise from his seat.

The phone rang and Dr. Stone said, "Wait a minute." He picked up the receiver and pushed a button. "Has it come through?" he asked. To Blake, he said, "I put a call in to Wisconsin."

"You shouldn't have done that. I don't want to talk to her."

"Okay," Stone said into the phone. "Yes, just wait a moment please." He put his hand over the mouthpiece and held it out for Blake. "It's for you."

Blake stood angrily in front of the desk and shook his head, waving the phone away.

"I told you I don't want to talk to her now. I don't have anything to say. I'm not getting back together with her. I only want to see my son. If she wants a divorce, she can have a divorce."

Dr. Stone held out the phone as if he hadn't heard a word, and Blake snatched it from him irritably.

"Cathy, I'm sorry," he began, "he shouldn't have call—"

And then he heard the voice on the other end and he stopped. He felt a rush of tears to his eyes and when he responded his voice broke.

"Tommy?" He felt a lump form in his throat. "Tommy, is that you?"

Blake couldn't be sure, but he thought he detected a gleam of triumph in Dr. Stone's eyes.

Leaning against the wall, his mind slowly clearing, Paul knew what he had to do. He had neglected to tell his boss a simple fact: while he and Blake had listened to Durkin's tape, they had been making a copy on the recorder David had left at his place. It was the evidence Marvin Botwinick's editor would insist on before publishing the story. Paul knew it was a path of mutually assured destruction and once he started down it there would be no turning back.

He had spent his whole life fighting for small victories in a corrupt system, trying to make things better, convincing himself he made a difference. But now the very justice system he had so fiercely defended would turn on him. After years of playing the game, he saw now it had been for nothing. It made him angry. David had been right, he had been right about so many things.

Once he went ahead with this, the life he had known would essentially be over and he didn't know what would take its place. But in the end, he had no choice. Not really. If the death of Wesley Durkin had taught him anything, it was that the price of having your dreams come true could be too steep, and the compromises you made along the way could be deadly as any bullet.

Paul pushed away from the wall he had been leaning against and followed the throngs of secretaries, paralegals and attorneys disgorging from their offices and crowding around the elevators on their way to lunch. He didn't look back at the conference room in the opposite direction. They would get theirs. The first thing he would do was put in a call to Marvin Botwinick.

He flowed with the tide through the open elevator doors into the car and felt others press in tight around him. Something in the corner of his eye drew his attention as the elevator began to descend and he stretched his neck to see better around the bobbing faces with their chattering voices.

A man in a trench coat in the corner looked agonizingly familiar, and though a hat was pulled down to obscure his face, warning signals touched off in Paul's head and he immediately became alarmed. He had put away many gangsters and murderers in his career, but he didn't think for a moment that this man was one of them. For the life of him he couldn't figure out who it was, and yet he was sure he had been in the man's presence only yesterday....

And then, the cloying scent of a cheap cologne met his nose and a sick sensation flooded his stomach.

Before he could utter a word the elevator reached the first floor and the passengers poured out. As he was herded forward Paul felt a hard nudge in his ribs and heard the voice and there was no doubt whom it was.

"Just walk slow or I blow you away right here. Nice and slow."

"Like I could do anything else. Thanks for the hole in my leg. Where are we going?"

"Your car."

Paul's Thunderbird was parked in the lot, but Blake had told him he'd be waiting out front so they could go to lunch together. Paul squinted at the brightness of the sun once they exited the building. The gun in Estes' trench coat pocket prodded his side. After a week of dry windless days the sky had lost its startling blue. Smudges of mustard yellow were building steadily at the horizon. Downtown traffic on the street was slow, edging along, and the smell of exhaust fumes permeated the air. As they walked, Paul scanned the curb for Blake's rental car. His hope was that Blake would see them first and realize Paul was in trouble.

Paul glanced over at Estes. His face, what Paul could see of it under the brim of his hat, was covered in sweat. He looked sick as a dog.

"You don't look so good."

"You won't either when I'm done."

Paul's heart sank when he saw Blake leaning against the bright new Buick engrossed in a newspaper. By the time he looked up Estes had already spotted him. Blake looked preoccupied but smiled at first, then his face fell when he recognized Paul's companion.

"This is a nice surprise," Estes said, as they approached Blake. "Both of you, get in the car."

They did as they were ordered, Paul on the passenger side and Blake at the wheel. Estes slipped in the back door behind Blake and sat heavily. He pulled his pistol from his trench coat pocket. His suit jacket was open and his shirt was wet with sweat.

"Drive," he said.

Paul angled his crutch the best he could between him and Blake, the staff with the crosspiece for his armpit poking into the back seat area. He looked over his shoulder at Estes.

"How many holes do you have in you? If you want to live, you'd better be making us drive you to the hospital."

"I'm already dead, remember?"

Blake started the ignition and pulled into traffic, which was inching along toward the next stop light. He observed Estes from the rearview mirror.

"You're just making it worse for yourself when they catch you," he said.

222

"You forget, nobody's looking for me. The LAPD likes to close its cases. The official story will be my body washed out to sea."

"So where are we going?"

Estes waved his pistol. "Head for the freeway. You're going to drive me to Tijuana."

"And then?" Blake asked.

"And then I'm going to kill you both for what you did to Agnes."

They hadn't driven a mile on the freeway when the midday downtown traffic slowed to a halt.

Paul glanced over his shoulder. Estes was still holding the gun, but his head was bobbing as if he was having a hard time staying awake. Or alive. His face was gray as dishwater and beads of sweat covered his skin like a pox.

While Blake's foot was still on the brake, Paul reached over and squeezed his knee. Blake glanced over at him and their eyes locked. They nodded almost imperceptibly to each other.

*Now.*

Paul gripped his crutch and rammed it backward into Estes' neck then grabbed for the gun while Blake whirled around and pummeled his fists in Estes' face. Blake kept hitting him and his head rocked back and forth like a punching bag, the hat toppling off. The gun dropped into the foot well and Paul scrambled halfway over the seat to snatch it up.

"Don't kill him." Paul held the gun on Estes. "I think we're going to need him."

Blake stopped punching his face and Estes' head hung forward. He didn't move. The stiff posture that had distinguished him was gone; his whole body sagged. His shoulders, once military erect, seemed soft. Blake lifted up his head. His nose and cheeks were smeared with sweat and blood. His snake eyes were half closed. He looked to Paul like a corpse in a morgue.

"Is he dead?"

Paul waited while Blake pressed his finger on Estes' carotid. It was a long time before he answered.

"Not yet anyway."

# Chapter 16

The sun was low in the sky, the horizon aglow with brush strokes of red and orange, and the shimmering ocean took on the rich blues of late afternoon light. Dappled sunlight filtered through the leaves and branches hanging over the park bench, providing shade for their faces, but the rest of their bodies soaked in the warmth of the sun.

It had been a long time since either of them had said a word.

Blake slapped a cigarette out of a pack and lit up, glancing over at Paul, who sat beside him.

"There's got to be another way."

Paul gazed out to sea. His eyes hung on the graceful slivers of white sails against the field of blue.

"I wish there were."

"I want to get those bastards as much as you do, but if you give your reporter friend that tape, you know they're going to release that surveillance file to ruin your reputation."

Paul chuckled hollowly. "I think that's a safe bet."

Blake watched him for a moment, studying his face before he spoke. "But I thought you wanted to be the next D.A."

"I did. But that's not going to happen now."

Blake reached over and touched him on the knee, but withdrew his hand when an elderly couple strolled past on the path in front of them that ran along the edge of the cliff.

They listened to the birds chirping in the trees for a while. Blake stared at the ocean, wearing a troubled look. He seemed to be struggling internally about something he wanted to say.

"Something else is bothering you," Paul observed. "I can see it in your face. What is it?"

When Blake answered he didn't look at him. "I spoke with Tommy today."

Paul sat up straight on the bench. "But that's good, isn't it?"

"It was the first time since Cathy took him." He nodded to himself and he almost smiled. "He's okay, he's doing okay. He misses his daddy."

That pride that Paul had seen before, the way Blake's eyes lit up at the mention of his son, returned, but it was laced with something that left Paul uneasy.

What Blake said next sounded like a prepared speech. "I've made a reservation. I'm flying out tonight to Milwaukee. I'm going to ask Cathy if she'll come back to California. It's been her home for ten years now. She has friends here, a life. I'll let her have the house. She can have it all. I'll just get a little place close by. Just so I can see Tommy."

"Do you think she'll do it?"

"I don't know. I've got to give it a try."

"If you can convince her it's what's best for Tommy. No matter what's gone on between the two of you, I'm sure she doesn't want him to grow up without a father."

Blake nodded. "She's a good mother. She'll want what's best for him." He hesitated before continuing. His forearms rested on his thighs and he gazed down at his shoes. "Even if I can talk Cathy into moving back, it won't be easy. We've got to be careful. I know her. She'd never understand." Finally Blake looked at him with his deep blue eyes. "About us."

226

"Jim, I won't be able to put the genie back in the bottle. People are going to talk. That file on me is going to be out there. And it's going to get ugly if the defense lawyers have their way when I testify against those bastards. They're going to do everything they can to destroy me. Anyone I touch is going to be tainted."

"That's why we've got to be very careful," Blake said quickly. "We can still see each other. Whenever we can, you know, we'll get together."

Paul stared at him. "But I'm in love with you." Suddenly he regretted not telling him before when he had the chance. Saying it now seemed too little too late. It was as if a door had already closed before he had even known it was open.

"I love you, too. This doesn't change anything." He dropped his cigarette on the ground and stepped on it. "It's just... I can't let anything get in the way of getting Tommy back."

Paul shook his head. "I want us to have a life together. I want us to live together someday. I don't want to spend our whole lives fearing that someone will find out about us. Doesn't it make you angry, the way they treat us? The way they make us hide? The way they always make us live in fear?"

"I have a kid," Blake said testily. "And I want to see him again. I can't afford to be angry."

"But where does that leave us?"

"Paul, no one can ever know about us."

Paul remembered what David had said to him and he felt like he had been struck by a bolt of lightning.

*You only loved me when no one else was looking.*

The park seemed to reel around him and he couldn't get it out of his head. *When no one else was looking.* They could love one another when no one else was looking. The bitter taste of it caught in his throat and he couldn't swallow.

"I want to be with you every day," Paul protested. "And I want to be with you every night."

"We can't, Paul. You know we can't."

It struck him how little he would be settling for. Hardly more than an occasional, furtive roll in the hay. But then, in their ten years together, had he ever offered David much more than that? His mind was still in a daze when he remembered something else someone had said. *You and I... we don't want the same things...* And then he realized that he had said those words himself.

"Jim, seeing you once in a while, that isn't enough for me."

"If we screw up I could lose Tommy. They could take him away from me forever." Blake's eyes grew wet and his lower lip quivered. "Don't make me pick between the two of you."

"It's not between Tommy or me, it's about the kind of life we're going to live. I understand you have to be discreet, nobody gets that better than me. But I've spent my whole life lying and being afraid someone will find out. What a terrible way to live your life. I don't think I can do it anymore."

Blake rose from the bench and his voice came out angry. "You think anybody's going to let me see my kid ever again if we live together? What court is going to give me visitation rights if you and I are shacking up?"

His eyes dropped to the ground and Blake looked weary and beaten. "Look, I should go. I've still got to pack." He hesitated. When he continued his voice was barely audible. "I'll drop by your place on the way to the airport, okay?"

Paul didn't answer, but when Blake headed around the bench past him Paul caught his hand. Paul stared out to sea as he spoke.

"Don't go now. If you do I know you'll never come back."

Blake's big hand felt warm in his, his hold firm.

Then he felt Blake's hand slip from his and Paul knew he was gone. He sat there for a long time watching the ocean. The afternoon grew dimmer and colder. A chill breeze flapped in from the coast and sent a shiver through him.

The setting sun left a trail of blood in the sky.

He was finished packing. His suitcase lay open on the bedroom floor. Just a couple of changes of clothes and a winter coat to weather the forecast of snow that weekend in Wisconsin. He crouched down and closed the suitcase, laying his airplane ticket on top.

He told himself that he had to keep his mind on Tommy. He couldn't let himself think of anything else. He knew he could get through it if he could just keep his mind on what he had to do and what he had to say to talk Cathy into bringing Tommy back to L.A.

As he rose his eye caught on the safe squatting in the corner. He took a step toward it and stopped himself. He shouldn't be doing this, not now, not with the way he was feeling. There was only one thing he should be thinking about now. But as it had so many times before when he was alone in the house, the safe pulled him in with a force of gravity he found he couldn't resist.

He sat cross-legged in front of it, his fingers spinning the dial. He cranked out the combination and heard the familiar thunk of the mechanism inside and the door creaked open. He hesitated a moment before opening it further, taking a breath. And then he swung the door open wide.

The safe was empty save for two photographs lying on its floor.

He picked up the one on top and held it in his hands. It was a five-by-seven in a cardboard frame. A young man in a Navy uniform from over twenty years ago looked back at him, so handsome, so full of hope. He ran his finger across the young man's jaw line and a single tear rolled down Blake's cheek. He studied the photo for a long time. He didn't notice he was gently rocking back and forth.

Then he laid the photograph in his lap and took the other one from the safe. He gazed down at it and his lower lip began to tremble. It was a harshly lit black-and-white photo of two naked men caught in the act in the back seat of a car.

He realized opening the safe had been a mistake. He should have just grabbed his suitcase and left. He should have fought off the urge to open the safe, fought off the way it pulled at him and drew him in. Now that awful feeling was roiling up inside him. If he just didn't think about it. He could get through it if he just didn't think about it. But he couldn't get the memories out of his head of what it felt like to be with him, to hold him, to lie intertwined and fall asleep in his arms. The memories of what it felt like to love someone.

He quickly put the photos back in the safe and was about to slam the door, as if that would shut off the flood of memories, but before he could he heard a wail erupt from his throat and a deep racking sob shook his chest. Tears flowed from his eyes. He balled his hands into fists and pounded them against his forehead until he felt dizzy. Anything to shut out the memory and the terrible emptiness that seemed to be forcing its way inside him.

When he was too exhausted to strike himself anymore, he sat there dazed, hunched over, his head hanging, for a long while. Then slowly, wearily, he remembered he had a plane to catch and he got up and closed the safe and spun the dial.

He picked up his suitcase and headed for the front door.

◇◇◇

Marvin Botwinick's explosive exposé in the *Times* the next morning rocked the city.

Reaction from municipal leaders came swiftly, first condemnation of the plot, then promises of restitution for those who had been overtaxed and vows to prosecute the accused to the full extent of the law. Charlie Barnes, the president of the California Real Estate Association, committed suicide before the police could arrest him. His family insisted he was innocent and had ended his life because of a terminal cancer diagnosis. Buck Chandler's doctors promptly announced he suffered from dementia; he was placed in a rest home, and whatever his culpability in the affair, he seemed beyond the reach of the law. Others indicted hid behind a veil of lawyers who loftily proclaimed their innocence and insisted that they would be exonerated in court. Paul thought the defense team was being a bit overly optimistic, especially since Dean Estes had agreed to testify against the conspirators and verify the authenticity of the tape in order to avoid the gas chamber.

D.A. Bulgetti had fired Paul the morning the story came out, then quickly leaked the surveillance file on him to undermine his credibility as a witness. Yet, so far, no one in the press had exposed him. But word would get out. It was only a matter of time. Paul only wished he'd had the satisfaction of being there to see the District Attorney shackled and dragged off to jail.

◇◇◇

231

Paul didn't hear from Blake after that afternoon in the park. At first he didn't know what to do with himself now that he no longer had a job. He had spent the last decade and a half thinking nothing but his career mattered. After the flurry of calls from the press died down, and with the trial not scheduled for months, his life became very quiet. Since he'd been pushed out of the District Attorney's Office, Paul had not received a single offer of employment, and the messages he left with law firms downtown which would have fought to get him just weeks before went unreturned. Word had gotten out.

He saw Jeannie for lunch occasionally; Pat was still too angry with him to come along. Much to his surprise, he found himself gravitating toward Watts and Jeff Dupuis' storefront office, occasionally at first, and then it seemed like he was going every day including weekends. There was always so much to do. He started out on little things, helping to draft briefs and giving advice to pro bono clients, but somewhere along the line he began to feel the cases were as much his as Jeff's. That passion he had lacked for so long in his career came back in a kind of righteous anger that never quite left him after the day's work was done. It was the kind of single-minded determination toward a goal that had characterized his first years as a lawyer.

One day Jeff had shaken his head when a new case came his way, a bar in Wilmington shuttered by the police on the charge that men had been caught dancing with each other.

"I don't know if I'll have time to take this on, not with all the other cases I have coming up."

"Why don't you go ahead?" Paul had said, not looking up from the legal pad where he was scribbling notes. "I can help you with it."

The lewd conduct trial of six of those arrested at the Black Cat began later in January. Jeff defended two of them. The question the jury had to resolve was, did public kissing on the lips for up to ten seconds at midnight on New Year's Eve constitute "willful lewdness and dissolute behavior in a public place?" Certainly it wouldn't if the defendants had been heterosexual, Jeff argued in court. Paul had sat in the back of the gallery and observed the proceedings. He hadn't been alone. A gay crowd attended to support the defendants. Paul had been annoyed with some spectators who wore flamboyant clothing and exhibited fey mannerisms, which he feared would influence the jury negatively.

A swaggering arresting officer testified that the bar patrons had attacked the cops, not the other way around. He waved a cast on his hand, claiming he had been bitten by a bar patron. However, during a court recess, the officer had taken his cast off in full view of the jury. It was a fake and the officer had perjured himself.

The jury convicted all of the defendants anyway.

Paul thought about Blake a lot. The things they had said. The things they hadn't. It all seemed so unfinished.

After a month with no communication, Paul finally decided to do something about it and got the address from one of his old contacts in the Police Department. One Sunday afternoon he made the trip over to Hollywood. As he pulled to the curb south of Franklin on Canyon Drive, he noted that it was walking distance from Blake's old place. It was a boxy apartment with a pool in the center surrounded by two stories of units looking into the courtyard. A gallery walkway circled the second floor.

He could hear laughing and splashing water as he climbed the stairs to the wrought iron security gate. An intercom to the left was flanked by overreaching birds-ofparadise. He searched for Blake's name, but before he could find it his attention was drawn by a familiar voice to the animated inhabitants of the pool, who were throwing an inflated ball back and forth.

Paul felt something happen in his chest and took a step back behind a climbing bougainvillea. Through the bars of the gate he could see Blake in trunks splashing in the water with a blond nine-year-old boy.

"Daddy!" the boy cried, "Catch!"

Paul stepped back farther into the shadows of the bougainvillea. Suddenly he didn't know why he had come and only wanted to get away. He remembered that night that seemed so long ago when he had stood leaning against his car in the rain looking up at Blake's house, the night that had given rise to the same conflicted emotions. How different his life would have been, he thought, if he had simply driven away.

Before he turned to go, he looked back through the gate one last time. Blake was throwing his head back in laughter as he tossed the ball back to Tommy. Paul was so close he could almost feel Blake's touch, and yet so far he might as well have been on the other side of the moon. Paul knew he would never stop loving him, could never stop loving him, not until the day he died. And he knew that love would be a terrible ache inside him, a beautiful burden that would follow him through the years, that would never let go, that would haunt him with the joy he had felt lying in his arms, and the empty promise of more to come.

He quickly made his way to the sidewalk and crossed the street to his car.

Blake stood by the gate looking out, a puddle of water around his bare feet, his hands resting on the bars. He watched as the red Thunderbird drove up the street and halted at the stop sign, its turn indicator light blinking.

"Dad, what are you doing? Come back in the pool!"

"I'm coming, Tommy," he called back. But he kept standing there a long time after the Thunderbird had disappeared down Franklin.

And then he wiped his eyes and composed himself before returning to his son in the pool.

Early one Saturday evening Paul dug a stack of photo albums out of the closet and sat looking at them on the living room couch. There were pictures of him and David going back ten years. The travels they had taken in Europe, the automobile trip to the Grand Canyon where they had stayed in a musty cabin at the edge of the precipice, Sunday barbecue parties with friends, the big blowout Paul had thrown for David's thirtieth birthday, the two of them exchanging gifts over the holidays.

In each and every one he saw their laughter and their smiles and remembered how genuinely happy they had been together. The only thing that had got in the way—that always seemed to get in the way—was their political disagreements. And even those were more about what tactics were most likely to bring about the changes that they both wanted. He had told David that they didn't want the same things, but now he realized that had never been true. They had just never been at the same place. David had always been so far ahead.

In the last month and a half he had picked up the phone a hundred times to call David, but in every instance he had never gotten past dialing the first few digits of his number. Now he set the album lying open on his lap aside, and picked up the phone. He dialed David's number and his

235

chest grew warm and he could hear the beat of his heart echo the sound of each ring. As ring followed ring without an answer, he felt disappointment harden his veins. Finally he hung up the receiver and got up. The afghan knitted by David's grandmother still hung over the back of the couch. David had never come by Paul's house to get his things, and somehow that had given him hope. Maybe David hadn't completely given up on him.

He went down the hall to the bathroom. Standing in front of the toilet peeing, he looked at the enigmatic expression on the cat in the framed *Chat Noir* poster. The moment Paul took the picture from the wall, gazing down into it, wondering what the expression meant, a striking memory flashed through his head. He and David lay naked on a lumpy bed in a *pensione* in a French village, spent after making love, a faint breeze flowing through the open window, their bodies covered in a sheen of sweat. The poster of the cat was propped up on the headboard above them leaning against the faded floral wallpaper.

"It's perfect," David had said, his palm resting on the fine hairs on Paul's chest. "This is a perfect moment."

And Paul realized now that over the years there had been so many, so many.

As he was hanging the picture back on the wall, the telephone rang and Paul quickly headed down the hall to the bedroom, a tingly excitement growing in his gut. Something told him that it was David. That David knew he had just called. That David was thinking about him, as he was thinking about David.

He snatched up the phone. "Hello, David, David is that—"

"Paul?"

Paul's chest deflated. "Jeannie... hi."

"Hey, you," she said. "I just wanted to ask you again about tonight. Pat and I are leaving in a few minutes. It's supposed to start at nine, but we wanted to get there early and pass out the picket signs."

Then Paul remembered. It was the rally in Silver Lake David had been organizing with PRIDE to fight police abuse. Though previous gay protests had never numbered more than a handful, this time activists promised it would be the largest gathering against police harassment of gays in history. It would be one of several rallies to expose LAPD violence toward minorities at different locations around the city, a coalition of hippies and blacks and gays and anti-war activists.

Paul hesitated. "I don't know if I can. I don't know if I should."

"Oh, come on. Everybody will be there. Why don't you come? What have you got to lose?"

And then he was driving into the night.

He sped down Sunset with a sense of urgency he didn't entirely understand, rounding the curves in Westwood toward the flats of Beverly Hills. When he came to West Hollywood, traffic slowed to a near halt on the Strip and he stretched his neck out the window to see what was going on. He could hear a din in the distance, like the beating of drums. Of course, he recalled, one of the rallies was scheduled on the boulevard.

As his Thunderbird inched slowly forward, the sidewalks began to come alive with more and more people, young people, roving the street, boys with ragged haircuts and beards, girls in jeans and colorful T-shirts, beads around their necks. Paul could feel the energy coming off them, the electricity of the night, and he pressed on, compelled forward.

Near Crescent Heights he could see masses of people, thousands, picket signs rising above them like sails, *STOP BEATING THE FLOWER CHILDREN* and *PIG HARASSMENT MUST GO!* Some drivers honked in support of the protesters, others blew their horns angered by the slowdown in traffic. Up ahead picketers on the sidewalk in front of the condemned teen nightclub Pandora's Box surged into the street, chanting, blowing whistles. He saw policemen with batons shouting and protesters shouting back.

There was something new in the wind, he could feel it. It was as if the whole world was coming apart and it was impossible to see what it would be like when it finally came back together.

The traffic was diverted around the ebb and flow of the picketers into the street, and once he was past the focal point of the rally, he pressed on the gas. He drove faster, eastward toward Silver Lake, his window down, the breeze in his hair.

He passed the bar New Faces and began to look for a place to park. He had heard the bar had already closed down, the victim of nightly harassment since the New Year's Eve raid. Across the street from the Black Cat he found a parking space. The Black Cat was still open, but its days were numbered, the owners drowning under a mountain of legal bills to defend their entertainment and liquor licenses, which were under attack by the authorities.

On the sidewalk in front of the bar with its art deco design and chubby-faced cat dominating the front window, a picket line of forty carrying signs condemning police harassment walked in a circle.

Paul sat in his car and watched. He spotted the sign he had seen David make at the Hub, carried by a young woman with long, straight hair. A collegiate man in glasses held a sign reading, *ABOLISH ARBITRARY ARRESTS*, and another waved one demanding, *NO MORE ABUSE OF OUR RIGHTS AND DIGNITY.* They were all so young, all so beautiful, and Paul thought if anyone could change the world, it was them.

While Paul had never seen a crowd this big of gay men and lesbians protesting, his heart went out to David who had worked so hard to get a lot of people to join the rally here in Silver Lake, where the focus would be on police harassment against gays. It would be a crushing disappointment and he knew David would be hurt and angry that so few people had cared. He spotted Parker and Billy in the picket line and climbed out of his Thunderbird.

It was only then that he could see the swarm of people in the parking lot east of the bar, hundreds of them. He'd never seen so many gay people and their supporters in all his life. There were Jeannie and Pat in the crowd, and on the corner Jeff was handing out leaflets explaining the reason for the protest to passers-by in cars.

As he began to cross the street, threading through slow-moving traffic, he saw David get up on the podium and take the microphone to address the crowd. He began to speak, and once again Paul was taken aback by what a commanding presence he had become.

Paul was halfway across Sunset when he seemed to catch David's eye. He stopped there on the pavement, as if in a spotlight. Their eyes met and David appeared to briefly lose his train of thought as he spoke. They stood in each other's gaze for an instant. Paul felt nothing but love and forgiveness from him. He was so overwhelmed with pride and love for David that his eyes filled with tears and he had to fight them back.

Then Paul proceeded across the street to join the protest.

## Acknowledgements

My deep appreciation goes to the following who led the way: Jonathan Ned Katz, *Gay American History*; John D'Emilio, *Sexual Politics, Sexual Communities*; Stuart Timmons, *The Trouble with Harry Hay*; Lillian Faderman and Stuart Timmons, *Gay L.A.*; John Rechy, *Numbers*; and ONE National Gay & Lesbian Archives. I thank you all.

A special thanks to Lloyd Brown. I am indebted to Peter Cashorali, Eric A. Gordon, Daniel Harris and Jerry Rosen for help on this book.

Made in the USA
Las Vegas, NV
02 July 2022

51001082R00134